SOME MORNINGS

J. L. LORA

SOME MORNINGS

Copyright © 2019 by Janny L. Lora.

All rights reserved. Printed in the United States of America. No part of this book may be used or reproduced in any manner whatsoever without written permission except in the case of brief quotations embodied in critical articles or reviews.

This book is a work of fiction. Names, characters, businesses, organizations, places, events and incidents either are the product of the author's imagination or are used fictitiously. Any resemblance to actual persons, living or dead, events, or locales is entirely coincidental.

For information contact J.L. Lora at:
P. O. Box 47022 | Windsor Mill, MD 21244
http://www.JLLora.com

Book and Cover design by Deranged Doctor Design
Copyediting by Nina S. Gooden
Proofreading by Katie Testa

ISBN: 978-1-950453-07-8 (Ebook)
ISBN: 978-1-950453-08-5 (Trade Paperback)
First Edition: October 2019

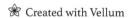 Created with Vellum

Some Mornings

J.L. LORA

For all those who get knocked down and keep getting up.

1

Sierra

Dear God, grant me the serenity to accept the things I cannot change, the courage to change the things I can, and wisdom so I don't speed my ass to the Bronx and kill this motherfucker.

"Edwin, you don't even have to leave the Bronx. I can pack up the kids and bring them up to you this weekend. Even if it's just for a day, it would make them happy. They just want to see you."

"Sisi, I told you. This is not a good time. Dania is delicate right now. The baby is riding too low and her morning sickness won't stop. She needs rest, care and attention."

Oh, I see. None of the things you gave me when I was knocked up with your two kids. All I got was cheated on and then called by your skank to rub my face in it.

But I swallow my resentment because I need him to see the kids.

"All I'm asking for is a couple of hours. Maybe Dania's mom can come stay with her and you can take Emmi and Eddie for ice cream or to the damned Rat. They miss you."

"You should have thought of that when you moved them over three hundred miles away from me."

I recoil like he'd sprayed kerosene over my skin. It wouldn't take a match for this shit to go up in flames. What I need is to keep it amicable.

"I moved down here because I got a good job. I couldn't afford the rent and the private school. Not on my own. Here, they go to a good public school and we live in a nice neighborhood. By the way, I still haven't gotten your check yet."

He clears his throat. "Um. I'm a little behind. With the pregnancy, and Dania not working, we have some added expenses. I need some extra time."

I grit my teeth so hard they may sink into one another. "How much time? You're four months behind."

"It's a rough time, Sierra. But don't worry, you'll get your alimony."

Oh, hell no. Fuck this.

"You don't pay alimony. The money I take from you is called child support, which the court decided your children need. Which you have not paid in months, and I've been overlooking it to keep the peace. I can't do it much longer. My funds are low from covering your faults."

And so is my patience.

"I have to go. I can't get in trouble at work or you won't get your 'court-appointed money.' I'll call the kids tonight."

A call beeps on the other line. "I'll tell them to expect your call."

And go to fucking hell.

"Yes?" My tone is rougher than I mean for it to be when I answer the other line. That's what a conversation with my ex-husband does to me.

"Hola, *bebé*." A husky voice croons from the other side.

I let my head hang back. I do not need this shit either. "Why the hell are you calling, José?"

He chuckles. "Seems like I called at exactly the right time. You sound tight, Sisi. You know I can make it better for you, give it to you how you like it.

Jesus, he's right. I need some dick. I need to get laid, slayed, piped, fucked, whatever.

I need a man's big and strong body pinning mine down, his hard cock sliding in and out of me until I'm sweaty, clawing, desperate and writhing for more friction. I need something to obliterate my bullshit reality for an hour. But I can't have that. At least not now, and never again with José.

"Come on, Sisi. You want it. I know you do. I can come down there to Baltimore and give it to you fast and hard, braced against a wall or bent over the couch." His honeyed voice drips with the memories of all my moans and echoes, of all the times he made my body tremble and seize.

My legs squeeze together, as do my eyes. I struggle against the urge to say yes and settle for a weak, "José..."

"Oh, yeah. There's my Sisi. I can be there before eleven and gone before the kids come back from school."

Kids, meaning mine. The word hits me like a bucket of cold water. I'm no longer almost clawing my thighs with need. Instead, my pussy has gone drier than a summer in Nevada.

My kids, Emmi and Eddie, are the two people I would do anything for. They are my greatest joys, who lately cause me the biggest pain. They're also the reason I say, "I have to go, José."

"Why are you being like this? It's always been so good between us. So sexy. Remember all those times on my couch or against my window, with the blinds open?"

I remember. *All too well.* It's why I'd been so horny seconds ago, but now my libido has gone straight into a coma.

"José, that won't ever be the same. Please stop calling. You're not going to wear me down. It's really over. Goodbye."

José fed my destructive side. He's the one I ran to when I got tired of my ex-husband cheating on me and making me look the fool. Every time Edwin had neglected my kids and me for a new piece of tail, José would shove all my pain away with rough strokes of his cock. I always left his place in Washington Heights in a good mood. I'd gotten my cheating husband back.

It never lasted.

It was never long before I was muffling my sobs in the shower and feeling like shit again because Edwin got with some new bitch. I would be pissed off and vindictive and looking to get mine.

Until one morning, at my sister's old apartment, when I came face to face with the truth. Edwin had cheated on me first, but I was a cheater too. I had let him turn me into one. The shame was so great I could feel nothing but disgust with myself.

Since then, I haven't been able to chill with José. No matter how much he begs. I can't even see his name on my phone without the skin on my face tingling.

That's why I hang up on him with no regrets. He'll call back. He always does. I won't ever answer him again.

I hit "info" under his contact information and scroll down to block the number, but my screen lights up with my sister's name. I haven't seen her in a couple of days. She's been working from the New York office.

"Hey, I was just about to call you—"

"Mom is threatening to come visit us." She blurts it out, not sounding as horrified as she should. Like she's not afraid to let our mom around her fiancé, Jax, or worried what her presence may do to us as humans.

"Tell her no. I don't fucking need this right now, Saona."

"Neither of us does, Sisi, but we promised her a move down here wouldn't mean we would stop seeing her. Maybe we can take a day trip to New York with the kids to visit."

"No, I can't do a trip to the city." Better said, I can't take my kids to the city. I can't stand to see them disappointed when they can't see their dad, because Edwin is too busy...*being a deadbeat asshole.*

"Are you okay?" My sister's tone shifts to concerned.

"Yeah," I lie. "I'm just not in the mood for a family reunion."

"I'm not fishing today, *Sierra*. Tell me what's wrong."

Ugh, I hate how well she can read me.

"Everything is a fucking disaster. I think the kids borderline hate me. I woke up at six in the morning to get them ready for school, cut the crust off their sandwiches, and find all the shit that disappears under their noses. Only to get attitude from Emmi and, 'I miss daddy' from Eddie.

My sister's sigh fills the line. "It's normal. He's their dad and they don't know what an asshole he is."

"I know, *Manita*. I do. But it's hard, when there's so much I can't and won't say to them. I called Edwin this morning and he told me he doesn't have time to come see them. They miss their daddy, and he made fifty thousand excuses when I offered to bring them up to New York so he can spend time with them." I shove a hand through my hair and take a few breaths.

My sister switches from voice call to FaceTime. Her frowning face, where I see so much of me and my daughter, fills my screen. "God, how can Edwin be such a dick? He just met that chick not even seven months ago."

"When has that ever stopped him? I'm worried about the kids. They don't understand that he has a new wife and a kid on the way. I can't keep covering all his faults. I'm exhausted from getting blamed, from being pelted with Emmi's attitude, and from dealing with his family's calls."

"I'm back home tonight. Why don't we go out this weekend and do something fun? Or maybe we can plan a trip to Disney with them."

Saona's the best sister and aunt anyone could ever want.

"Jax would kill us. The bar is so busy at night that he's going out of his mind. I'm shocked he hasn't quit his day job yet."

Saona shakes her head, but there's always a hint of a smile whenever his name is mentioned. "He's hardheaded. I hate how much he works. He would be at The Birthmark all the time, if we didn't have you and Juan helping out."

"Yeah, he would."

Saona taps a pen against her bottom lip, right over the black beauty mark she's had since birth. "Do you think maybe you should take the kids to see someone? They've had a lot of changes in the past year and a half. And, unlike when we were kids, we have the means now."

I glare at her with narrowed eyes. "You mean you have the means."

My sister glares right back at me. "You need to get laid. You're way too bitchy. *We* have the means to take them to a counselor."

"I'm sorry." *I am.* I just hate that she's always having to help me, but if I tell her that, she will pitch a fit.

"I mean it, Sisi. And you should go out with someone. It's not good for you to just go from your house to work, to driving the kids around and back."

"I can't think about that right now… José called today. He wants to come visit."

Her eyes grow round. "Oh. What did you say to *El Tiguere*?"

"You sound like *Mami*, calling him that. Of course, I told him no. I can't bring myself to be involved with anyone, least of all him."

She nods. "I understand, but I'm going to give you the same advice someone once gave me. You're single and gorgeous. You should be fucking everything that makes you feel like an absolute Dominican goddess."

I laugh. "Don't throw my words in my face. The difference is, you don't have kids. It's easier to pass the biscuit around when you don't have little ones. Anyway, I'm not ready. I don't know anyone here and it's not like I have the time to break in someone new."

Her eyes grow round again. "Oh, crap. I have an eight o'clock meeting. Hang in there, Sisi. I'll be home tonight. We'll talk." She hangs up.

I need to get a grip and get back to work. These books are not going to get themselves done. But I'm going to stay the course for now. I need to take care of my kids and make sure they're okay. I don't need a plaything, a man, or anyone who can get complicated. Maybe I can upgrade my *Pleasurizer* to the 3.0 device.

The shattering of glass tears through the silent bar. I'm out of the office chair in seconds. I'm from the Bronx, so a little shattering glass doesn't scare me but it sounded too close for comfort. I grab the bat Jax keeps in the office and tiptoe my way to the back of the bar.

If it happened inside, someone is going to get their head cracked open. All the lights are on and nothing's out of place and then it hits me. *There are no windows back here.*

The rumble of an engine comes alive and my heart thumps my sternum. It's loud and *oh shit*, I know that sound. That's my baby. I run down the hallway and throw the back door open. I halt over gray pieces of broken glass, only to be left in the dust as the back of my 4Runner disappears at the end of the alleyway.

Heat rushes to my head, clouding my vision. My hands go tighter around the bat. *This is not happening to me.* I stomp my foot and it crunches over the broken glass. My head and body do a frantic one-eighty and turn looking for something, anything, anyone that can explain this.

There's no one, so I turn to the gray Baltimore sky and let it rip. "Are you fucking kidding me? Someone did not just steal my fucking car."

2

Matt

Fuck Calvary Street, the dirty buildings and boarded up windows. It looms like a beacon of death. My stomach does that pitching thing when I turn into it and I hold my breath. *Ten seconds*. Then I won't have to see it. We can take a different route out of the neighborhood after we're done with this service call.

I'm not worried about the 10-16, one of our regular domestic disturbances, that I'm about to encounter because I'm so caught up on turning onto this fucking street. I'm glad I'm driving. It gives me less of a chance to dwell on it. I can fly through it and hold my breath. It's been over fourteen years but it's always the same. Not much has changed on the block. The deli with the best damned sandwiches in town is still standing. People still sit on the bench to wait for the bus. The same old lady still peeps out of her first-floor rowhouse. I sink my foot harder into the gas, passing the fried chicken spot where Ryan used to work. I don't even want to smell it. It would stay in my nostrils for days, souring my mood even further.

"Take it easy, Hunter," Wicker says from the passenger seat.

I don't even turn my face toward her. I don't want to catch a glimpse of the store sign. "You're telling me to take it easy? The same person who said she doesn't do speeds under sixty?"

"I don't. Except for this street. There are a couple of walkers in this neighborhood who I went to high school with. They're usually high out of their minds and not paying attention."

"Walkers" is my partner's special word for our city's drug addicts. They move a lot like the zombies on the *Walking Dead,* coked—or *methed*—out of their minds and shuffling along without a sense of direction. It's trendy and popular to talk about the opioid crisis but no one takes any action. Like talking does anything to solve it.

"That's nice of you to be worried about people, Wicker. I like it when you have your coffee. You become kinda…human."

She snorts. "Look who's got a sense of humor today. Since when are you Mister Witty?"

I shrug. "About the same time you became concerned about pedestrians instead of trying to sweep East Baltimore with our squad car."

She laughs this time. "I'm not that bad. I just like to get where I'm going, fast. No need to dilly-dally."

The banter dies as we turn onto Morris Place. There's another police car outside and I barely put the car in park before we jump out. All the flashing red and blue lights have gathered a crowd around the perimeter.

"What have we got here, boys?" Wicker's tone is sober and as normal to me as her odd sense of humor.

"Your regulars are at it again. We knocked twice and no one's opened. We don't want to knock the door down, in case he decides to harm the kids. Dispatch said wait for you, since you've got experience with them."

"Who called it?"

Officer Johnson hooks a thumb toward a group of teenagers about ten feet behind us. "Those are friends of the teenage son. He texted them and they called us."

Wicker tilts her head for me to go. She doesn't talk to the teenage boys unless we need to pump them for info. I hear their account all over again. In between each, "Um…" I get that the father came home drunk, beat on the mother and wouldn't let the family members leave. This couple always fights and gets physical. I hope she presses charges this time.

I signal to my partner and we head to the door. It's my turn to lead, so I take a long breath and knock. And everything goes molasses slow. My heart, time, Wicker's breath. A domestic disturbance can morph into anything. A teary couple swearing they'll never mistreat each other again. An abuser turning into a little bitch after he was big and bad, beating his smaller or weaker partner. It can also blow sky high when you have an aggressive offender who is out to prove himself, even to law enforcement. Whether he's trying to take a cop out or commit suicide-by-cop, this situation has messy potential in it.

I hate messy potential. I spend my life staying away from it.

I also hate having to pull out my service piece, even as my finger hovers over it and I blow a mouth full of air. Footsteps echo in my ears as the world fades. In my immediate world, there's only Wicker, with her wagging fingers by her hip, whoever is on the other side of this door, and me. I don't even graze my piece until it's necessary because once the Glock 22 is out, death looms larger than it usually does around me. But I unfasten the safety strap from the holster.

Hope for the best and prepare for the worst.

I'm grateful I updated my life insurance information for Hayden and RyanAnne. My nieces depend on me, as does my brother. The smaller stipend to care for any of his outstanding necessities was a good idea. But who's going to be there for him if I'm gone?

That's why you're still needed in this world, Hunter. And Wicker is counting on you, so stop thinking.

I pat my vest, reassuring myself it's where it's supposed to be. A sturdy wall between my chest and whatever a suspect wants to shoot my way.

The click of the lock, sharp like the cocking of a revolver, makes my heart jump and Wicker suck in a breath. Untrained ears couldn't tell the difference, but everyone's safety hangs on us knowing what one versus the other sounds like. That's why our fingers are still stalking but not pouncing on the grip of our pieces. The door creaks open and the seconds tick by without a face.

My fingers fold around the grip, its porous surface pressing against my palm. "Open the door slowly."

My words are measured but I say them with enough force to let them know we're not playing.

One…two…three…four…five…six seconds and the door creaks open. The sweaty man is standing there, staring between Wicker and me with bloodshot eyes. The cheap scent of Wild Turkey permeates the air. The bottle in his left hand is almost empty, so he probably drank and bathed in most of it. My true concern is the SIG in his right hand.

My pulse slams against my wrist. My breath lodges in my throat and, next to me, Wicker twitches. It's slight, almost imperceptible. *Shit. Fuck. Damn…it came to this.*

My service weapon is in my hand before I can blink, pointed straight at him. "Get down on your knees and put your gun on the floor."

"Now!" my partner yells.

Time keeps on ticking and Wicker clears her throat in our signal for situations like this. It's a miracle I can hear her over the rumbling in my chest, but I do. And I nod.

"Put the fucking gun down and kick it our way. Don't make me have to shoot you." Her voice is so even-tempered that it would fool the whole world.

Not me. After eight years, I know her breath like my own. I can taste her fear. She doesn't like to pull the trigger either. But we both would, in a second, to protect each other.

"Fucking do it," I snap.

He does as he's told, then lowers himself to his knees. I follow his progression, feathering the trigger of my Glock with my index finger. My heart is beating so fast it hurts. This must be what a heart attack feels like. Except I know this pain too well. I know I won't die and that it will pass. Hopefully, without anyone else dying.

I don't breathe until the gun hits the tip of Wicker's boot.

"Put your hands on the back of your head." I wait until he complies. "Now crawl to me."

He does as directed, mumbling, "It's not loaded. I just wanted to scare them."

I step forward, my gun turned in the direction of the hallway. Behind me, Wicker slaps the cuffs on him and follows. Beyond me, in the hallway, a teenage boy with huge eyes is holding his mom and two little siblings.

I blow a mouth of hot air and lower my gun. "Come on out. You're safe."

Two hours later, after a meat-lovers omelet for me and the biggest hot chocolate I've ever seen her drink, Wicker looks over the diner table at me. "Next case better be a hot male stripper we need to help find his thong."

As if she summoned our next call, dispatch gets on the walkie. "Dispatch, unit thirty-eight, what's your twenty, over?"

My partner rolls her eyes. "This is thirty-eight. Ready and willing in the village. Over."

"10-8-51 in progress near your location."

Wicker lets her head hang back for a second, then slaps a twenty-dollar bill on the table. "On me. You paid last time." She turns her mouth into the radio. "Copy. On the way."

As we walk to the car, I look up to the sky and thank my mom for watching over us. This could have gone really bad but I know she's protecting me. And I wonder why. Hayden and RyanAnne would get more if I were gone. Wally would probably do better without me as a crutch.

"It better be a male stripper's car," Wicker reiterates.

And I nod. We've all got to live for something.

Even if it's just for others.

3

Sierra

"Drink this."

I peel my face away from my hands and get nose-stabbed by a whiff of pure, smoky alcohol. I recoil. My gaze shifts from the shot of Jameson to Jax's wrinkled brow. My sister's fiancé's face shows the type of concern I never saw reflected in my ex-husband's. Or José's, whose only face I know is the one that offers dick-delights. *Delights that, had I taken him up on, I wouldn't be here right now.*

I take the glass and throw it back. The liquor perforates the knot and clears a path down my throat, making my eyes water. "Thank you."

"It's going to be okay, Sisi. The cops are coming and so is Juan. He's taking over for the afternoon. We're going to file a report. Then we are going to my house, so you can take Saona's truck until they find yours."

"No way—"

Jax shakes his head. "I don't want to hear shit about it. Neither does your sister. She and I can manage with one car. You have to pick up the kids and drive them around to their after-school stuff."

My face starts to tingle and I can't hold his gaze. I drop my head back into my hands. Am I even an adult anymore? I can't even seem to do the regular things without my sister and her man's help.

"Hey—"

I shake my head. "I can't talk. I can't even look at you."

"That's a first. Customers usually take one look at me and blurt out all their issues." His voice drops at the end, as if in genuine surprise.

"You're not a bartender right now, Jax."

"I'm behind the bar and I just served you a drink. What does that make me?"

I shake my head and look up again. He's leaning against the bar. His smile is teasing but the worry is there, lingering in his eyes. I'm so happy my sister found this guy. "My super nice brother-in-law."

"If I'm super nice, you should talk to me."

"My life is just fucked. Nothing's as it should be. I can't seem to do anything right on my own."

"What are you talking about? Anyone's car can be stolen. It's Baltimore. Besides, you're the best manager this bar could ever have. And you kick ass as a mom."

I scoff. "News flash. My kids hate the shit out of me."

"They do not. It's hard because—"

We both turn as the front door swings open and a tall police officer with enviable curls walks in. She looks around, her fingers hooking into the belt of her uniform pants. Her eyes move past me and rest on Jax for longer than necessary. "Someone reported a car stolen?"

Jax comes from around the bar and she's still got her eyes on him.

I climb off the stool and wave in front of her face until her brown eyes are staring straight into mine. "Yes, it's mine."

"I'm officer Wicker and that's my partner, Officer Hunter." She moves aside as another police officer steps in. He towers over her by a foot. He has a shaved head and quarter-sized, water-blue eyes I would know anywhere. They're a flashback that floods me with memories of long chats, teenage angst, hormones, and hanging out on the rooftop of my Bronx building. *It can't be...*

"Matt?"

He blinks a few times and even shakes his head. "Sierra? What the hell are you doing here?"

It is him.

"I work here. What are you doing in a cop's uniform?"

He looks at his partner, who's staring at him with interest, and clears his throat. "My family moved to Maryland years ago. So your car got stolen, huh?"

The abrupt change has me blinking fast, but I recover. "Yeah. It was parked in the alleyway behind the bar."

His partner moves further into the room, looking around. "Do you have cameras?"

"Yes, the monitors are in the office," Jax answers.

"Let's go check them out," she says.

I start to follow them. There's no way I'm leaving her with my sister's man. She's looking mighty thirsty and eyeing Jax like he's a Big Gulp.

"Sierra, you show me the alleyway," Matt says.

We make our way to the back and as soon as we're at enough distance from his partner, he places a heavy hand on my shoulder. I turn to face him. His warm eyes and that bashful smile take me way back.

"I'm sorry I cut you off. Not many people know about my old history and I don't share."

I shrug. "No worries. You're on duty. And that's the craziest statement in the world. Dare-Me-Matt is a cop. Who the fuck would give you a badge?"

His laughter is instant, bubbling from deep inside, and triggers my first smile of the day.

He takes my arm and rushes me out the back door. "I'll have you know, I'm a respectable police officer now, Ms. Torres. I catch hellraisers."

"Ten years ago, you were the… I forgot we can't talk about that. I'll have to keep that as our secret, I guess."

He leans forward until we are almost nose to nose. "It will go into the vault with all those other secrets we kept before."

The chill bursts all over my spine and makes my nipples tingle. *What the fuck am I doing? Am I flirting? That's a no-no.* I turn around, unlock the deadbolt and throw the back door open. The cool October air washes over my skin like I'm on fire.

"This is where my car was parked. It's a white 4Runner, twenty-fourteen. I have my plate numbers on my phone." I go through all the details, answering all his questions.

"This is good. We can go back inside now." He holds the door for me.

We step back in the building but he stops me a few steps from the office door. I turn around and he hands me his phone. It's open to the dialing screen.

I frown. "What is this for?"

The way he's staring sends a shiver over my skin. "Enter your phone number."

"This is how you write your report?"

He shakes his head. "Officer Wicker will write this report. You'll have to give her your number when she asks."

"How come you don't just get it from the report?"

"I stopped breaking the law a long time ago. I'm one of the good guys now."

And he looks it too. Long gone is the wild hair, the baggy jeans, and the hoody sweatshirt. His uniform is neat and pressed. His shoes are so shiny I can see myself reflected in them.

He's still through my survey of his body, but those eyes are ripping my clothes off.

It revs the blood in my veins. "What happens if I don't enter it into your phone?"

"Then I won't call you."

Oh shit. I stare at his phone and back at him.

"Let's go find my partner and tell him," his partner's voice rings out.

Matt doesn't move but my fingers do. By the time they join us, I've handed it back to him and he's put the phone away.

"Guess who?" his partner asks. A giddy smile plays about her lips.

"Regulars?"

She nods like a sugar daddy at a twenty-five-and-under club. "Petey and Doug. Mr. Hamilton here has state-of-the-art cameras. Faces clearer than their mugshots. He also gave me all we need."

Matt shakes his head. "Let's go get those bastards."

"This is a nice little bar, and if the wings are as good as Mr. Hamilton said, we'll be back." She puts on her hat and winks at Jax. Then she turns to me. "We'll be in touch about your car. Don't get your hopes up. They've probably trashed it for parts already."

Matt holds the door open for her but his gaze is still on me. He nods, slow and nonchalant, like he used to when he saw me by the bleachers with my friends. That nod meant I would see him again. That he would climb up the fire escape to knock on my window.

And damn it if my chest doesn't vibrate at the prospect.

4

Matt

"Dude." Wicker inclines her head for me to look at the suspect.

I don't want to. *At all.* The last thing a man wants to see is another's nuts and bolt. I shoot a longing look to the pile of dog shit a few steps away—it's more appealing—and turn to the perp. He's still yelling into the glass of our squad car, without an ounce of self-awareness.

"Sir, I handcuffed you in the front so you can pull up your pants. I find it concerning that I've made this request three times."

He shoots me a puzzled look so I point at his exposed, pale junk.

"Oh. My bad, man." He reaches down and pulls up his boxers and then his pants. He nods to Wicker. "Excuse me."

"You still got more to pull up," my partner points out.

"Nah, shorty. That's as high as I wear them."

"I'm not your shorty, Justin Bieber. I'm a police officer. You will address me as Officer Wicker. You're already in trouble for assaulting the nice young lady in the car. Don't make things worse for yourself."

"What nice lady? She's a hooker that I had already paid to..." he trails off, blinking a few times like a dumb ass who realizes he just admitted to soliciting.

Some Mornings

Wicker rolls her eyes at me and gets on the radio. "What's your ETA?"

I chuckle. "Mr. Whitten, this is the third time you've been caught for soliciting. I don't think the judge is going to be kind to you this time. If I were you, I would call a good attorney."

"This is a setup," he yells.

"Did I bring this woman to you? No, you went to the corner and paid her for sex. And you admitted it on police camera." I point to the device pinned to my badge.

Ten minutes later, the backup squad car takes him away. "See you in court, Biebs."

"You're wrong for that, Wicker."

She starts walking toward the driver side of our squad car. "You smile now?"

Shit. Nothing gets by her.

"I'm in a good mood."

She smirks at me and leans over the top of the car. "You sure are. Ever since we took that 10-8-51 and you're not the only one, Hunter. That bartender is something else." She bites her lip. "At first, I'd thought I'd gotten my wish, because he definitely should be a stripper with that body. Too bad he's engaged to 10-8-51's sister."

I freeze. 10-8-51 is the code for stolen vehicle. Sierra Torres' stolen car in this instance. "How the hell do you know that's her sister's fiancé?"

She shrugs and opens the door. "He told me when we were in the office. He said I can come for free wings because his fiancée would love to meet us. Since you seemed to know her sister from way back when."

I'm pretty sure she added the last part, so I ignore it. "You did not hit on that man."

"Not overtly." She smiles and dips inside the car.

I get in on the other side. "Someone's going to complain."

"I'm a female officer." She laughs like that explains everything, and it does. Men take her flirting as a compliment. She never goes too far but Wicker does like to tease.

The woman in the backseat knocks on the partition. "Where ya dropping me off at?"

"On South Carey. Lynda, you need to stop picking up these johns. There're only so many chances we can give you for keeping us informed before it starts looking suspicious."

"I would give up all the johns for you, Officer Hunter."

I don't have to turn around to know her tongue is half hanging out.

Wicker sighs. "Jesus, Lynda. Are you propositioning an officer?"

"Don't get jealous, Officer Wicker. I can turn you out too, if you let me."

Wicker slams on the brakes, sending us both toward the dashboard. "Get the fuck out. Next time, we're hauling you into East Madison."

She barely waits for Lynda to get out before she speeds away.

I try not to flip out. "You know if you hurt her, we're going to get in trouble."

"She needs to be home, taking care of her kids, instead of turning tricks."

"Wicker…"

Our radio scanner goes off with a new service call.

We have a 10-40-2 at ninety-one Scotts Street in Ridgely's Delight.

Oh shit. I hope it's not—

"Oh, damn, I hope Ms. DelRay's not dead." Wicker says.

I grab the radio and respond. The dispatcher gives me all the details on the welfare check. Every so often, we get to check on Ms. DelRay. She's a sweet old lady with crazy energy for her age.

We ride in silence. And though it's nothing new to check on someone and find them dead, it's something I still don't get used to. People think all police officers do is stop perps, issue tickets, spray Luminol on walls, and interrogate people. Except, most of the time, there's no bad guy, just everyday life. Someone can be dead for days while no one notices because that person lives alone.

I don't want to think about it so I turn my attention to who Wicker calls my 10-8-51. *Sierra Torres.* Not her car, which I'm one hundred percent sure has already been divided amongst every junkyard within fifty miles. I think of the woman. The woman whom I met as a girl. Not, a girl, *the girl*. Every guy in the neighborhood's dream. That badass chick who we all dreamt about and beat off to.

She'd been my best friend. The one I'd climbed fire escapes to go chat with. The one whose secrets I'd known.

The one I had a wild crush on and got to make out with for the best seven minutes of my young life.

She's still hot as always, but she's not as skinny. And there's less anger in her eyes. She looks a little tired or stressed but my God, that smile still stirs something in my chest.

We arrive at Scott Street and I shelve my thoughts for later. I can't wait for my shift to be over so I can call her. The fire truck is waiting for us and so is Ms. DelRay's daughter. We make it to the door and Wicker grabs her flashlight and knocks.

No answer.

My stomach knots as we give the order and they break the door down. Wicker and I get to go in first. The smell is the first thing that hits me and I cover my mouth and nose. *Marijuana. Jesus, did some junkie hurt her and take over her place?* My partner coughs and we rush the living room.

And I wish to God we'd never gone in. On the couch is an old man smoking a joint. On the coffee table are two pairs of discarded hearing aids. And on the floor, between his legs, is sweet, eighty-five-year-old Ms. DelRay going to town on his junk.

I turn around and head to the door to stop her daughter from coming in, leaving Wicker to handle things in here.

Half an hour later, we are at the Pitt beef joint. I've managed to purge the image of that sweet old lady, who reminds me so much of my late grandma, deep-throating someone. Then I take one look at Wicker and we start laughing. I have to put away my fries.

"That ten-sixteen aside, it's been a good day for you," Wicker says. "I haven't seen you smile this much in a while. You going to call her?"

And there goes the laughter. "Who?"

She rolls her eyes at me. "Ms. Torres, you know? 10-8-51?"

I'm saved from answering her by another call from the dispatcher. This time it's an accident off the downtown exit. All available units are called to the scene.

Probably a pileup.

On the way there, I think of Wicker's words. It has been a good day. I haven't thought of Wally or Ryan. At least not in my usual walking-the-ledge kind of way. And that has Sierra's name all over it because when I walked into that bar, it was high school all over again.

And I need more of that. I don't want to think of the pileup I'm driving toward, or of my brothers, their wasted lives, and the children they'd left behind.

So, I keep my mind off what I'll find, by thinking of the call I'll make tonight and the smile that put me in a better mood all day.

5

Sierra

"So, it's true? Dare-Me-Matt is a cop?" Saona asks, her eyes blinking fast.

I nod. "Crazy, right?"

"Yes," she breathes out. "I couldn't believe it when Jax said you knew the officer and his last name was Hunter. I kept saying it can't be the same guy. All the neighborhood guys hated the police. Remember that?"

Oh, yeah. I remember. His brothers were hoodlums and Matt and José were wannabes. Matt wasn't like the other boys, though. Yeah, he had that don't-fuck-with-me exterior but he was the nicest guy...to me. "His partner was eyeing Jax like a hungry she-wolf."

"He told me she was friendly and he invited her to come try the wings with her partner." My sister steals a look into the kitchen and tilts her head for me to follow her gaze. Jax slides out from under the sink. He turns on the water from the faucet, then starts replacing all the items. Saona turns back to me and we share a smile. It's *déjà vu*, something we share every time he comes to my house to fix something.

Our dad was like him. He was the family fixer. He would go to his sisters' houses and repair whatever was broken. They never had to pay anyone. Neither did my mom. Even after they'd separated, he would come and fix things. He used to do it for Saona and me.

A good man takes care of his ladies.

I never knew how meaningful that was until he was gone. Until I was married to a man who couldn't hang a picture without fucking up the entire wall. A man who couldn't even put his children's cribs together.

Saona won't have to go through that with Jax. This guy has renovated their house on his own. The warmth in her eyes tells me she gets it. Like me, she knows all too well what it's like to be married to a waste of skin.

"Sooo...what does he look like now?" Saona's voice brings me back from the memories. There's a slight tug at the corner of her lip. She's trying hard not to smile.

"He's...grown up." More than grown up. Jesus, his shoulders are wide and it's like he fills a room with that body. His smile has been playing over and over in my head.

Saona leans forward on her elbows, her eyes drifting to the kids finishing their homework near us, and back to me. "What was it like to see him again?"

I asked myself the same thing on the way home, and whenever I've gotten free time. Matt represents a different time for me. He was a respite in my teenage existence. Seven magical minutes in our classmate's closet, but a world of confusion after. I was so young back then.

"It was—"

"Why can't we go see Daddy this weekend?" Eddie grumbles, drawing my gaze away from Saona.

I go through my repertoire of excuses—he has to work late, he's out of town, he's working on a surprise for you—but my daughter beats me to it.

"Cause *Mami* hates him now. She kicked him out the house and he had to go get a new family, since she won't let us see him."

Emmi's words cut through my skin like a scalpel. My mouth's

frozen open and I don't know what to say because everything that bubbles up my chest is nothing I should say to my innocent baby.

"Emmi, that is not true." Saona says, her hand pressing against my daughter's shoulder. "Your mom would never do that. Things are a little difficult and everyone's adjusting but you'll see your dad soon. Saying things that you know in your heart are not true about your mom doesn't help. It hurts everyone."

"I just miss my daddy," my daughter mutters.

Tears sting my eyes. I open my mouth but close it again.

My sister's hand squeezes my thigh but she continues to talk to her. "I know, *cariño*, but your mom is doing the best she can and your dad is working a lot."

For the next few breaths, we are in silence. I'm struggling to keep a tight rein on my mouth.

"Hey, isn't there a Sweet Frog nearby? Why don't we go get some fro-yo for everyone?" Jax asks from the kitchen door, like the savior he's been for the past few months.

My kids jump from their places and rush to get their jackets on.

I can't look up from my dinner plate even as my brother-in-law touches my shoulder.

"Saona, go with them." My sister starts to shake her head but I stop her. "Please. I just need some time alone. I'm sorry to impose on you both, but —"

"*No seas ridicula*. We'll take them and talk to them."

I wave them all away from the door and then I collapse behind it, with my back against it and my head on my knees. I close my eyes and breathe until I'm no longer shaky. I wish I could cry, but the tears won't come. Because now I'm pissed off and when I get to this stage, I don't cry. A year and a half ago, I would have already been on my way to the Heights, to José's living room couch.

Except, Edwin didn't cheat on me today. He didn't hurt me with his newest chick. We divorced and I got sole custody, by his choice, but he gets to keep our children's hearts and their smiles. All I get is dumped on by Emmi, his family, and my mother.

My phone pings and I crawl to grab it from the table by the stairs. It could be Saona and they need me. My screen is full.

José, five emails.

Mom, two messages.

Unknown, one message.

The top one is from Saona and I unlock my phone to check it out. *I'm bringing you one. Reese's Pieces and Nutella and I'm going to load it.* There's a cookie emoji, then an ice cream one.

I send her a kissy face emoji and go to close my screen but it lights up with José's nickname, *El Tiguere*. What my mom used to call all my guy friends back in the day.

I tap the decline button, go through my contacts, and block his number like I meant to do earlier. The phone rings again right after that, this time from an unknown number. He's onto me sending his calls to voicemail. I stare at it and hit answer. "José, I don't want to talk to you. Stop calling."

There's a brief silence on the other line.

"I guess it's your lucky day, then. It's not José."

I know that voice. It's deep and just like this morning takes me back to another time. I clutch the collar of my shirt. "Matt."

"The other *tiguere*."

I laugh. "You remember my mom called you that. She hated you on sight."

"Your mom hated everyone who got close to you girls."

"She still does." *Except for cheaters. She loves those.*

"And with plenty of reasons. You girls were going places. We were a bunch of degenerates."

Yeah, I was going so many places that I ended up nowhere.

"Are you calling me to tell me you found my car in a million pieces?"

He sighs. "No, we don't have anything as of yet. This is not an official call."

Oh.

"Why are you calling from an unknown number? So your wife won't find out?" I *pfffft* after.

Some Mornings

"I'm not married or engaged or in a relationship, and I texted you the number earlier. Should I take it as a sign that you ignored it?"

The timber in his voice is so rich it makes me all tingly. In places that can't afford to be tingling.

"What? No, I'm sorry. I had to pick up the kids and drive them around. We came home and Saona and Jax brought us dinner. It's just been one thing after the next all day."

"Sounds like it. You should have some ice cream. Orange crème, no frills. I could always get a smile out of you with that."

Apparently, he still can. "I can't believe you remember that."

"I thought I'd forgotten all of this. It came rushing back today. When did you move to Maryland?

"Six months ago, when my divorce was final." I don't tell him how hard it was to make the decision or that there are days, like today, when I question if this was the right thing to do.

"So, how many kids do you have and how old are they?" he asks.

My chest squeezes thinking of them. Of how my daughter hardly looked at me at the table. "Two. Emmi is eight going on twenty-one and Eddie is six."

He chuckles. "Ah. So your daughter is a mini you?"

"Don't even say that. God forbid."

He laughs out loud this time, in that soft, hearty way that brings back images of chats outside my window by the fire escape, of thumping hearts when my mother would come in the room. I can still picture that smile that used to send the girls to giggle together in the bathroom.

"Where's your ex-husband now?"

Damn, he wastes no time.

"In New York, with his pregnant new wife."

"Are you still in love with him?"

"No." *And I'm not elaborating.*

"What about José?" He's going way too far with this. I'm not one of his suspects.

"What?"

"Are you in love with José, Sierra?"

My back stiffens at the way he says my name. I don't owe this dude shit. "Why is that any of your business?"

"Because I don't want to trip over him again to get to you." His voice is sure and firm, like a cop's should be, but it's the twinges of street that still linger in it that set my heart pounding. And has my pussy so impossibly wet...

Oh no. Because not tripping over José means he plans to hang around and start something. *And nope. Not going down this road.* I can't afford it right now.

"I have to go, Matt. My kids are coming back soon and I have dishes to wash."

"Okay. We'll talk again tomorrow. Good night."

The line goes dead and I can't do anything but stare at the phone. He hung up. Just hung up like it's nothing. No insisting or begging.

So much for being interested.

6

Matt

I can't shake the brother's cries. They've stayed with me all night. There's nothing like crying for a dead sibling, when you know they went before their time. There's nothing like the impotence of a wasted life.

The last thing on my desk was Sierra's report, with her address. I'm pretty sure Wicker dropped it on my schedule today on purpose. She knew that I wouldn't let this wait until tomorrow. And it became my excuse to be here right now. She didn't sound okay last night and God knows I'm not okay today. My hand hovers over the ignition and I tell myself to turn on the car and go.

This is not a good look. You could just call her and tell her this over the phone.

Instead, I'm sitting in my car like the kind of guy I lock up on an everyday basis. Granted, I'm more like the poor sap I give a summons for following around the girl he likes, rather than that dirtbag who terrorized his ex-girlfriend for two days straight.

I just need a glimpse of who we were back then. Of the friendship we shared, before my life had gone to shit.

Sierra doesn't want to reminisce. She thought you were José. She didn't even answer your question about him straight out. But you're here, like a teenage boy with no clue. Go home, Hunter.

I don't. Instead, I grab the plastic bag, open my car door and walk down her driveway just as she steps out of the nifty, white Range Rover. She's wearing a bun on her head, a terry cloth house robe, and an are-you-shitting-me look so sharp it takes me back to junior year of high school. Even in her disheveled state, she looks every bit what her mother one day shouted to José and me that Sierra was: *too good for you.*

Today, she looks almost like a girl next door, with her rounded eyes and a hand that flies to smooth her hair. But God, those eyes. They flame over me like a gasoline fire.

"What the hell are you doing here, Matt?"

No, she's not happy to see me.

"I came to give you an update on your car and to see if you were okay. You didn't sound like it last night."

"What's the update?"

"Your car was stripped for parts," I blurt out, and damn, I could kick myself for being callous.

She makes a growling noise, turns on her heel and walks toward the door. I follow because, apparently, I am looking to be brought up on charges. I can see the captain calling me in for a friendly chat and explaining, like he had to do with Caldwell, that even police officers can be accused of harassment.

She stomps up the steps and I'm right behind her.

"Sierra."

She stops in front of the door and whips around. "What? You already told me about my damned car. What more do you want?"

Yeah, I crossed the line and need to get the fuck out of here now.

"I...I'm leaving. I'm sorry. I'll call you tomorrow for the update. Here, I thought you could use this."

I thrust the plastic bag into her hand, turn around and head to my car. My heart is in my throat and my face is burning. This is so stupid. Who does something like this? I freaked her out, caught her in her pajamas coming home from taking her kids to school. We're not in high school. You don't really know this Sierra.

I am almost at my car when a firm hand wraps around my wrist. Her hands, like her cheeks, have always been warm and she's always had so much strength in those long, delicate fingers.

"Matt."

I turn around and stare at her. "Look, I'm sorry. I shouldn't have come. It was a dumb idea. I warn women all the time about things like this and here I am like a dumb—"

She shakes her head fast. "I'm sorry. I'm having a shitty morning. My kids bickered, screamed… They blame me because they can't see their dad. My daughter slammed the door to the car. Then, you show up and I look like shit and you bring me orange crème."

"It's not the same brand, but I hope you enjoy it." I pull my hand from her wrist.

She holds on tight. "Don't go. Please. Come share this with me."

I shake my head and pull my hand free. I've already embarrassed myself enough. I go around the car.

"I dare you," she yells, stopping me dead in my tracks.

"I'm not that guy anymore. I don't take dumb dares."

"I don't believe you. You stopped." She's smiling now and God, if that doesn't take me back to evenings on the fire escape outside her window. Usher and Mariah playing in the background, while her sister did homework with her headphones on.

"I thought you would say something else."

"No, you didn't." Her lip disappears behind her teeth. "Don't make me beg. Come on."

She walks to the house and doesn't look back. There's no doubt in her mind I'm going to follow. As much as I tell myself to have some dignity, get in the car and drive away, I'm right on her heels. She opens the door and holds it for me.

I close the door behind me, engaging only one of the deadbolts, and follow her. We go through a long hallway, passing the modern living room with the big sectional on the left and then into the open-concept dining room and kitchen. Everything is white, the walls, the cabinets, the big sink. It's a nice contrast to the honey wood floor and black counters.

"It's a nice house."

"Thanks. I'm renting." She points to one of the stools on the other side of the granite counter.

I sit down and lean in with my elbows. "I really don't do this. I just wanted to check up on you and maybe invite you to coffee."

She smiles over her shoulder. "Ice cream is better."

"How come you didn't move into the city, closer to your job?"

She opens a cabinet and pulls out two bowls. "I would have loved to. My sister lives downtown, near the bar. I wanted to be near her but the schools are not so good there."

Oh yeah, her kids. "Catonsville is the better district. Good choice."

She would freak out if she knew how bad the truancy is in some of those schools, or the three times we'd been called to the elementary school closest to that bar because some kid had brought a knife.

She scoops the ice cream from the jar and puts it in bowls. "Saona and I did a lot of research on the school districts. Btw, this is way fancier than what we used to eat back in the day."

"I don't trust the no-frills anymore. It's full of high-fructose corn syrup and shit like that. So, your sister is still a cute nerd?"

Her smile widens. "She's a human resources executive now, like a movie one. You know those women who are pretty and handle their business? Saona's a boss."

There's so much pride now. Just like back in the day. "Let me guess, you would still drag down the hall and beat anyone who messes with her."

She drops the spoon. "Of course, you remember that. My mom was so pissed. She still brings that fight up from time to time."

"But no one messed with Saona again. That's how you got your badass reputation."

She snorts. "You know very well this badass went home and cried. I wouldn't come out because of the scratches on my face."

I can't forget that.

"You used to pass notes through the window, telling me how beautiful I was and how the scars were barely there."

She hasn't forgotten either.

"You were, Sierra. You still are. Even sexier now." It's the truth. She's filled out from that skinny girl. She's a woman with all the right curves.

She looks away, grabs us spoons, and places one bowl in front of me. She stays on the other side of the counter but leans into it. "If my kids were here, and not hating me, they would complain that it's not fair I get to eat ice cream in the morning."

"That's the advantage of adulthood."

I offer my spoon like a wine glass and she clinks it with hers. We're still chuckling when she dips the spoon into the bowl, scoops some of the crème and puts it in her mouth.

And I nearly black out.

It's not only how her mouth closes around the spoon, securing it against her lips, like she's unwilling to let it go. It's not how her eyes squeezed shut like she found Jesus. It's not even the moan in the back of her throat that I can feel vibrating all the way into my spine. It's all of it that has my cock twitching in my pants. That has me out of my seat and around the counter before I remember myself.

She's blinking fast, no doubt wondering what the fuck I'm doing. Then her gaze goes to her feet.

Oh, shit, I fucked up again.

I take a step back and she takes one forward. And we're there, staring at each other. I'm swallowing hard and her mouth opens.

And then she moves closer, her hands bunching on my shirt. My heart takes off, galloping fast like an untrained horse on the run. She climbs on her tiptoes and crushes her open mouth to mine.

I wasn't expecting that, but I'm not dumb enough not to go with it.

7

Sierra

Jesus Christ, Sierra. Stop now.

But I can't. Not when his tongue swipes against mine and his hands are firm on my back. I pull him closer, pressing myself against him, sharing the orange crème taste in our mouths. Thinking is futile. Because my body's hot, his body is hard, and his fingers are digging into my skin.

Yes. Dig deeper.

His hand glides up my neck and settles at the back of my head, tilting it up. He takes control of my mouth, leaning into my body, making me feel how big and strong and hard he is.

The most amazing electric currents flow into my pussy and I need this so much right now. It's been so long. I take a step back and pull him with me until my back is pressed against the counter. I arch against it, using it as leverage to rub my crotch against his hard—*and oh my God*—feels-so-thick hard-on.

He moans and his hands fly to my ass, squeezing and pressing me against him until we're those two kids who dry humped for seven minutes in Angie Navarro's living room closet. My hand sneaks under his sweatshirt, past the T-shirt so I can get my hands on that hot skin, on all the muscles that make him different from that sixteen-year-old boy.

His chest is like sleek concrete and I splay my fingers all over it.

And I can't wait anymore.

I feel my way down to his back pocket and pull out his wallet. I yank my mouth from his. "You got a condom in here?"

His mouth is still open, his eyes glazed, but he nods. "Yeah."

I push the wallet into his hand. "Get it, then."

He fumbles with it, and I undo his belt, slide down his zipper. He's got the foil in his hand but is just staring at me. I smile at him, reach inside his pants, and my whole world unhinges.

"Ay, *Jesús*, that's big."

His laugh is rough but in his eyes is the gleam of an ego that has been stroked. I massage my fingers down his length, giving his lower ego the same treatment. I pump him until he's pushing against my hand.

He groans. "Damn, if this doesn't take me back."

"I don't want to take you back, Matthew. I want to take you deep, all the way, 'til I can't take no more." I hook my fingers on my pajama pants and push them down. I turn around, leaning on the counter, bucking back against him.

His dick grazes my skin and gold stars float around my eyes. I bend down deeper, as if I could roll out the welcome mat wider.

The rip of the foil fills the room and my walls flex in anticipation. I can't wait until he fills me. But he doesn't touch me or move. I wait and then turn. His head is bent and he's just staring.

"What the hell are you doing?"

His gaze scorches over me. "I'm having a look."

Then his hand flexes and cracks hard into my ass cheek, yanking a gasp from me, and setting off a tingle that bounces from my clit to my nipples.

"That was a touch. Now, I'm going to have a taste."

What? No! "Come on, just—"

He drops to his knees and I can't even finish because his lips graze the area his hand just swatted and he runs his tongue over it. His hands are on my cheeks. His breath waves down over my ass and grazes my folds.

The tremors echo all over my skin and I can't help myself. I bend more, push my ass higher. It's an invitation or maybe an order.

See. Eat. Fuck.

He slides two fingers between my folds, gliding them front and then back until the tingle becomes too much. My mouth flies open. I brace my palms against the cold granite and try to grind back but he removes his hand.

I groan. This guy is so frustrating. Screw this, I can relieve myself. I take a hand off the counter, only to find it trapped in his.

"Come here." His voice makes me jump.

But I'm obeying without question, pushing off the counter and looking back at him. My heart stumbles and crashes against my ribs. *Dear God.*

He's sunk to his knees, his cock is out, sheathed inside the condom and pushing straight up. My breath hitches. My inner thighs tremble. He pulls on my hand and I'm brain dead but my body knows what to do. I finish discarding my pants and slide down to my own knees, facing away from him. I back into his lap, impaling myself slow and measured, looking back into his eyes. His cock travels deeper and deeper, and my mouth opens wider and wider. His hips roll and I press my palms against the vinyl floor I'd spent an hour cleaning last night.

He moans but it's more like a, "Yum." Like he can taste me and it's so good. And God bless his cock. It's so big and it strokes the right way. The head is so fat and it rubs the exact spot.

And he goes there again, slow. And again.

"Faster," I rasp out.

His hands shoot to my waist, and off he goes, flicking his hips against mine, flesh slapping flesh. My world tilts and my vision blurs and everything implodes inside me. And I'm moaning, loud, like I never do.

He pounds faster, this time between hisses and moans. I'm feeling too much, each tap of his hips against the ripple of pleasure. He takes one hand off my hip and wraps it around my neck. I gasp and his index and middle fingers slip into my mouth. The same fingers he slid through my folds. The pulsing between my legs intensifies and I latch on those fingers with my lips, pressing my tongue to them.

He releases a strangled grunt. And then stills in a long sigh.

I'm limp, not even thinking as I let him drag me up, tilt my head and kiss my lips. He settles me on the floor and goes to dump the condom.

I should stand. Tell him I have to work. Send him on his merry way. But I just watch, like I'm high on something.

Oh good God. He dickmatized me. I need to get him the fuck out of here.

He drops to the floor and pulls me between his legs. This is a no-no but it's been so long since a man held me that I flip away common sense.

"I didn't see this coming," he says.

No shit. "God knows I didn't either." I try to get up but he holds on tighter.

"Stay."

I shake my head. "I have to go to work soon."

"Are you giving me the hit-it-and-quit-it cold shoulder?"

I laugh and then surprise myself by saying. "Not exactly."

"We're going to do this again, Sierra."

I shake my head again. "I have kids, Matt. I can't go meet you somewhere whenever you want and I don't bring men into my house." I wince because that's not true. I'm sitting here between his legs with no pants on. "I mean..."

"I know what you mean. You don't want to expose your kids. I respect that." His lips graze my ear, sending a hot shiver down my spine. "But we need to find a way. Unless you're good with leaving things here."

I can still feel him inside my walls, that magical stroke, those hands on my hips. I shake my head and I don't know if it's to say I'm not done or to tell him again that I can't. I want to feel like this, like I'm more than a cook, maid and driver to my kids. Like I'm a woman, not just a mom.

But things are kind of fucked right now. The last thing my kids need is to see me with a man who's not their father while they're dying to be with him. I can't do that to them. They're number one and most important. Even if I have to shove the woman into a box, I have to be their mother.

"Matt..."

He places a finger on my lips. "Don't say no. You need a distraction and so do I. Let's be each other's escape, even if it's just a couple of sweaty hours in the morning."

My insides quiver. Hours of this? That would be decadent. A treat. No messy commitment, and my kids don't have to see him. I need this...so much.

"Yes, but just this. That's all it can be..." My mouth hovers over his. "...and only in the mornings."

8

Sierra

The second we go through the school door, Emmi turns to her brother. "I'll see you later, Eddie." Then begins to walk away. "*Bendición?*"

She doesn't look at me, just asks for the blessing over her shoulder like a second thought.

Heat flushes over my neck and my teeth grind together. *No, she didn't.* I could let it go, but the hell I am.

"Emmi," I squeeze through my teeth. "Come here."

The door attendant shoots one look from me to my daughter, who's now walking back the five steps between us, and away. It's like she doesn't want to see what's about to transpire.

The defiant look on Emmi's face is offset by the wariness in her eyes. That's what ticks me off. She knows she did something wrong but she continues to try me. I'm not going to let her get to me.

I put my arms around her, give her a sound kiss on her soft cheek, and the customary blessing. "*Dios te bendiga, mi amor.* I love you. Have a wonderful day."

She steps back, eyes wide. Then smiles, really smiles, like my little *ride-or-die* chick who'd disappeared the day her father moved out of the apartment in the Bronx. "See you later, *Mami.*"

My chest inflates and I can't help but smile too. *That's my baby.* Maybe this is a step to things getting better. I turn to Eddie. "Let's go see the guidance counselor."

We walk through the hallway and I'm happier. My heels are clicking along the floor, competing with my son's fast chatter. "And that's the gym over there. Today we get to play kickball. I love kickball. I'm going to play with Michael and Ethan. You remember them, right, *Mami*?"

He's at that age where he repeats things. He doesn't stop talking about Ethan and Michael. He's had a couple of playdates with them. Their moms are the nicest ladies I've met here. I know where his gym is and we go to the park to play kickball with his aunt and uncle once a week. But I listen, smile, and nod. Because I love the sound of his voice and he talks to me. *Always.*

We step into the counselor's suite and are asked to wait in the sitting area.

"You smell good, *Mami*, like flowers," he says.

"Thank you, *mi amor.*" I put my arms around his shoulders. He's really the sweetest boy.

"And you look pretty too. You dressed up today."

"Well, we always dress up for meetings." But my smile falters because, yes, I make it a point to dress up for meetings with the school, but the perfume and the makeup and the heels are more for the meeting after than this one. I got ready this morning, specifically so Matt could peel these clothes off me. I want him to see me pretty and smelling good, as opposed to all raggedy like our last two times. I don't want him to think I've let myself go. I want him to kiss, smell, lick his way down my body while I'm wearing my pretty underwear. Just like he texted he would.

I can't wait to be with you.

I can't stop thinking about my morning escape.

I can almost hear his text messages in that deep voice of his. Heat shoots straight down between my legs and I'm ashamed of myself.

Here's my son being sweet, and then here I am, thinking like a straight-up *sucia*.

I'm wiping this make-up off my face before leaving the school, and putting on the flats in my car. I don't even know why I dressed up. It's not like we have the dress-up type of thing going. It's a fuck and see you in a couple of days kind of thing.

"Ms. Torres?" Ms. Lane smiles at me and I'm taken aback by her. Since when had counselors start dressing up like Ann Taylor mannequins and wearing fake lashes at eight in the morning? "Mrs. Foley will escort Eddie to class. Today, it will be just us."

Eddie hugs me. "*Bendición*?"

I hold him tight and give him my blessing, before I thank the secretary. He waves and disappears through the door with her.

I straighten up and follow Ms. Lane, wondering what Mrs. Lachey, my guidance counselor, who'd wore khaki pants and a polo, is doing these days.

She motions for me to sit across from her, then points in the direction of the suite. "This is the second time I've heard Eddie say that to you. I asked him, but he says that's just something you all do?"

I nod. "It's a cultural thing. You always ask your parents, aunts and uncles, and Godparents for a blessing when you greet them and when you're leaving their presence. The answer is always *God bless you*."

Her perfectly lined lips dissolve into a smile. "I love that."

We sit down and go through the preliminaries. "This is just a routine meeting to go over the children's progress. We want to talk to you about what we observed. Eddie is a kind, helpful and dedicated student. He works well with others in class and is always sharing things with his classmates. The teachers tell me he tries to give everyone his lunch all the time."

I smile. *That's my sweet boy*.

"He misses his dad a lot. Both of them do. Emmi is under the impression that they don't see him because of you."

My heart flops to my gut. "It's really not. I try but he…"

I shove my eyes closed and breathe. When I open them, she's staring at me.

Probably thinking how to document this.

Her eyes go warm. "Divorces are hard, Ms. Torres. We, as adults, understand. Children don't always. She sees you all the time but not him and he has a new family. That's causing some resentment because she thinks his new daughter is a replacement for her."

My stomach clenches and my hand shoots to press over it. *My poor baby.* In my head I'm on my feet, screaming what a motherfucking piece of shit Edwin is. I can't say any of it out loud because she will go and document that.

"Tell me what I can do. Please. She's always angry with me. I know she blames me but I call and ask him to come. I even offer to bring them up. It's never a good time for him."

Ms. Lane nods. "Unfortunately, that is not uncommon. It's also typical for the children to miss the other parent, even if he is not hands-on or is hardly ever present. You should take them to see someone. I can recommend a good family counselor."

"Yes, please. I'll do anything."

I go through the rest of the meeting with a knot in my throat that won't me breathe well.

Even the cool October air fails to break through my lungs. By the time I get to my house I'm worked up. The ten-minute screaming fit inside the car, with the windows up, did not help. No matter how many swear words I got to unleash. I had to fling my iPhone in my bag so I wouldn't call Edwin and tell him what a son of a goat he is. I have to remind myself that for a couple of hours I can put this on a shelf.

Release and relief are waiting for me.

But Matt's not here yet. His car is not in the usual spot. I jump out of the Range Rover, speed-walking in my heels on my way to the porch, only to stop dead in my tracks. There are flowers on the chair next to the door.

Matt.

Some Mornings

But what the fuck. Why would he bring me flowers? Oh my God, he came and left.

My shoulders sag and I want to cry. "I needed my escape today."

I pick up the flowers and go inside the house. I don't go past the foyer. I just stand there with my back against the wall and my nose pressed against the bouquet. I do love the scent of fresh roses and try to hang onto that.

I can't blame Matt for leaving. He worked all night and was most likely exhausted. *He never seems too exhausted to fuck, though.* I need to get over it. There's always the day after tomorrow. When he works night next.

I'll just go to work early and keep my mind occupied. I'll call Saona and tell her about the meeting. Yep, that's what I'll do.

The knock on the door makes my heart thump. I look into the peephole and all I can see is body and the stubble I would recognize anywhere. The one that deliciously scrapes over the skin of my thighs.

My body is thrumming and I'm tighter than guitar wire. I can almost taste him, feel him. I fling the door open and yank him inside. The roses are crushed between us as I pull him down to my mouth. Even with my heels, he's taller than me and I try to push myself up higher. I love his soapy smell. Did he just shower? Who cares? Every damned thing about him makes me so hot right now.

"Fuck me, Matt. I need you and I can't wait."

That's how I find myself bent over on the stairs and bracing on the third step. My ponytail is wrapped around his hand and my hips bounce back against his every slam.

He's pulling a bit too tight but I don't even care. Not when I'm so spread for his attention and he's ripping gasps from my throat.

This probably doesn't look pretty. It's dirty and primal. *Exactly how I need it.*

9

Matt

Damn, this woman can wear a pair of jeans. Those thighs, that ass, man, that waist. Skinny jeans are the most underrated invention in history. They get us, men, remembering the names of garments. Because everything inside them is so memorable.

Sierra looks up and smiles, more like smirks. She knows how good she looks. I'm happy to see the anxiety gone from her eyes. A couple of hours of hard fucking could take the stress off anyone. I'm feeling pretty liquid myself right now and not at all like the guy who'd spent the night canvasing an area after a homicide.

"Would you like some coffee?" she asks. "I set up the pot before I went to the school."

I nod and she sashays her way into the kitchen. Her hips sway a little more than usual, with a slight jiggle. That jiggle is what ass-men live and die for.

I stretch out my legs and press my back against her couch. There's not a thing out of place in her living room. Except the coffee table we pushed from the middle.

I won't fuck on my couch. My kids sit there.

Her words from the second time I came over still make me chuckle. Her mouth is so fresh, her attitude so hard, but it was kind of sweet. She's always thinking about them in some way or another. She's a good mom.

"What are you smiling at?" She's at the door with the mug in her hand.

"All your rules about sex in this house. We can do it on the living room rug or the kitchen floor but never on the furniture."

She laughs, makes her way to hand me the coffee and then drops on the floor next to me. She presses a kiss on my cheek. "Thank you for coming back."

"You're welcome?" I'm the one who should be thanking her, on my knees. These few hours with her did what neither coffee nor the shower after my shift could do. It helped me forget.

Forget the eyes of the young man who bled to death in a cold alleyway. I can't unsee the rats scurrying under the dumpsters while we canvased the crime scene. A scene way too familiar to me. I can't remember how many young kids I've seen lying dead in my lifetime. No one saw anything today. Just like no one saw anything twelve years ago. No one here ever sees anything.

"I'm serious." Sierra brings me back to her. "I really needed my escape today and thank you for the roses. But you know, you don't have to bring me something every time you come by. The pastries were okay last time since we ate them after, but...I'm clear as to what this is and I'm not expecting anything more."

And back to reality.

I sip and don't look at her. "Yes, I know. You've made it clear, Sierra. We're just about the fucking."

Damn, why did I say that?

She whips around to look at me. "Why are you getting mad? I'm just saying you don't have to bother with this."

She's letting you off the hook. Thank your lucky stars and go home, Hunter.

"I'm not mad. It is what it is but for the record, I never said it was a bother."

"I know you didn't. I'm just saving you the trouble. I mean, you already bring what I want." She strokes my thigh.

That should stir my dick but all it does is stoke my annoyance. *Time to go.* I put the mug on the coffee table and get up. My T-shirt is on the floor by the door. I go around her and grab it.

She snatches it from my hand. "What the hell is going on with you?"

"Nothing. All is good. This was good. I should be thanking you as well." I hold out my hand.

She frowns. "But you're not. You're sulking for God knows what reason."

I recoil like she doused me with iced water. "I don't sulk. Give me my shirt."

"Not until you tell me why you're so pissed off."

"I had a long night, Sierra. I just want to go home and sleep."

She shakes her head. "You weren't that tired just a minute ago. Shit, I bet I could've gotten another round out of you."

"What can I say? It hit me." *After you reminded me that my job here was done.*

She sighs. "Come, sit down."

I shake my head. "No. You have to go to work, remember?"

She pats the floor next to her. "Sit."

I drop down next to her. "Can you at least give me my shirt?"

She stares at my chest and flings it across the room. "I want to ogle you some more."

My lips twitch no matter how hard I fight it. "You want me for my body."

She drops a hand on my bare stomach. "It's just so big and hot. There's just so much of you." Her fingers trail up my torso. "Tell me why you're mad."

My stomach tightens, the muscles flexing under her digits. I can't tell her what I don't know. *Why am I mad?* She's sticking to the plan. Every man knows that's fucking ideal. We've all dealt with a casual date that turns clingy. I have the opposite.

I reach for her hair. "It's nothing. I really am tired. It was a long night at work."

Her forehead wrinkles deeply. She's not buying it. "What happened? Did you have a bad case?"

I shove the boy's lifeless eyes and the images of those who knew nothing away. I tug on her ponytail. "You don't want to know."

She leans until her nose touches mine. "I do. You listen to me ramble about my kid issues all the time."

I can tell her about my seven o'clock case, but public urination is not something anyone gets worked up about and I don't want to lie to her. Even if she just reminded me that we're just fucking.

"A kid got killed in an alley downtown last night."

Her mouth falls open. "That was *your* case? I saw it on the news this morning."

I nod. "Yeah, we got called to the scene around nine last night. Didn't leave until about three in the morning."

Her hand splays on my chest, her face is closer. "I'm sorry."

I swallow and shrug it off. "It's part of the job."

"Still awful. How old was he?"

"Seventeen. His mom is a teacher."

She presses a hand to her chest. "Jesus. That's horrible. His poor family."

The breath halts in my throat. *Yeah, poor family*. They'll have to bury him. Live without him and with the pain that they couldn't save him no matter how hard they tried. And it will destroy them. That's what gang life does.

"Matt." Sierra's hand goes to my face.

I stare into her big dark eyes, into her strained gaze, and my pulse sets off in my throat. I take her wrist in my hand. It would be easy to tell her everything and have her say nice things like she used to when I got suspended and my mom gave me hell. But we're not sixteen anymore and that would overstep what we have. I don't need to ruin her day with this kind of thing, anyway.

I kiss her hand and release it. "I'm okay, but we should get going."

She moves aside, way too fast, and we both get on our feet. I stride across the room to grab my T-shirt and shrug it on, along with the weight of her gaze. Sleep will clear my head.

She follows me to the door. "I'll walk out with you."

I was hoping for a clean break but stand around as she opens the closet by the door and pulls out a leather jacket.

I take it from her hands and hold it out for her. "Leather? It's October. Can you be any more New York?"

She smiles over her shoulder, tilting her head. Her face is so close, I can feel her breath on my chin. I could kiss her if I wanted to.

And I want to.

But I step back.

Her gaze drops to the floor and shit if this is not weird.

I hold the door for her and we step outside. The breeze coats me in her flowery scent and makes her ponytail sway as she locks the door. I really love that ponytail.

"You forgot the top deadbolt," I remind her.

She nods and locks it but doesn't look at me. I've made her uncomfortable or upset or both. That's not what I want at all.

"Don't be mad at me for overstepping, but you smell delicious. Whatever it is you're wearing, it's really nice."

She tucks an errant strand of hair behind her ear. "Thank you."

"And you look beautiful, Sierra. I didn't say this before because I didn't get a chance."

The impish smile is so her. "Yeah, I kind of jumped you." We stand on the porch, staring at each other. "Matt, I'm sorry. I know it pissed you off when I said you didn't have to bring me flowers. I didn't want to make it weird. I just wanted you to know I don't have expectations—"

I put my fingers over her lips. "There's one expectation that you should always have. I'll always treat you with respect because we were friends. We *are* friends. Just because we're sleeping together doesn't erase the time you sat by the bleachers when the cops were after Wally. It doesn't erase the afternoon you held my hand in the hospital when Ryan got jumped as part of the gang initiation. I don't forget those things. I never will. So, no. I'm never going to treat you just like any other pussy I'm pounding. I'm going to treat you like so much more."

I kiss her cheek and walk away. The two minutes it takes her to get into the car and drive away are long and heavy.

I said too much *because I stayed too long*. I need to put more distance between us so this doesn't happen again.

10

Sierra

I wish Matt had not said those things at the door. I keep thinking about them. They've been with me through the work hours, the wait in the car line to pick up the kids, even as I made dinner and prayed that the kids' call with Edwin went well.

It didn't. Emmi is back to giving me the side eye. Eddie didn't eat all his dinner and asked to go to bed early. He doesn't have a fever or cough so I don't worry. We go through his prayers and I lie down in bed next to him until he falls asleep. My mind is on the porch, on that conversation I shouldn't be thinking about. On the friendship we had. On the seven minutes in heaven I can't forget and the naked hours together that change the way I see my days. On whatever this is turning out to be...

I don't think Matt told me the truth, at least not all of it. He didn't text me all day yesterday or today. Which wouldn't be a problem if I weren't used to him texting me throughout the day. Why did I follow him up with the texting? I should've kept my distance, kept to the morning fucking. I wouldn't be in this fucking antsy predicament.

My sister is done with Emmi's braid when I go into her room. "Look at this superstar."

I go sit on the other side of the bed. "You're going to look so beautiful tomorrow in the dress *Abuela* sent you."

Emmi's cheeks darken, making her cinnamon skin glow. "Thanks, *Mami*."

I live for these glimpses of her. When she looks at me like I'm not the enemy. Like she used to before things changed. I go find her bonnet and stay with her for fifteen minutes. That's all she allows me anymore. It's a good, day though. I've gotten a smile out of her.

Downstairs, Saona goes to the fridge and pulls out the lemons and puts them next to the rum she brought over. "*Punta Cana,* for the win."

It's been our new favorite since our last trip to the Dominican Republic.

I pull out the tumblers. "I'm ready for it."

Her smile, so much like my Emmi's, triggers my own. "You should be at the bar, flirting with your man."

She shakes her head. "It's always busy there lately and Juan is helping him. They don't need me."

I tsk-tsk. "Jax would be so mad if he heard you. Oh, by the way, the insurance paid off. I should be able to pick up a car this week and give you yours back. I'm going to miss her, though. She's a honey."

She squeezes the lemon into the tumblers and adds ice. "You can keep her for longer. Jax and I can manage. And don't forget my job pays for my Uber rides."

I shake my head. "I don't want to get used to her. She's so fancy." Her Range Rover is a freaking dream. If I can find an older model, on my budget, I would snap it up in a second.

We go sit in my living room. The post-season Yankees game is on in the background. She sits cross-legged as she used to when we were growing up. The way she did when she wanted me to tell her about the boys I hung out with or show her the clothes I bought and Mami never got to see.

She takes a sip of the rum and shakes like she got a chill. "Sooo good. I've been waiting for this conversation all day."

"Sad fact? Me too."

She frowns. "Why sad fact? It's good, right?"

My body heats with images of yesterday morning. How I had to brace myself against the banister, because of how hard I'd come. I'm pretty sure my nails are still imprinted on his back. "It's really good."

Her palms flip up. My daughter gets way too many mannerisms from Saona.

"He's different."

"How so?"

I shrug. "I dunno. Maybe I'm weird. I had a booty call for a while and there are rules. José and I didn't talk about our lives, the kids or the side-chicks he had all over the city. I would go to the Heights, get my dick and a 'see you when I see you.'"

"So, you and Matt talk? Before or after?"

"Both."

She takes another sip and stares at me. "Why does that bug you? There's nothing wrong with it?"

I sigh. "Because it's not normal. We're not dating each other but here we are making conversation. I told him he didn't need to get me flowers and he got pissy. And the most fucked up shit of all, I've been in my feelings all day because he was holding something back."

I don't tell her how my heart races whenever my text notifications ping, only to get disappointed when it's not him. I can't tell her, or anyone, that. Sierra Torres doesn't do that kind of shit. I'm the one that does the brush off.

"Flowers and conversation, but you're not dating? Wait, don't tell me, are you cuddling too?"

My mind goes straight to our after-moments when I am sitting between his legs in the kitchen or getting spooned on the living room rug. The flush starts at my neck and geysers over my face.

"Oh." Saona's smile is so wide.

Shit.

"Stop smiling like that. This is not a good thing."

"Why not? You're single. So is he. Neither of you is hurting anyone, and he is a nice guy because he's bringing you flowers and talking and not just trying to dip it and bounce."

Some Mornings

"He *is* a nice guy but I wish he wasn't. I can't entertain this kind of thing right now. The kids are hurt and confused as it is. Especially Emmi. What kind of message would I be sending her, introducing her to some new strange guy?"

"That you're a woman and a human. *And*...he's not a stranger. You guys were friends a long time ago—" She looks down at her phone and smiles.

She always gets giddy when Jax texts her. She grabs her iPhone and texts back.

I side eye my phone and tap the screen. One message, from our relatives group chat. Nothing else.

This sucks.

"What was I saying?" my sister asks, then waves her hand. "I forgot. Anyway, just go with it. Enjoy it and don't complicate things by overthinking and trying to get him to be an asshole like all the other ones you knew before."

It makes sense but I can't help but think this is going to get more complicated. It's been a day since he texted and my hand is itching to break my hard-and-fast rule against texting first.

I don't do that. *Ever.*

I'm still thinking about it after Jax picks her up to go home. My phone is on the shelf when I shower, after I wash my face and moisturize. In my hand as I check on the kids one last time. No messages.

I tiptoe out of Emmi's room and turn toward Eddie's. I find him at the door. He's rubbing his eyes with one hand, his Spiderman pajama top hiked over his belly.

"*Mami*, can I sleep with you?"

I smile and hold out my hand. I can't talk or he'll never go to sleep. I turn off the hallway light and we climb in my bed. The late-night news is playing on the TV and I put my phone next to my head on the pillow. He snuggles to me and I kiss his forehead. It's cool, so I know he doesn't have a fever.

His fingers scrape lightly over my arm, like he's done since he was a baby. He does it whenever he sleeps with me. His breath evens after a while. I hear all sorts of awful situations going on in the city. The repeated sentence of the night is: Police were called to X block of Y street. Is Matt on any of those calls? I hope he's okay.

When my phone vibrates, I grab it quickly so it doesn't wake my son.

Matt.

The fluttering in my belly is instant. So is the quick catch in my breath. And that makes me mad. I'm not that girl. I don't think about a guy all day or worry because he shut me out or because it's been thirty-seven hours and fifteen minutes since I last heard from him.

I unlock the phone and read the message.

Can I see you tomorrow?

My heart thuds because yeah, he wants to fuck and God, I want to see him. But this is going too far. I never missed or worried about José's calls or texts. I'm not going to start now. This is not that deep. I'll answer tomorrow.

I flip the phone away and stare at the TV. *Cirque du Soleil* is in town. I'll buy tickets for me, the kids, my sister and Jax.

Eddie's head moves around. He's restless. I stroke his forehead until he stills.

And this is why I can't have anything complicated in my life. I wouldn't be able to do this, to hold my little man or let him sleep with me. The thing with Matt is nothing but a good time in the morning. Nothing more.

11

Matt

Sure.

I stare at the word. It stands out from the ones below. Sierra sent that one-word answer around six in the morning. Six hours after I sent my text and an hour before I got off work. So I stayed extra time, filled out the nightly reports and ignored Wicker's raised eyebrow. At eight thirty, she sent another saying to meet her here around nine because she has an errand to run after she drops the kids off at school.

Now I've been sitting here, like the chump Wally always says I am, staring between the word and her door. "Sure" makes me feel anything but. She's most likely pissed I haven't called in two days. I know how this works. I've had girlfriends before. Calls and texts are important. They're a requirement.

Not that she's my girlfriend. She's far from it. She doesn't even want me treating her decent.

And you said things you shouldn't have.
And you left the ball in her court.
And she didn't call either.

By late last night, I couldn't wait anymore. I had to know what she was thinking. I had to make a date to see her.

Her answer came in the morning and so did a little relief. Until she said nothing else. She works at eleven, so that gives us less than two hours together.

The white Range Rover comes flying down the street at twenty-after-nine and pulls up into the driveway. She needs to stop speeding.

I step out of my car as the back of hers lifts. She comes around in her yoga pants and matching jacket, looking like one of those athletic wear ads on Instagram.

"Hey, sorry. I took advantage because I was right there and hit the supermarket." She climbs on her toes and kisses my cheek.

"It's okay."

I grab the four bags and she hurries to open the door and hold it for me. "Thank you."

In the kitchen, she works fast, putting everything away. I sit by the counter, watching, waiting.

"Were you waiting for long?"

"I got here at eight-thirty." She opens her mouth, her intention to apologize all but clear. I hold up a hand. "But don't feel bad. I had to have a long talk with Hayden, my niece, about the stuff she posts on social media."

She stops, absently rolling a garbage bag into a ball. "That's right! Wally's little girl. I still can't believe your crazy ass brother is a daddy."

I smile through the pang in my belly. "Daddy" is a loose word here and both my brothers were always crazy. She just doesn't know how much. She doesn't have to know either. "Hayden is the reason I have an Instagram and a Snapchat account. I monitor what she posts daily to make sure she doesn't get in trouble. Also because if you want to really know what your kids are up to, you look at their social media."

"Oh," she says with her pretty mouth in the surprised shape of a parent who realizes social media is in her future.

"You have no worries yet. Your kids are pretty young." I need to get her off this conversation. I don't want her to ask more questions.

Her face is scrunched up. "Yeah, but they have iPads. I monitor them but it won't be long 'til they ask."

God, she's pretty.

"Come here, Sierra."

She blinks a couple of times but then her gaze drops to the floor. She puts the bag she's holding in a drawer and comes around the counter. Her head is high as she stands between my legs, the rosy scent in my nostrils, her hands reaching for my face.

And my chest shrinks. As hard as my dick is, I can't get through my head...

Her mouth swoops over mine, her tongue slipping between my lips. And I forgot what I was going to say. I press her to me. I need to feel her tits against my chest and her ass in my hands. I hoist her onto my lap. Her yelp is short-lived because she starts grinding against me.

"I love it when you're on top. I want you to ride my—"

A phone goes off. We don't acknowledge it and it keeps ringing. I'm feeling my way down her chest, trying to pull her zipper down. She's fucking my mouth with her tongue, begging me to hurry up.

"Ms. Torres, this is Mrs. Foley from Catonsville Heights Elementary—"

That's her kid's school.

She flies off my lap, runs around the counter and grabs the phone. "I'm here."

Her breath is choppy and I'm amazed at how fast she moves and how she can even talk. I'm still catching my breath and flipping my palm, trying to ask her what's up.

Her eyes are moving around the room and she beelines for the other end of the counter and grabs her purse. "I'll be right there to get him. Thank you for calling. I'm sorry it took me so long to answer."

As she hangs up and looks at me, there's an apologetic look in her eye. "Eddie's sick. I should have known something was wrong when he didn't eat much last night."

"I'm sure he didn't look that bad or you wouldn't have dropped him off."

She shakes her head. "He didn't have a temperature and he was dying to go to school today. They both were. I should have known."

"If he didn't look sick or feel warm, how could you?" I don't understand why she's blaming herself. Then again, I don't have kids.

She looks away for a second and then back at me. "I'm sorry. Can we raincheck? Maybe tomorrow before your shift…"

Her lips press together and I try not to latch on to the fact that she knows my schedule by heart.

I nod. "Let me know if you or Eddie need anything."

She gives me a smile as we walk to the door. I help her into the car and linger, wanting to ask her if she needs me to come with her. She waves and drives away. I make my way to my car slower than usual. Maybe I should hang around. What if she needs help getting him into the house?

Her kids don't know you and she wouldn't want that anyway.

I get in the Camaro and drive home. I'll text her to check on Eddie. There's a text message from Hayden.

It's just a pic. People are the ones making it dirty.

I loosen my grip on the steering wheel or I'm going to yank it out. Kids are so fucking dumb sometimes. What part of she's fifteen and shouldn't be posting photos of her naked back doesn't she get? Why do I need to explain every two months that there are perverts who target young girls?

I don't have time for this.

Tomorrow's Ryan's anniversary. I'm going to the cemetery in the morning and then I'll go see Sierra. Maybe I can convince her to have lunch with me before I go see Wally in the afternoon. She can be the break between fucked-up traditions.

Maybe this is a blessing because I'll need her to take my mind off everything tomorrow.

There are six text messages from Hayden by the time I get home.

Society puts women in boxes and we need to break with those norms.

I should be able to express myself in the way I want to.

No one has the right to judge me because of what I wear or don't.

I stop at the third and dial her number. I don't let her speak. "You are right. No one has the right to judge you by what you wear. Society is misogynistic and fucked up but my job is to protect you from pervs out there who could harm you. Also, I want you to get into a good college and I don't want people to use what you post to harm you. I also don't want to block all your phone privileges. Now, either you delete the photo right now or I'll have a techie wipe your phone and LoJack your number."

All of which is illegal and I'm not really going to do, but she doesn't need to know that.

"You're worse than a dictator." She hangs up the phone.

But the image is gone. In its place there's a new post. She's sharing some quote about despots who fear freedom.

I text Sierra, asking her about Eddie.

She sends a medical mask emoji and a baby one, along with a teary face.

He has a little fever but I gave him meds and he's resting. Thxs for asking.

I tell her to let me know if she needs anything.

She sends me a kissy face emoji.

Tomorrow, I'll tell her where I want those kisses.

12

Matt

I gunned it here at eighty-five, my Camaro roaring like a beast. Like I can't scream. My skin is jittery as fuck as I open the door to my car. I hang back and breathe.

Go home. You have no right making her part of this shit.

But I can't because today, like every October twenty-second, I'm back to twelve years ago. To the same nightmare that keeps destroying our lives. Every step I walked to Ryan's tomb is the same. An abomination. Eighteen-year-old boys don't belong in graves. They shouldn't die for senseless shit. They shouldn't inspire more death, more waste of lives. They shouldn't leave broken families and babies without their fathers.

I push it away, push out of the car, push my feet through Sierra's driveway, go around the white truck. The air brushes over my uniform. I won't have time to go home and change after I head to visit Wally, so I'll be wearing it all day.

I take the three steps up to her house in a single jump. I take two breaths at the door. I don't need to scare her to death.

Shit, I forgot the cookies for her and her kids on the counter.

I knock on the door and it takes her a couple of minutes to open.

Some Mornings

When it does, I can't believe what I see. She's in her robe with her hair half on her face. Her skin is a pallid mixture and her eyes are sunken.

"Oh, man. I forgot to call you. I'm sick." Her voice is croaky.

I nod. "Yeah, I can see that."

She leans on the door frame, like she can barely hold her own weight. I reach out to touch her face and it's hot. I open my mouth but a little head pops out from under her arm to stare at me. He's got her eyes and pretty skin. My breath halts and my gaze flies from his to hers.

"*Mami*, we have to go. We're already super late," a little girl's voice says behind her.

Ah, shit. Her kids are here.

"I have to take them to school. I'm running late," she says.

"*Mami*, are you getting arrested?" the little boy asks.

What?

"No, baby. This is my friend, Officer Hunter."

I look down at my uniform and try not to laugh. "You must be Eddie. Nice to meet you."

I offer my hand and he shakes it, offering a little smile. Little kids love cops. It's why I love going to the schools to talk to them. A little girl comes to stand next to him. I'm taken aback by how much she looks like her mother.

"And you must be Emmi." I offer my hand to her too.

She nods and shakes it. "Nice to meet you." Then she turns to her mom. "*Mami*..."

Sierra shoots me an apologetic look. "I'm sorry, Matt. I really have to take them. They have a school party they can't miss."

She looks shaky and glassy eyed.

I move closer. "You can't drive like that."

"I have to."

"Give me your keys. I'll run the kids over to the school."

She shakes her head but it's Emmi who speaks. "But you're a stranger..."

"You're very smart, Emmi. You should never go anywhere with

someone you just met, but your mom has known me since we were kids. And I'm a police officer. You see this?" I point to the badge on my shirt. "This is my badge and it lets people know I'm one of the good guys. I'm here to serve and protect. Right now, your mom is in no condition to get behind the wheel so I'm going to take her car and drive you. I don't want you to miss your party. Would you let me?"

She looks from my face to her mom's smiling face. Sierra nods at her.

"Okay," Emmi says. "Eddie, come get your book bag."

"You don't have to do this. I can call an Uber."

"It's fine. You go call the school and tell them I'm dropping them off. Give them my badge number." *Because you'll still worry and I get it.*

The kids hug her and there are some Spanish words exchanged. Something about blessings.

At the bottom of the steps, Eddie turns around and yells, "I'm sorry I got you sick."

She's still leaning against the door frame as I help them into the back seat and when we drive away.

"You and my mom have been friends for a long time. How come we never heard of you?" Emmi's tone is the same as Wicker's when we're questioning someone and she smells bullshit coming out of the suspect's mouth.

Shit. How do I even explain this without stepping on Sierra's toes? I go with a modified version of the truth. "I used to live in the Bronx when we were kids and we saw each other again when her car was stolen."

"Yea, *Baby* got stolen but *Mami* said we are getting another car this week. This is *Titi* Saona's car. I like it a lot but *Mami* says we can't keep it."

"This is a really nice car, Eddie. I'm sure your mom's next car will be too."

"How come you came to the house?" Emmi asks like the junior detective she apparently is.

"I came to check on your mom. I'm glad I did." I look in the rearview and she's staring right at me. *Good God, she is her mother's child.*

"Are you going to come back for us?"

Shit, what do I say? "I'm going back to make sure your mom is comfortable and if she's still not well by then, I'll pick you up."

"Thank you, because *Titi* Saona is working in New York until tomorrow." Then she nods and looks out the window.

I've never been so happy to see a school in my life. I don't mind answering children's questions, but I don't know what Sierra would want me to tell them.

Mrs. Foley meets us at the door. I tell her I may be back later since I'm not on the list to pick them up but that Sierra will call them.

"That's Officer Hunter. He's our friend," Eddie tells the secretary as they walk away.

I smile and linger until a car behind me honks the horn.

I make it back to Sierra's house in five minutes. I knock and the door flies open. She never moved from the spot and she's clutching her phone tight in her hand like she expected something to go wrong. I should be offended but I can't be. She's protective of her kids. *As all moms should be.*

"Everything went well?"

"Emmi questioned me like I was a perp caught on the make, and Eddie rambled and then told the secretary that I'm a friend."

Her chuckle is so lackluster it's almost pitiful.

I hook a hand under her arm and guide her toward the stairs. "Come on, let's take you to bed."

"You don't have to do this, Matt. It's sweet you took the kids to school but I don't want to impose and I don't want you to catch this."

I measure my words. "Yeah, you look like a walker on *The Walking Dead* but I cleared my schedule for a few hours to be with you. So I'm going to do just that." I lean closer to her ear. "In case you get better…"

She laughs. "That's a pipe dream."

"Who are you to judge my dreams, walker?" At the top of the stairs, she points me to her bedroom.

Her bed is rumpled but other than that, everything is neat and in place like the rest of the house. Like the bedroom she used to share with her sister back in the day. This one doesn't have posters of Jared Leto and Ricky Martin or stuffed animals on the dresser. There are area rugs, magazine-style curtains, and art on the walls.

I can't keep my gaze off the wooden headboard I would definitely fuck her against. "Your bedroom is nice." I help her onto the bed. "Do you have medicine?"

She nods and points to the door on the other side of the room. It's the bathroom, all white like the kitchen. I open her medicine cabinet and grab the Theraflu. I check the expiration date and it has two good months. I pour the measure into the cup and hand it to her. When she's done, I leave it on the nightstand.

She grabs the remote from the nightstand on the other side and hands it to me. "I'm going to knock out for a bit and don't want you to be bored. You can lie on the bed."

I don't know if it's because she's sick, but she's way too mellow when we've broken so many rules today. I've never been to her bedroom before. Not only did I meet her kids but she let them be alone in a car with me.

I take off my service shirt and drape it over a chair and then shrug my shoes off and place them under the chair. I climb on the bed next to her and put my phone on the nightstand beside me. Her lashes flutter and it won't be long until she goes to sleep. I flip around the channels and land on *Dead Pool,* setting down the remote between us.

Her hand wraps around my wrist. "Thank you."

Her breath evens out faster than I expected. I close my eyes and wake up to my vibrating phone.

It's a text from Hayden.

Dad's in solitary confinement.

Every year, this is the day from hell.

13

Sierra

Cold medicine always gives me nasty sleep. I think I'm awake for hours but I'm dreaming and end up waking up with a mixture of exhaustion and overstimulation. Matt's voice pulls me out of the fog. I can hear it in my crazy sleep trance. He's in my bed with his back to me, whispering.

"Honey, I'm sorry. I wish I could find a way to make this better for you. It shouldn't be like this." His back stiffens and the hand on the bed bunches into a fist. "Please don't cry, sweetheart. Don't get like that."

His voice is soft and pained. Whoever that is must be important to him.

There's a burn in my chest that has nothing to do with the cold or the Theraflu or the overstimulation. Who is he talking to? Who is this woman? Not that it's any of my business, but I borderline hate her already.

"Sweetheart, listen to me. You're not responsible for what he does. I know you're disappointed, but you'll get to talk to him again soon. This doesn't last but for a few days."

I hold my breath and try to focus but I can't make out what is being said on the other side. All I can tell is, whoever this woman is, she's bawling and talking at the same time.

"Okay, I understand. I'll call to check on you later." He pauses, running a hand through his hair. "Hayden? Love you, sweetheart. Your dad does too. He's just...talk to you tonight."

Hayden? His niece.

The air flows out of my body in a way that has me stiffening and him turning around. Our eyes meet for a brief moment but he looks away.

"I'm sorry. I didn't mean to wake you."

I shake my head, trying to push away the shame of getting caught listening...and catching feelings. "You didn't. Cold medicine always does a number on me. I don't sleep for long after taking it. Is your niece okay?"

His lips curve but it's more a grimace than a smile. "Yeah."

"What's going on with your brother?"

"You know. Shit here and there." His head bobs upside down. "Let me get you some juice and something to eat."

He tries to push off the bed but I'm not letting it go this time. I grab on to his wrist.

"Matt, you met my kids today. I trusted you to drive them to school. I trust you to lie in my bed as I'm sleeping medicated. This is the third time your brothers' names have come up and you've tried to dodge my questions. I think it's your turn to trust me."

He stares at my hand for a bit, like he's considering yanking his arm free but he leans back against the headboard. "Today is the anniversary of Ryan's death."

My heart drops. *Ryan's dead?* I gasp. "When? How?"

"Thirteen years ago. I'll tell you from the beginning because what you heard just now is part of it. The reason we had to leave the Bronx in the middle of the night so many years ago is because Ryan got into it with one of the Crows gang members. He stabbed the kid in a fight. My mom was worried that they were going to come after us, so we had to leave and we couldn't tell anyone. We came down to live with my aunt in Dundalk."

His family had disappeared one day. No one knew why. "No wonder we never heard from you again."

He nods. "I wanted to climb the fire escape that night to say goodbye but my mom said no. When we got here, her boyfriend back then told us not to contact anyone because it was too dangerous for Ryan and us. Wally already had Hayden. His girlfriend moved down too. All of us kept the no contact rule. Ironically, it was Ryan that broke it. He contacted his girlfriend. She blabbed. Two of the Crows came down here and waited for him when he got out of work at a restaurant downtown. They killed him in the alley behind his job."

"Oh my God." I sit up with my hand tighter around his wrist.

"Wally found out where they were, went there and killed both of them. He's serving a life sentence. I go see him every two weeks but on October twenty-second every year, we spend time together no matter what day of the week it is. Except today, because he's in solitary confinement."

He's calm, speaking matter-of-factly, as if it's not the story of his family he's telling. As if his eyes don't look a million miles away. And that's what breaks my heart and builds a knot in my throat. He lost his brothers. I don't know where I would be without my sister. We got through our father's death together and each other's shit-show marriages. He's had to live all these years without his.

"I'm so sorry." I scoot closer, my hands moving up his arm. "That had to be so hard for you and your mom. Where is she now?"

He looks away to the window. "She's gone."

My heart drops into my stomach and the pain is physical and fast. I wrap my arms around him. "Oh, Matt."

His arms stay at his side but I hug him tighter. He needs it and maybe I need it.

And then he crushes me against him. "I'm tired. I'm so tired of this. He's not learning or maturing. He just keeps getting worse."

"Wally?"

He nods against my head. "I don't judge him. I would've gone with him to kill them. I was that angry."

I'm rubbing his back up and down. "But you didn't."

"Because of my mom. She held onto me so tightly and told me she wasn't going to lose me too. She knew who Wally was. She loved him and went to see him every chance she could until she got sick and died. But she always said, 'I know who he is.' She couldn't stop him from doing what he was going to do."

My heart is breaking for her all over again. These were her babies and she'd lost one to death and the other to the system. I would've held onto Matt too.

"And I know too, Sierra. I keep waiting for him to start doing better, try to make something of himself in there. To be an example for Hayden and Ryan's daughter."

I pull back to look at him. "Ryan's daughter?"

"The girlfriend he had here was pregnant. We found out at the funeral. Her name is RyanAnne. She lives in North Carolina with her mom." The smile comes through in his voice.

"And you help out with her like you do with Hayden." He doesn't have to tell me these things. I just know them.

"She's my niece. I can't do anything for my brothers but I'll do whatever I can for the girls to have better lives." His voice is soft but there's so much emotion in those eyes, such sincerity.

"I'm glad your mom held you and kept you from going anywhere. I bet my life she was proud of the man you became."

"She was. I decided to become a police officer because of the ones working my brother's murder case. They asked questions and people swore they didn't see or hear anything. That's what set Wally off. But the officers kept asking. They would check on us. They came to the house to talk to us when Wally got arrested. Sgt. Mason asked me to walk outside with him. He said he didn't want to see me end up like either of my brothers. That I needed to choose the life I wanted and choose it carefully."

His eyes are dry, and if his heartbeat wasn't pummeling my chest and his hands holding me like he would a raft, I would think this was an easy conversation.

"You're a good man. You're always respectful and good. You chose well, Matt."

His jaw drops and his eyes well. "Your mom was right back then. I was a hoodlum. It could easily have been me instead of Ryan and Wally."

I shake my head. "You did dumb shit, like we all did back then. But you never hurt people, not even the girls who used to follow you around like lost puppies."

He chuckles. "That was never you. You liked the hardcore boys like José."

How did we get here?

"José was there. He was a way for me to torture my mom, but we didn't talk. He doesn't know how to hold a conversation. I liked hanging with you on the roof or the fire escape lots more. We talked about all kinds of stuff and you weren't always trying to grab my boobs. I was heartbroken when you disappeared. It was right after Angie Navarro's party. I thought things were heading somewhere different with us after that day…after the spin-the-bottle game."

He frowns and I can tell he doesn't believe me.

I continue. "I rigged the bottle. I wanted those seven minutes in the closet with you."

"What?" his eyes are big as saucers.

I shrug. "I had it bad for you then."

He shakes his head. "You did not."

"I did. I always wore lipstick around you and made sure to push my chest out. It was taking you too long to make a move. I had to do something…"

"Damn," he says, and we laugh.

"I always liked bad boys, but neither José nor my ex-husband would have done what you did today. None would have taken my kids to school and understood how much I would worry. None would have taken care of me. You chose well Matt and, without meaning to, this time, so did I."

A unicorn may have flown out of my mouth because he's staring at me like he can't believe me. "What are you saying?"

I swallow, because I'm about to put myself way out there, and I don't ever take this kind of first step. "I'm glad you met my kids today, and if you want to, I want you to come back for dinner, on a day I'm not dying. I want them to get to know you better. *I* want to get to know you better."

14

Sierra

My sister's gaze is frozen on me and her hand completely misses the shelf. The bourbon tumbler slips from her fingers and crashes to the floor.

She doesn't bat an eyelash. "I'm sorry. I think I heard you wrong."

I grab the short broom and dustpan we keep next to the garbage can behind the counter. "I said what I said."

Saona doesn't try to move, even as I sweep around her feet. "Sisi, you're going to let him take you and the kids to Cirque and dinner. Tonight?"

I nod. "I was going to buy the tickets and take you. I mentioned it to him and he said he would do it and take us to dinner after. So, we're dumping you."

She shakes her head. "I'm...quite okay with that. I just need to know more."

I shrug and proceed to sweep the glass.

She sidesteps the glass to loom over me. "*Now*, Sierra. It's bad enough that I had to find out about the kids meeting him through Eddie almost two weeks later. Thank God for his little blabber mouth. I can't believe you kept this development from me for so long."

I lift my head up and she's wearing her serious face. I laugh. She's been a bit short the past couple of days. "He was so sweet when I got sick. He took the kids to school and came back to take care of me."

She smiles. "He's a good guy. He always was, underneath all that crazy Dare-Me-Matt shit he used to do."

"He is but how do you know that?"

She dips her head. "Because he always listened to you, and you guys talked about all kinds of stuff. He wasn't just talking about your boobs and asking you to let him feel them."

My mouth falls open and my brain falls down the hall into the past. Saona was always so still, studying with her headphones on. "I knew you were listening."

Her fingers press to her mouth. "I wanted to learn what to do with guys. Fat lot of good it did me."

I laugh. "You didn't need any of that. You had so many guys after you. You were just married to the books."

"Eh. Anyway, did you tell the kids you are going with him?"

"I…did. I've been preparing them, little by little. Two days ago, I told them we were going out with my friend Matt. Eddie was excited, asked me if Matt was going to wear his cop uniform"—I shake my head—"Emmi was another thing. Like the twenty-one-year-old she is internally, she asked if Matt is my new boyfriend and informed me that she's not going to call him Daddy. Ever."

Saona's mouth falls open. "She's so damned smart. What did you tell her?"

Pride explodes over my chest because, *yeah, that's my smart girl*, but then my chest constricts just like it did when she asked. "I told her that we are friends getting to know each other more. That we're just hanging out for now. It won't be long until she starts asking more questions, though."

"I believe it. But…if you've taken this step…he's a good guy and there's nothing wrong with you both continuing to get to know each other."

"*Saona*, you're getting way ahead of yourself. I like him and he's a good guy and I am willing to hang out in public, but—"

She shakes her finger at me. "Don't *Saona* me in that tone. You introduced him to them and you're going to dinner. There are natural progressions to things and, like you once told me, he seems a come-correct kind of guy."

The stirring in my chest is unbearable and I try to cover it from her and from me by rolling my eyes but it's there, intensifying. I was impulsive when I set this up. Stupid heart and feelings drove me. "I'm scared, *Manita*."

"Why? It's a good thing. You're trusting someone, which, let's be honest, you have not done in years. You trust guys to get in bed but not with the things that really matter."

I nod. She has never been more accurate than in this moment. "But why do I feel like I'm on the verge of throwing up?"

She smiles. "Because it's a big leap. They're your babies and you're the most awesome mom in the world."

I scoff. "I am not. Granted, my goal is to do seventy-five percent different than what our mother did, but awesome mom? Nah."

"Shut up, you are. You put those kids ahead of anything and anyone. Which is why I was so surprised when he got to drive them to school."

I chuckle. "I didn't want to but I was sick as hell. He didn't give me a choice. But you know what? He's so correct with everything. He had me call the school with his badge number."

She pulls out the garbage can so I can dump the glass. "Everything happens for a reason. You needed a push and the universe gave it to you. I wish you had told us you were sick but I'm glad he was there."

"I didn't want to put that on Jax. You were out of town and the guy is running himself ragged. I didn't want to add that to his schedule."

She shakes her head. "You know he would have gone anyway, right? He's like *Papi*, family first."

"And that's why I didn't call. He worked late the night before. He always does when you're not around to take him home."

She leans against the bar. "Yeah, that's one reason why I told corporate this week that I want to start limiting the trips back and forth to once a month, starting in December."

"Oh, good. I'm glad. I bet Jax is excited about that."

"He is excited." Her hand drifts to her belly and her smile widens. The light makes her cheeks glow into a pretty shade.

My heart flips. *She's pregnant.* I take a breath because I need to let her tell me. "What's the other reason?"

She laughs. "You know already. It's all over your face."

I drop the damned broom and throw my arms around her. "Holy shit, you're going to be a mom."

My throat closes and the tears start coming but I don't let go of her, even as I sniff.

"You're crying? Sisi, you almost never cry."

I nod and take a shaky breath. "My little sister is having a baby. Of course I'm going to cry."

She pulls back and wipes my tears. "I found out last week. After I left your house the other day, I got home and threw up. It happened while I was in New York again. So I peed on like five sticks. Jax was on FaceTime. He didn't want to miss a second."

I sniffle, grab a napkin and blow my nose. "I bet he's crazy happy."

"He is. We had a long talk about him overworking and he's going to quit his job. He told me last night. He's going to call a meeting with you and Juan because we are going to buy the locale next door and expand this to a full-blown grill."

"Oh. I like that."

"As it turns out, he's had his eye on that for a while but wouldn't tell me"—she rolls her eyes—"And you have to help him run it." She dips her head, as she does every time she ropes me into something.

This is a no-brainer though. I get to work with my family, who helps me out. I would walk on coals for these two. "Of course I am. He needs me."

Her head bobs up and down. "And I need you. So we'll pay for a babysitter after school for the kids and we'll offer medical to you."

Some Mornings

"That works for me."

"Now, let's talk about what you're wearing on this date."

I sigh. "Saona, it's not a date. The kids will be there."

"I know. He's taking the three of you on a date. So, your outfit has to knock his breath right out but also look like you're not trying."

15

Matt

I'm blasting the air conditioner in the car in early November. Otherwise, I would be sweating like the husband on a missing woman's case. I take the exit closest to Sierra's house at eighty miles an hour and tell myself to calm down. *Why did I fucking tell Wicker?* I didn't need to tell her about going out with Sierra or ask for her opinion on gifts for the kids. It was bound to blow up in my face.

"You're acting like a boy on his first date," she said like an annoying younger sibling looking to stir the shit.

I played right into her game too, getting flustered and frustrated.

So what if I'm excited? I like Sierra. I always have. This is not the same as the mornings. Yeah, there's a risk she'll tell me to fuck off. There always is with a woman. *Especially this woman.* She's made it clear her kids come first and the fact that she's giving me a chance to be up close with them feels like a huge deal. Wicker's damned words keep playing in my head.

You need to watch what you're doing. You're dating her kids now, too. You mess up and you'll be on the train to Gofuckyourselfville in no time.

I did not need to hear that right before I went home. I woke up twice, thinking I overslept. It's the kids who are messing me up. I don't want to ruin this. It's one thing to take them to school when she isn't feeling well. It's something altogether different to take them to school than it is to have dinner with them. Ample time for conversation equals higher risk of me fucking up and them hating me. *And being on the train to Gofuckyourselfville.*

I park behind Sierra's car in the driveway and grab all the stuff in the passenger seat. I'm ten minutes early but it would look weird if I sat in the car and waited for five o'clock. I climb her steps in two long skips and knock on her door. The gift bags and the flowers at my side make this feel like a regular date, like something normal. Except it's something I stopped doing a while ago, when I realized my family history was too much to impose on anyone.

Sierra's going to lecture me over the flowers but I don't care. I wasn't going to bring something for the kids and not her. Plus, it's a date.

A date.

She opens the door and I take her in, all of her, fast. The skinny jeans, the white-as-morning-cream sweater over her cinnamon skin and that smiling mouth that I want to devour. The breath catches in my throat.

"Hi," she says.

"Hi," I manage to mumble back as I thrust the bouquet of flowers at her.

Her eyes go round but the smile that blooms on her lips is prettier than the peonies. "Thank you."

She bites her lip and takes a peek over her shoulder, then climbs on her toes and presses her mouth to mine in a kiss that should be brief and barely there, but serves to remind me that I haven't kissed her in a week, that I haven't fucked her body in way longer than that, and that I've been needing her all this time. The Sierra withdrawal is real.

My whole body combusts as her mouth slides over my cheek and her nose settles at my neck. "You smell good."

My free hand settles at her hip to pull her closer. "And you look like you taste delicious."

"You're going to have to come back in the morning to find out."

My cock twitches in my pants. "Sierra."

"I know, I'm going to behave—"

"*Mami*, I can't find my purse."

"You left it on my dresser," Sierra yells, stepping back just as Eddie appears at the top of the stairs.

"He's here, Emmi. Hurry up." He runs down the stairs. "Hello, Officer Matt."

I extend my hand to him and he shakes it. "We're friends, Eddie. You can just call me Matt."

"Okay, Matt."

"This is for you." I hand him the gift bag. "I hear he is your favorite player."

He smiles—"Thank you"—then tears through it and gasps. "Look, *Mami*, an Aaron Judge bobblehead."

Sierra is smiling and nods. "That's so cool."

Emmi runs down the stairs and Eddie holds the bobblehead up to show his sister.

"Hi, Emmi, you look really pretty." I hand her the present I have for her but she doesn't smile. She frowns and looks from her mother's flowers to the bag in my hand.

"On dates, the guy is supposed to bring something for the girl. Why are Eddie and I getting gifts?"

I fight the urge to look at her mother for help. If I'm going out with these kids, I need to handle myself. I can't look at my partner every time I need an answer. I can't show fear either. Kids, like perps, can smell fear from a mile away. So I look her in the eye and tell her the truth.

"It's true. That's what happens on dates. But this is more than that. It's not only a date but an opportunity for you, Eddie and I to get to know each other better. I was thinking about the two of you and I saw those things and decided to get them. It's just a little something

Some Mornings

from me. If you would prefer not to accept this gift now, I'll understand. I can hold onto it for when you're ready."

She stares at me for a few hair-raising seconds, then smiles, reaches out and grabs the bag. "Thank you."

She pulls out the junior designer book, her smile widening. "Look, *Mami*."

At least Wicker was good for something.

As we walk out of the house a few minutes later, Sierra winks at me. "Nicely done."

I drive this time and it all goes by in a blur. Eddie's chatter over my Camaro's rumbling. Emmi asking questions about when we were younger and telling her mom she's going to design an outfit for her aunt Saona in the book I gave her. Through the show, the kids sit between us. Emmi next to Sierra and Eddie next to me.

He chats and his awe over all the moves is in his rounded eyes and gasps. It is contagious. He tells me, "I want to be an acrobat cop when I grow up."

Whatever that is.

Whenever we talk, I catch Sierra watching us. I know she has to be evaluating our interaction. I smile at her, trying to reassure her all is well. She doesn't seem to relax until we're at the restaurant when both the kids are pelting me with questions.

"Can I ride in your police car with you one day?" Eddie asks.

"Maybe in a year or two. You're still too little for the front seat," I say.

"But I can go in the back seat."

I think of some of the shit I've seen go on back there. Literally. Suspects who have peed or shit in that back seat, trying to prevent us from taking them to central booking. Hell no, this innocent little boy will never ride in that backseat. *Never.*

Sierra chuckles like she can read my mind. "Eddie, my job in life is to make sure you never ride in the back of a police car, even if it's pretend. No riding in the backseat of a police car for either of you."

"But why, *Mami*?"

Emmi rolls her eyes. "Because that's where the criminals go. Don't you know anything?"

"Oh," Eddie says. "I'm five, Emmi, I'm not older like you."

I try not to laugh. "You know, I have a couple of books at the station for kids who want to be cops. I'll drop them off for you guys."

"You think we can be cops?" Eddie asks.

"Oh, yeah. I can see you as an officer and Emmi can be a detective."

Her eyes go round. "Me?"

I nod. "You always ask the right questions. And Eddie, your mom says you're always looking out for people at your school. Those are qualities all cops should have."

I look at Sierra and she is staring at me. What the hell is she thinking? Then her phone goes off on the table.

"It's Daddy," Emmi says, reaching for it. "I want to answer it."

"No, you talked to him first the last time. It's my turn," Eddie grumbles.

Sierra answers it. "Hi, Edwin, we're out to dinner. I'm going to put them on the phone so you can say hi, but we'll have to call you when we get home."

Her words are fast and she doesn't give him the chance to answer. She passes the phone to Eddie and shoots me a look that seems like a mixture between pain and apology.

"It's okay," I mouth.

"Daddy, hi. We went to see the acrobats and it was so nice. They did all sorts of stuff in the air like they were flying. Now we're out to dinner. Daddy, I think I want to be an acrobat and a cop."

Sierra is sipping from her drink and Emmi is almost ready to snatch the phone from her brother.

"No, it's just me, Emmi, *Mami* and our friend Matt," Eddie says, pointing at each of us with his finger as if his dad can see it.

I hold my breath because, *Oh shit.*

Sierra closes her eyes. She can see it too. This is not good.

"No, Daddy. He's too big to be in my class. He's a police officer and

Some Mornings

his car is soooo loud... Okay. Bye, Daddy." He turns to look at Sierra. "Daddy wants to talk to you."

She smiles at her son and takes the phone. She listens for a while and she's staying calm, despite the flames burning in her eyes. Emmi starts to tug at her shirt. "I think Eddie told you. Matt's a friend. I've known him since I was younger. He's a police officer here in Maryland. Your daughter has been patiently waiting to talk to you."

She hands the phone to Emmi, who repeats everything Eddie and Sierra said before. Except for telling him that no, she hasn't been left alone with me. Sierra's mouth drops open and she's about to move to take the phone but I shake my head.

Part of me is a little offended but if I were their father, I would want to know these things too. I've seen awful things in my job and understand his worry. I just wouldn't question the children first. That's an asshole move. My job right now is to diffuse the situation so it doesn't ruin our evening.

Emmi's squeal draws our attention back to her. "Mami, Daddy wants us to come to New York next weekend if you can take us."

She smiles but it doesn't reach her eyes. "That's great, *mi amor*."

Emmi hands her the phone. She listens again, the heightened color in her skin the only indication of how close to blowing up she is.

"Eddie, we are spending time with Daddy. He's going to tell *Mami* to ask the school if we can have a couple of extra days off and then he will be driving us back."

Eddie turns to me and repeats everything like I wasn't here when Emmi was saying it.

"No, I can't drive them up but Saona has a work event she has to attend. I'll ask her to drop them off to you."

She cuts off the call after that. The kids are chatting with excitement, oblivious to the fact that their mom is like a dynamite keg. The food arrives and they talk to me. A lot. But she barely says a couple of words.

Damn, the bastard ruined the night.

Sierra

I press a kiss over Emmi's forehead and linger, staring at her face.

The heat in my skin cools down and my teeth unclench. I sigh.

Even in sleep, she's still smiling. That's what has me pushing my anger down. She and Eddie are so excited about going to see their dad. I can't ruin that. So for their sakes, I swallow the bile, close the door to her room and tiptoe down the stairs, swearing to myself that I am not going to call Edwin and tear him a new asshole.

He put me on the spot, knowing full well I would not disappoint the kids. Something tells me his invitation to New York has more to do with Matt than his new desire to see his kids. I should have turned off my phone so they couldn't have seen his call. We could've called him back.

I breathe again. It's not doing me any good to dwell right now. I need to salvage the rest of my evening. Edwin's not going to ruin that.

Matt is sitting on my couch watching the game. His back is so ramrod straight it's got to hurt. He's so proper, but in a way, he's always been that way. He never touched me or got fresh in any way when we were in high school. Most guys had always been pushing the boundaries, trying to cop a feel. That's why I'd had to kick so many in the balls.

Not Matt, though. His touches were always sweet, friendly, even though in my heart I'd been begging for so much more. Except for those seven minutes in Angie Navarro's closet.

"You can relax, you know? They're already asleep."

He looks up and smiles. "I didn't want them to come downstairs and find me slouching."

I nod, turn off the hallway light, and climb onto the couch next to him. His arm drifts to the back of the seat. "You did great today. They like you. They opened up to you and had a good time."

He turns his head so he is looking into my eyes. "You didn't, though."

A statement, not a question. I swear that is the cop in him.

"It's not that…"

He blinks but says nothing. *Yup, cop.*

"I don't like him using the kids to manipulate me or jab me."

"Why do you think he's doing that? He's their dad. I would have a lot of questions if they were my kids and were hanging out with someone who is a stranger to me," he says.

I shake my head. "But I'm their mother. I would never bring a stranger around Emmi and Eddie. Or, as he suggested, leave my kids alone with a strange man."

"He just doesn't know me."

No, he's a fucking asshole. But I'm not going to say that to the guy I'm seeing. That's what a lot of men would call a bitter-bitch red flag and need to move on.

"I don't mean to gripe. I'm just…it's hard. Now they're going over there and they're so excited—"

He stops me with his hands. "You're not griping. It's normal for you to be worried. Divorces are hard. I've seen the toll it's taken on some of the guys at work. It doesn't always end well. I've also been called to step in after these kinds of situations. It's like these parents don't think about their kids…"

"How can they not?" I blurt out.

"I love that about you. You always put your kids first. You were pissed off all evening but you hid it from them. You smiled and tucked them in, even as you were practically chewing on glass."

"That's what moms do, Matt."

He shakes his head. "Not all. I could tell you stories of the things I've seen…you're a great mom."

God, I'm starting to like this guy so much.

I dismiss the thought because nope, I'm not going to analyze this shit right now. I have a lot to think about but, as worried as I am about the kids taking this trip, I can make the most of it. I've been needing some me time but I can also have adult time and not have it be on the floor.

"So, my sister is going to take the kids up to New York. They'll leave on Friday at noon. Jax is going with her so I have to help Juan run the bar Friday and Saturday night. You should come by and flirt..."

He smiles. "Deal. And I'm off Saturday. I can take you to dinner."

"Oooh. Maybe I'll let you take me home, then."

His eyes darken. "Maybe you should give me a preview of what that looks like."

I look up toward the stairs and back at him. "Okay, but it will have to be a PG preview. Not going past second."

Matt tilts his head toward the TV as Gary Sanchez rounds the bases and slides into home plate. "Lucky bastard."

He places his hands behind his head and shoots me a your-move look.

I chuckle and crawl into his lap. "You're not going to get as dirty as he is but I think you'll like this much better, and come this weekend, you'll be luckier than Gary."

"I like the sound of that."

My hands cradle his face, my thumbs making circles over his freshly-shaved cheeks. I whisper against his lips. "I want the scruff back. I love how it feels on my skin."

His mouth drifts open again but I don't let him talk. I kiss him, soft and lingering, tasting his tongue, flicking it with mine. I wiggle my hips and he gets the message. His hands settles at my waist and he presses me against him, branding his erection on the crotch of my pants.

"*Mami?*" Eddie's voice is accompanied by fast footsteps down the stairs.

I fly off Matt's lap to sit at his side and he readjusts the bulge in his pants so fast I gape.

"Do you have practice at this or something?" I ask him over the pounding in my heart.

He shakes his head, his eyes as nervous as mine. It's almost cute. He opens his mouth but my son appears at the door, rubbing one hand over his eyes.

I hold out a hand. "You can't sleep?"

He shakes his head. "I'm too excited to sleep. Hi, Matt. You're still here."

"Hi. Yeah, your mom and I are watching the game. You want to watch with us for a little bit? Maybe you'll get sleepy."

Starting to like him? Yeah, right. I'm way past that. I'm hot for him. God, I'm so easy. He's nice to my kid and I'm ready to spread myself like a cheese platter at a networking session.

16

Sierra

It's been busy all night and I thank God, *San Miguel*, and the full court of holy angels for it. I spent part of the day staring at my phone and waiting for a call from the kids. I figured they would miss me and want to talk to me. When the call didn't come, I spent the rest of the hours bummed because maybe they're not missing me. They've been wanting to be with their dad so bad, they don't even remember me.

I got two calls today. One from my sister, telling me that she dropped off the kids and warning me that Eddie told my mom I have an adult friend named Matt. I had little to no time to react to the news, not to mention prepare myself for the confrontation. My mom called right after the kids left her house.

"You have a man-friend, Sierra? And you bring him around your kids? Around your daughter, especially? Did you learn nothing from me? I never exposed you girls to a man who wasn't your father."

She never brought a man around us. *She never had to.* She had already broken our home by cheating on *Papi*. I didn't say it, I don't need the hassle of a fight with her. I remained calm for as long as I could and when I felt my patience beginning to snap, I told her I had to be at work and ended the call.

And back I went to feeling sorry for myself until I got the text from Matt.

Work sucks. Life sucks. I'm counting the hours 'til I'm sitting at the bar staring at you.

It made me smile. It made me put on my tightest T-shirt.

Hell, it has me staring at the door every certain amount of time. Between waiting for my kids to call and waiting for Matt to walk through the door, I'm fifty shades of pathetic.

I keep busying myself in every way possible, from wiping the counters after spills, to taking the drinks to people after Juan makes them. I'm filling up the dishwasher for the umpteenth time tonight.

Juan comes to stand next to me. "I need to know how Saona was able to pull Jax out of town on a weekend."

"He's texted me like five times already. They're at a gala for her job, but he's worried about how things are here. But to answer your question, I think my sister could talk him into anything."

Juan chuckles. "You're not wrong about that. He was willing to quit his job, sell the house and move to New York, just to have a chance with her. But look at them now. They own this bar, are expanding it and having a kid."

A customer motions for him on the other side and he heads that way. I take an inventory of what we have and replace the empty bottles. By the time I return to check on the dishwasher, Matt is sitting on the other side of the bar.

My heart skids and crashes against my chest. He's wearing a black T-shirt and leaning against the bar. I look from his muscled arms to the crooked smile on his lips. *This. Man. Is. Hot.*

"Hi."

"I'm later than I thought I would be," he says.

I shrug, like I haven't been low-key watching the door since the clock hit nine. "It's okay. What can I get you?"

His gaze does a slow drift down my body, leaving a trail of heat in its path.

"From the menu," I say.

"Of course." His smile widens and he points at the blackboard with the house specialties. "The Between the Sheets looks promising but I'll go with the Dark & Stormy."

"Good choice. It's one of the best drinks. Jax has his own recipe with a little twist to it." I signal to Juan, holding up my index finger, and lean against the bar, closer to Matt. "How was the rest of your day?"

"Same ol'. Hayden's back to posting pics on the 'Gram. Well, that's not entirely true. She's guilty of letting her dumb new boyfriend take the pic. I had to call him and subtly threaten to break his legs if he doesn't remove the pic. Then he told his daddy, and I had to outright tell his old man I would beat the shit out of him if his son didn't delete the image."

"What were they doing in the photo?"

His jaw clenches. "She was on his lap and they were making out."

"Like we were the other day when Eddie almost caught us," I reply without thinking. It earns me a glare. "She's a teenage girl. Wait, let me finish. She's going to do dumb things. Don't let it bum you or get to you because the more she sees you react, the more she'll do it. Trust me, I was like that with my mom."

"So I should let her and that stupid boy post these dumb things?"

I shake my head. "Hell, no. If it were Emmi, I would have done worse. I would have gone there and beat their asses. But once you make the threat, hang back. Don't dwell."

His shoulders sag a little. "When does this shit end?'

"When she turns twenty-five."

He laughs and snatches my hand in his. "How about you? I didn't get a lot of chances to text you today. How are you without the kids?"

"Saona said they were happy when she left them. I called Edwin once today but they were at The Rat (Chuck-E-Cheese) and texted when I was coming to work, in case he's trying to reach me and I don't answer right away. I'm trying to give them their time with him..."

"But it's bugging the hell out of you."

"It sounds crazy. He's their dad."

"But you're their mom." He squeezes my hand. "They'll be okay and back soon."

"I know. I tell myself that all the time."

He tugs at my hand and leans over to whisper. "I'll just have to become a really good distraction. Keep your hands and mouth busy. I have official handcuffs I can put to good use."

His eyes don't stray from my face but the tingle sets off like a fuse, spreading through my body. I lean forward, pushing my chest against the counter. "I'd like that."

His thumb circles the pulse point at my wrist. I feel it way lower, like he's touching me in all my sensitive areas.

"Drink," Juan yells and I pull back.

Walking all the way to the end of the bar, I have this feeling like his gaze is burning over my back. I tell myself it's ridiculous but when I turn around, he is looking at me. The night needs to end. I need to go somewhere with him. My house. His house. The back of my car.

My pulse is bruising my throat when I get back to him.

"This place is nice. I told Wicker she could come but that you would drag her out if she flirts with your brother-in-law. She had a date with some guy but she dropped me off."

I narrow my eyes at him. "Jax can handle himself with Officer Thirsty. He's not like other guys. He's friendly to the female clients but he's all about my sister."

"He told her that."

"But she met him just once…wow, she wastes no time."

"She's forward and strong. A little like you."

I bite the corner of my lip. "So, you have a type when it comes to women and partners."

He shakes his head. "No one's in your league, Sierra."

My heart pumps hard. I can't help it but I temper it down. What he said is the kind of thing that should have me scoffing. Whenever a guy gasses you up this way, there's something behind it. I flash back to getting flowers or a spa treatment from Edwin for no reason. Or him telling me how beautiful I am. It was all right before the shoe dropped. The gifts always came days before one of his side pieces called to tell me he'd been with them. The compliments were meant to get me in his bed. I still wonder why he'd needed to sleep with me when he'd been fucking half the Bronx.

But why am I not scoffing? Why am I feeling all blushing and tingly, like a high school girl who doesn't know better? I can't afford to be that. Matt is a nice guy but I need to keep my feet on the ground. He likes my company and my body and wants to fuck me like I do him. I need to not make it more than that in my head.

I look down the bar and the empty glasses on the counter become my escape. Because I need a little space from him. "Be right back."

Matt

Okay, how did I fuck up now?

As if I wasn't already feeling a little stupid about telling Sierra she's in a league of her own, she hasn't been the same since. She's way too quiet. I know she is working but a man can smell the unique scent of a brush-off, in a field of flowers or near a pile of dog shit.

Did I come on too strong? Was I creepy in the way I was looking at her? I mean, I can't help it. I've been thinking about her all day.

I don't think she liked the fact that Wicker dropped me off at the bar and that I'd left my car at the station.

After closing the bar, we wave at Juan and head to her car. I stop her before she goes around to the driver side. "I'm not good at guessing, so whatever I did to piss you off, just please tell me."

Her lips go flat. "It's nothing. I'm fine."

"Yeah, right. Nothing says fine more than when someone who was hot one minute won't even look at you the next."

She steps closer, pressing her body to mine. "You know I'm moody. Don't make more about this than it needs to be."

I should press her against the back of her Jeep and commit my first Class A felony, public indecency. But I don't want to do that. Instead I take her shoulders in my hands. "Why do you do that? Why do you always try to use your body when I make you uncomfortable?"

She flinches. "I do not. Isn't that what you're here for? Am I wrong? Aren't we going to fuck tonight?"

Damn, I love the way she says *fuck*. It's blunt and up front, like Sierra herself.

"We *are* going to fuck. Right after we clear the air and you tell me what I did. Is it because Wicker dropped me off? That's an easy solution. We can go pick up my car at the station."

"No, we don't have to do that." She tries to turn away but I hold on tighter.

"Did I stare at your tits or your ass too long? I apologize. I'll try to temper my excitement when I see you."

"Stop being an asshole."

"I can't stop being an asshole if I don't know what I'm being an asshole about."

She growls. "I just don't like empty compliments. They bring back bad memories."

"Empty compliments? You think me telling you no one is in your league is an empty compliment?'

Her gaze drops to the floor and shit. *She does think that.*

I can stand here and tell her it's not. I can defend myself, but she won't believe me. This is not the place for this talk anyway. I let go of her and take a step back. "Give me your keys."

"Why?"

"I'm going to drive. We're going to my house tonight. We can talk and fuck there."

She nods but it's unsure and unlike her. *Fuck, I hate this side of her.* I like her angry and mouthy, not this wary and mistrusting.

She hands me the keys and I go around and open the passenger door for her. She starts to get in but I pin her against the car. "I don't lie. I don't say things because I think you want to hear them. You *are* in a league all your own. You always have been."

I press my lips to hers when her mouth drifts open, then let her get in. We are silent on the ride to the house. I take the exit and turn through the darkened roads. I'm close to a large commercial avenue but tucked into a little, almost country-looking, suburb.

We pull up the long driveway and she turns to me. "You don't live far away from me."

I shake my head. "Two exits away." I get out of the car and open the door for her.

It's pitch-black except for the light on the porch. I open the door and turn off the alarm. She's right behind me, her boots tapping along the hardwood.

"It's really nice in here." Her eyes are everywhere. On the walls, the big glass window into the woods, my kitchen.

"It's okay. It doesn't feel as nice as your place. You have furniture and stuff on the walls."

"I like it, though. It's nice without any knick-knacks. How long have you lived here?"

"Eight years. I bought it right after I came out of the academy. There was a homeownership program and I took advantage of it."

She smiles. "That was smart."

I nod. "Thanks. Do you want something to drink?"

"Are we talking?"

God, I love her smart-ass mouth. "Yes."

"Then I'll take a drink."

"You used to love talking to me. We would chat for hours," I say.

"Facts. But I've been wanting to be naked with you for days."

"We'll get naked, I promise." I stare at her, wanting to say to hell with the talk and fuck her right here on my couch.

But I plan to fuck her for a long time. Not just tonight. So I ignore the twitch of my cock and force myself to go get the drinks.

I grab two beers from the fridge. On my way back, I pause. She's staring out the big window onto the deck. Beyond it, you can see the lights of the city. Her fingers are pressed into the glass, her hands cupped so she can block the light coming from behind her.

"This is a nice view," she says.

I agree. Then again, I'm staring at her ass. She's entranced by the city in the dark and I can't see anything past her. She turns around smiling. Most likely because she caught me ogling her.

She tilts her head toward the bottle. "Corona, huh?"

"I have a profound passion for Latin things."

She rolls her eyes. "I hope your Spanish has gotten much better."

"It hasn't. I kept up with the lessons but my pronunciation sucks in the worst kind of way." I hand her the bottle. "The view is better from the deck. Do you want to see it?"

She nods and I lead her out the glass doors. It's chilly (but not cold) and she's still wearing her jacket. "Damn. This is great. I can't believe how peaceful this is."

"Why?"

"I'm a big city girl. I've never known anything but the noise of the Bronx, but since moving down here, I've gotten used to the quiet at night."

"It grows on you."

She nods. "It does. I mean, don't get me wrong. I still miss the city. I hate the chicken shit drivers who cut you off but don't have the guts to stare you in the eye when you catch them at the light."

"Jesus, Sierra. Do I need to have a talk with you? As a police officer? Do you know the stats on road rage crimes?"

"Ugh. Stop it, Officer Hunter. I'm not getting out of the car. I want them to know I see them. If you're that big and bad to cut me off, the least you can do is look me in the eyes."

I laugh. Because she's crazy and I dig her crazy. I also like her aggressive side.

"If you don't stop staring at me like that, I'm going to start taking my clothes off."

I take a swig of my beer but don't take my eyes off her. "How is that even a threat?"

"You want to talk."

I swallow slowly and I can almost see her patience beginning to dwindle. "I do. And then I am going to let you take your clothes off. Here."

"We don't need to talk, Matt. I'm good." She shrugs off her jacket and throws it on the deck rail.

"I want to know why you went all weird on me earlier."

"I wasn't all weird. I was working. I guess I forgot that when you came in." Her mouth takes a sassy upturn.

"Thank you. But one second you were about to jump over the counter and the next you were ice cold. You didn't look happy when I told you Wicker dropped me off either."

"I wasn't mad. It's just..."

I wave my hand for her to continue. "...just? Was it wrong for me to say that you're in a different league than anyone else?"

"Yes." Her reply is so quick, so loud it takes me aback.

"Why? It's the truth. I've never met anyone like you..."

And now I trail off. *Why the hell did I say that to her? Why can't I ever keep my cool around her?*

"I'm not special or unique, Matt. I'm like every other woman, like every other mom. Every time people want something from me, they throw compliments. They want to make me believe I'm someone different, unique, but they'll step on me like they would anyone else. Edwin swore I was hot in bed. Like no one else he'd ever had. He said I was the best mother any man could want for his children."

"Sierra— "

"But he cheated on me, like men do to average women every day. He shamed me and tried to cover it with flowers, with gifts, with compliments. Until I couldn't take it anymore..."

I don't move from where I am. "Do you think that's what I'm doing?"

She shakes her head. "No. And when I gave you shit about the flowers it wasn't because I thought you were like him. It was just me saying you don't have to butter me up. It's not necessary. I'm putting out anyway."

We drink in silence for a while. She begins to rub her arms against the chill.

I put my bottle on the floor by the door and walk to her, trapping her against the rail, pressing into her body until she shudders again.

"It's not about buttering you up. I've never wanted to fuck anyone like I want to fuck you all the time. Since I was a kid. And I've already fucked you and know I will get to again. It doesn't stop me from wanting to. If I see flowers and I think of you, I'm going to get them because my mom always said if something makes you think of someone, it's because it's meant to be theirs."

I capture her lips with my mouth, curling my hands around her lower back, leaving not even a whiff of air between us. Her mouth tastes like beer, with a sweet aftertaste.

"If I tell you how good you look, how sexy you smell, how you're in a league of your own, it's because I've found only one person who makes me feel all these things. Someone I left behind years ago. I'm a lot of things, Sierra, but I'm not a liar and I'm not a user."

"I know," she whispers.

"Do you?"

She nods. "That's what scares me."

"You don't need to be scared. You just need to let go of the past. I'm not going to be Edwin. I'm not going to cheat on you. I'm not going to mistreat or hurt your kids. I just want to be with you. You opened the door, now you have to step out of the way to let me in."

She swallows. "Okay."

I kiss her lips like the chill is not playing on the back of my neck, until she moans. Then I slide my hands and cup her ass, hoisting her up. Her legs wrap around my waist.

"As much as I want to see you naked on my deck, I think it's time we take this inside."

17

Sierra

I shouldn't drink Chivas. It brings out the freak in me. I tilt my head back, take another shot, and place the shot glass next to my phone on Matt's nightstand.

He smirks at me from the door, the handcuffs hooked on his index finger.

Ho-ly shit.

He stalks into the room. His gaze is hot, burning over me, melting my insides. "Hands up."

I lift my hands above my head and press them together. "I hope to God you're not this eager when you arrest people."

He shakes his head. The smile vanishes from his lips but the sinful gleam in his eyes makes my skin tighten around my body.

"Let me know if they're too tight." He closes the handles over my wrists. I test the resistance and they're full-on binding. I'm at his mercy. I don't know if it's the alcohol, the way he's staring at me like he's going to eat me alive or that I want him to, but I'm wet. Like dripping wet. So wet my walls are quivering.

His hands close over my wrists and desire jolts over my skin. My hips buck up. His knee parts my legs farther and he kneels between them. I lift my hips and he pushes himself deeper and I get my contact but he's got his jeans on. I need him naked. Now.

Last night and today are going to spoil it for next week when the kids come home. We'll have to go back to the mornings and keeping my moaning under wraps because of the neighbors. His hands skim down my neck, past my shoulders. His fingertips brush my nipples. I try to arch against them but I'm not fast enough. His touch has gone south, his hands gripping my waist.

"I had so many plans. Now I can't decide which way I want to fuck you."

"Pick a fantasy, cowboy, and let's giddy up." I lick my lips because I've been wanting to taste him all evening. He took me to dinner before my work shift and I can't wait to have my way with him.

The blue shirt makes his eyes more intense and it clings to his body the way I do when he holds me tight. He took his time licking the spoon after dessert, eyes on me, and God if I almost didn't come right then.

I want him to moan like he made me moan until the sun came up this morning.

"I want you in my mouth first."

His hands pause on my belly and he turns those scalding hot eyes on me. "Yeah?"

It's sweet that he's trying to be nonchalant about it.

"Lose the pants."

He lets go of my waist and his fingers go to his fly. He climbs off the bed and slides the pants down his legs, pushing his boxers along with it. His cock springs free, harder than concrete. *God, I know just how hard it gets.*

I rub my legs together. If my hands were free, one would be right between my legs. "Those pants look so good on you."

"Thanks." He smiles and kicks his pants off.

"But they look better on the floor."

He places a hand on my knee and slides it over my thighs. My skin tingles and heats.

"You going to uncuff me or what?" I pant as his fingers reach the juncture of my thighs and he strokes me.

He shakes his head. "You don't need hands for what we're going to do."

My insides quicken and pulsate. *Jesus.*

Matt straddles my legs, his lips finding mine, in a slow kiss. When his tongue sneaks into my mouth, I catch it, sucking it, laving over it.

"Hmm," he moans.

"Come on, baby. Bring all that to me." I look down his body and he follows my gaze.

He climbs on his knees and scoots forward. I lick my lips and my mouth drifts open. His fingers sink into my hair. He loves to pull my hair tight. And I lose myself, with my chest under him and the weight of his cock on my tongue. I suck him into my mouth and I love the hiss that pours from his lips.

I love how big he is, how he fills me, and the tender way he strokes my hair back. Only to pull it again, and stroke, and tell me how good my mouth feels while whispering promises of how he'll return the favor.

"I can't wait to have your clit between my lips, to suck it and bite it how you like it."

That is how I like it.

The ache between my folds is too great but making him feel this good is as big a pleasure as exploding against his tongue.

The vibration of my phone against the wooden nightstand startles me. Few calls can get through my Do-Not-Disturb phone feature. The screen lights up with Edwin's name. Last night, I added his name to the feature in case something's going on with my kids and he needs to reach me.

I tap on Matt's thigh and he snaps out of his trance, eyes wide and confused. "Sorry, I got to answer that."

His gaze flashes to the phone and frowns like he is trying to register what it was.

What the fuck? Did he not hear it?

"Can't you call him back? It's two in the morning and..." He looks down at his cock, still glistening from my mouth and then back to my eyes.

I shake my head. "It could be the kids. Sorry."

He breathes out, nods and grabs the keys on the nightstand next to my iPhone. He places the phone on my belly and reaches over my head to unlock the handcuffs.

Edwin hung up but the second my right hand is free, I dial him back. Matt is now sitting next me with his dick uber hard. I run my fingers down his length. "I'm sorry. I promise I'll finish that."

He half groans.

I'm about to tell him how deep I'll take him when Edwin answers the phone. The sobbing in the background drops my heart down my chest and into my stomach. I know those sobs. *It's my Emmi.*

Sierra

"What's wrong with Emmi?" I can't help the agitation in my voice.

"She won't stop crying and has been wanting to talk to you. I told her we shouldn't bother you because you were working."

How fucking considerate.

"Why is she crying, Edwin?"

Matt is sitting back on his heels, facing me. His forehead is wrinkled.

"I don't know. She won't tell me. Just that she needs to talk to you."

"Put her on."

His footsteps echo over the phone line and he says, "Here, it's your mom."

I'm going to address his exasperated tone when I get a chance, but all thoughts of him go to the wayside when I hear Emmi's voice.

"*Mami?*"

"Hey baby, what's wrong?"

"You didn't call me." Her voice quivers like it did when she was three and started Pre-K.

"I did. Your dad said you were working on a project for your baby sister and then you went out to The Rat, I mean Chuck-E-Cheese."

"I was... *Mami*, I want to come home."

The words are barely out of her mouth and she starts crying harder. My heart nose dives. *Why does she want to come home?* They both wanted to be with their dad so badly. I need to see her face. I need to know she's okay.

"Don't cry like that, *mi amor*. Hey, is your iPad charged?"

She sniffles. "Yea."

"Give your dad his phone back and call me on FaceTime in two minutes."

"Okay. Here, Daddy."

"They want to go home," Edwin says and God, how I fucking hate him right now. He's not even trying.

"Yes, I know. Saona's coming back tomorrow morning. I'll ask if she can bring them back with her. You can go to bed. I got this."

As always.

I cut off the call and shoot a text to Saona apologizing for the time and asking her if she can pick up the kids and bring them back. I'll call her in the morning to follow up. I grab Matt's T-shirt from the end of the bed and try to push off.

"I'm going to the living room to talk to Emmi. I don't want to bug you with this."

His hand closes around my wrist, hard like the cuffs but warmer. "Stay. I don't mind."

"I don't want to answer why I'm on your bed or your house at this time of night."

He nods. "I get it. I'll be quiet."

My chest expands like it can't fit in my body anymore. He's such a good guy. What other man would be this understanding? None of the ones I know. There's so much I want to say to show him how much I appreciate that. But it's not the time, so I settle for a little smile. "Thank you."

Emmi's call beeps through and I settle back against the headboard. Matt switches the nightstand light just as her face appears on my screen. Her eyes are wet and swollen, like the day her father left the apartment we shared as a family. That day, she cried for hours and refused to eat dinner.

She looks just as miserable now.

"What's wrong, *mi amor*? You're not feeling well?"

She shakes her head, her bottom lip quivering in that babyish way she's yet to lose. "I want to come home."

"You don't want to stay a couple more days with your dad?"

Her gaze drifts up, then down and back to look at me. "I just miss you so much."

My chest squeezes. My kid doesn't know how to lie but she's trying. "I miss you too. I can't wait 'til you and Eddie are back."

"Really?"

"Yes. Did you think I wasn't going to miss you, silly?"

"*Güela* said you would be too busy with your new man." Eddie's face appears next to hers.

My daughter's eyes widen. "Eddie! We're not supposed to repeat that."

Tension breaks out in my spine, jagging at my muscles. My gaze flies to Matt's. His eyes shove closed like he doesn't want to see my reaction, but his hand massages my leg. *Güela* is what my kids call Edwin's mother, a fact I would choose to forget if she were in front of me right now. She dared to say that to my kids?

"I'm sorry, *Mami*. I know we're not supposed to listen to adult conversations."

I use all my wherewithal to put a smile on my lips. "You're right. You shouldn't eavesdrop because the conversation is not for you and you can miss the context. Your grandma is just confused. I am not, and never will be, too busy for you. You two are the most important people in my life. You can call me anytime."

"Can we come home?"

"Of course. *Titi* Saona and Uncle Jax will pick you up. If they can't, I'll drive up to get you. Why do you want to come back so quickly? You were looking forward to spending time with your dad."

Emmi looks away but Eddie shrugs. "We don't like it here. We have to be quiet all the time because Dania's head hurts. And I don't like this living room bed. It's cold and it's too big in here."

"Why are you sleeping in the living room?"

"The other room is the baby's room. It has all her stuff." Emmi answers. Her voice is soft but the tone scrapes over my jagged nerves. It's all starting to make sense. The counselor's words echo in my head.

She thinks his new daughter is a replacement for her.

"You know, just because your dad is having a new baby, it doesn't mean anything's changed. He loves you both just the same."

Emmi nods. "Yeah, he says that. A lot."

But you don't believe him.

"We don't like it here. Everything's glass and I'm messy and I miss you." My son's bluntness makes me smile.

"I miss you, too," Emmi says.

"You'll see me in a few hours. Why don't you guys lie down now?"

"Can you stay on the phone until we fall asleep?"

I nod and smile. "Where else would I go?"

"*Mami*? Can we get *locrio and maduros* when we get home?" Emmi yawns. It's three in the morning and the exhaustion is clear on their faces. I don't dwell on how agitated she had to be. I can be there for them now and tomorrow we'll have a long conversation about what happened.

"Of course, baby."

I hum the way they loved when they were kids. They're not real songs, but stuff I make up as I go along. Only my kids are comforted by my tone-deaf humming.

Matt is lying on his side. He's breathing is even. I feel bad that he has to deal with all of this but I need to be here for my babies.

I wait until their breaths even out too. There's light snoring from Eddie, and Emmi's mouth goes slack. They're asleep. The minute I click off the screen, I push off the bed and make my way downstairs. It's been a while since I've done this pacing thing and I don't want to wake up Matt.

I manage to keep the burning in my stomach from my voice but I hate this so much. The kids were so excited to be with their dad, and I

Some Mornings

had hoped it would be everything they'd wanted. I didn't want to keep calling so they could have this time with Edwin. But I was just being a naive idiot. Like always, he made a fool out of me.

He hasn't changed. This wasn't an attempt to bond with them or spend time. He's probably been ignoring them. It was in Emmi's eyes. I hate that she feels replaceable. I hate Edwin for not reassuring her. I hate that he and Dania are such bastards. They wouldn't let them sleep in the baby's room.

I stand by the patio doors, looking out. I'll need to call the counselor and set up an early appointment on Monday. I want the kids to talk to her. Maybe she'll want to make the sessions more frequent. Jesus, *I didn't want this.* I didn't want them to be disappointed.

The tapping of large feet on the hardwood fills the silence but I don't turn. Shit, I woke him up, and this has to be the furthest from the dirty-sexy night that had been unfolding before the phone rang.

Matt's body presses against mine, his hand around my waist. His knuckles brush up and down my belly. Maybe I can still salvage this night for him, make it worth his while. I want to turn but he holds me tighter, with both hands this time, and kisses the back of my head.

"What is that thing they want with the maduros? Sweet plantains, right?"

I chuckle. "Yes, maduros are fried sweet plantains. *Locrio* is rice cooked with meat. It's their favorite meal."

"Sounds delicious. I want to try it." His thumb brushes back and forth against the skin of my chest. "You okay?"

I start to nod but it's hard faking anything when you're held this tight, when our bodies are almost fused.

"I'm sorry. This is not what you signed up for. I just don't like anyone snubbing my kids, making them feel like they're a second thought. He asked for them to come to New York but he's paying them no mind. He has them sleeping in the living room. He knows Eddie hates that. When the room is too big, he needs an adult there. He thinks monsters could be hiding when there's so much space."

"I'm no kid expert, but yeah, he should have set them up in the room. Even with an air mattress."

I nod because I can't do anything else. Even a single man with no kids gets it.

"I never hated him for the things he did to me. I got mad and I got vindictive but I never felt this kind of hatred that creeps up every time he doesn't make the effort to see them. Did you hear how happy he was to just return them? It hurt my heart when they left on Friday. He thinks nothing of letting them go and Emmi has been missing him so bad—"

I hate the catch in my voice and I don't know when I start crying. I hate crying. It doesn't do shit for anyone. Ever. I try to press my lips together and breathe but I can't seem to stop. Even as he turns me around and crushes me against his chest.

18

Matt

"I can't believe I overslept like this. I'm like a clock."

Sierra's been rushing, getting dressed and ranting since her sister texted her that they were midway through the Jersey Turnpike. We were having a lazy morning. Ideal, if you ask me. Naked in bed, touching each other.

But now her kids are coming home and she has to go cook for them.

I had planned my Sunday with her but I get that they need time together.

"What are you doing the rest of the day?"

My gaze drifts to my phone. I just got a text that Wally came out of solitary today. "My brother's out of the hole. I'll go visit him and have another long talk. Remind him of how his actions affect Hayden. It's been a while since I've seen him and he's always touchy after one of his bouts in confinement."

Her gaze goes soft. Gone is the rush and excitement for her kids. She moves to stand closer. "You're going to be okay?"

A surge of blood rushes through my head. *Of course, I'll be okay. This has been my life for years.* I don't say any of that. Instead, I put my hand on her shoulder. "You don't have to worry about me. I've done this plenty of times. This is not his first extinct on the hole."

Or the last.

"Still... Why don't you come by after? We can watch a movie or the game with the kids. You can taste my *locrio*."

She means it. It's in her big eyes and I love that about her. She has such a caring heart, but today is about her kids. She'll have things she wants to talk to them about and reassure them. She doesn't need me there making it awkward. I wouldn't know what to say anyway. "No, you have to find out what happened from the kids. They'll want their mom all to themselves. I'll come back home and pass out. You didn't let me get much sleep."

"Oh, you're going to complain about that?"

I fling my phone on the bed and snatch her against me. "Never. I don't want to intrude and I don't want to bring my family drama over there."

She pulls back but doesn't go off like I expect her to. "I brought my drama to you and you hung in there. We are much more than fucking, Matt."

There's an odd rumble in my chest and I tell myself to let it go, but I ask anyway. "What are we, Sierra?"

She stiffens. "I'm not going to label it, but it's much more."

An odd pang of disappointment settles in my stomach but I shrug it off. "I'll take the three of you out again this week."

Her eyes narrow like there's a lot she wants to say. "I'll let it go, this time..."

"Thank you." And I kiss her before she can say anymore.

We finish getting dressed and I walk her to her car, pinning her against the door. Our time alone is too short and I do want to see her later, but who knows what I'll find when I visit Wally.

Normally it's heavy when I talk to my brother. He's always contrite and things can get messy.

It's better I keep all that mess to myself.

Some Mornings

Matt

I force another breath, losing track of how many times I've had to do this in the past few minutes. This is never easy.

There's twenty-five minutes between my house in Catonsville and Jessup Correctional Institution. But my body and emotional temperature drop as if I've gone five states north. I take the forty-minute scenic route to get there but return home like I'm trying to get away from an erupting volcano.

One would think after ten years of coming to JCI once a week, I would be used to the heavy air and the gray walls contrasting with the bright orange of my brother's inmate uniform. The desperation in the room should be as normal as the temporary contrition on Wally's downward face.

It's always the same.

Wally always comes out of the hole a new man who's embarrassed, apologetic, and changed in the most profound of ways. He swears on our mother's life…again.

It's a blessing mom died years ago or she would have dropped dead from all the promises her eldest son can't keep.

He stares at me with a subdued expression. "I can't keep on this way, little bro. I gotta change. I'm going to get my degree for Hayden. I want her to be proud of me, like she is proud of you."

The pain in his voice doubles me over as it always does. It is an organic feeling, like the hope brewing inside me.

It's not real, Hunter. You're a cop. You know repeat offenders. You know better.

But this is not a perp…he's my big brother. So I rein in skepticism and let hope soar. "This is good. This is the right thing, bro. Hayden needs you so much. If she sees you doing this great thing, it will have a positive impact on her."

His nod is forceful, like the shoplifter Wicker and I arrested two nights ago. The time before, when we busted him for stealing underwear at Walmart, he had found Jesus. He was going to church and everything. This time he got caught stealing at Target. His Bible had been inside the canvas bag he'd just stolen.

Stop thinking about that.

Wally continues, unaware of the turn my thoughts have taken. "They have a good program. They tell me with my GED, I can qualify for it. When my parole comes up, I'll be ready for it. Who knows? Maybe this will go toward getting my sentence reduced."

A wave of nausea rises up my chest but I push it down. I can't even say anything because he won't get his sentence reduced.

"There're so many programs," my brother tells me. "They're helping prisoners who show potential for rehabilitation."

And contrition. And good behavior. And disposition. And who are not double first-degree murderers.

"Wally—"

He holds up a hand. "I know what you're going to say and I can't change my past. I can only go forward from here. I'm going to start doing better and maybe I'll write to one of those celebrities. You know, the ones who are working toward prison reform. Maybe one of them can get me a reprieve. Come on, don't bring me down."

I shake my head. "I'm not trying to bring you down."

"Then don't. I don't need 'buts.' I need someone to motivate me and tell me I can do it. I need you, Matty. You're my hype man. But I'm going to do it no matter what, you know?"

I nod, slow and measured. The last things he needs are my doubts tripping his path to redemption. "I know you can do it."

He smiles and continues to tell me about his plans. He wants to get a law degree. "I'm not trying to practice or nothing. I just want to help people who become criminals when they didn't know any better. I can start now. I can start helping out with the *Scared Straight* program."

The hope breaks out from the tight rein I've got on it. *He's thinking of helping kids.* He can tell them so much from his own experience. "That's great. You would be really good at that."

His eyes light up. "I think so, too."

I get caught in his excitement, in the words flying a mile a minute out of his mouth.

Then he looks over my shoulder. His gaze goes cold and vacant, like I'm no longer across from him. I ignore the chill in my spine and turn around. Across the room, another inmate is staring our way, mirroring my brother's expression. I turn around and Wally is still staring at him. I shift in my chair to cover his line of vision.

"Bro."

He blinks a few times but his face relaxes. He now stares into my eyes as if someone shut off a switch.

"Who is that?" I ask.

He shrugs, like it doesn't matter. "Some asshole who thinks he's big time."

"You don't care though, right? You have other plans. Don't let anyone derail you."

He nods. "You got no worries with me, Matty. You can go home to your nice pad and rest. Enjoy your freedom. These assholes can't get to me no more. I know how to handle this."

His words chafe my skin, making my spine stiffen. The sickening sensation stays through the last few minutes of the visit and hovers over me as he waves goodbye. Long gone is the excitement he had when I came in. As he goes through the door, his eyes are still planted on the other inmate.

The man smiles at me as I'm heading out, and his companions turn around and do the same. I don't give a shit about them. Except I have a feeling that, thanks to this man, my brother's promises will last a shorter amount of time than usual.

The familiar weight settles in the back of my neck and the pressure builds in the back of my head. I need to get the fuck out of here.

I head for checkout and make my way to my car. I need air and it's like I have not taken a real breath in over an hour. I sit in my car, giving myself the customary five minutes. I inhale, gripping the steering wheel, but my breathing doesn't even out. I said and did the right things but, not for the first time, they were hollow to my ears, to my heart. This time, I ask myself why, and the question comes hard and fast. I don't believe them.

I don't believe him.

Heat flares over my face and I wheeze from the thought, using the steering wheel to steady myself. The shame coats my mouth with bitterness. I need to get it together. My brother has lost everything. I can't stop believing in him now. I must be tired.

Go home to your nice pad and rest. Enjoy your freedom.

His jab found its target. I didn't miss it, like it didn't miss my side.

I hit the start button and my Camaro's engine roars to life. I put the car in drive and exit the prison as fast as I can without speeding too much. I need to breathe this out, get rid of the dark taste coating my tongue.

I'm heading to my empty home to spend the rest of the day in my basement, in the dark, watching TV and drinking beer. My thoughts will clear out. I never think well when I'm this close to the prison. I hit the radio button for my favorite satellite station. I need something to fill the holes between thoughts.

I can see if Hayden can come around Christmas time. Wally needs to see her, to bolster this new goal of getting his degree. And she needs him too. I need to bring them together.

And then what? What happens when he gets angry again? When another inmate challenges him? Whenever he remembers Ryan?

How many more times can I do this?

Today I was so close to telling him how full of shit he is, but I can't do that. It won't help him in any way. I can't turn my back on him. He has no one else. Hayden's too young and the more I can protect her from all of this, the better.

The thoughts race in my head and my foot presses down on the gas. I'm gunning it at ninety, Carnage playing on my satellite radio station.

Sometimes the real satisfaction
Is not in the human interaction
Sometimes what we need to learn
Is just to watch the world burn
Burn burn burn burn

The base makes the whole car vibrates with every "R" and the sound is trapped inside the vehicle, drowning my worries until I can't hear them. I keep a steady foot on the gas and sing along. With every mile my breath flows easier and the knot in my chest eases. Why can't I ever breathe around my brother?

The ringing of my cellphone blares through my speaker, jolting me. My foot flies off the gas while my heart bruises my sternum. Sierra's name appears on my dash and my fingers fumble to adjust the volume and answer.

"Hey."

"I know I said I would let it go. But it's not me this time. Someone here wants to talk to you," she says, her voice breathy and quick.

"Hi, Matt," her son says.

"Hi, Eddie. Welcome back. Did you have a good time in New York?"

"It was okay. Daddy's busy getting ready for the new baby. Do you want to come to dinner tonight? Mami's making *locrio*. It's me and Emmi's favorite."

"Emmi and mine," his mother corrects.

"Emmi and mine favorite," he repeats.

"I would love to Eddie, but I'm tired."

"We can watch the game. The Giants are in town and they're so going to win," he says, adding, "You can nap on the couch before the game."

It makes me chuckle. "Your mom doesn't like people sleeping on the couch."

He's silent for a few seconds. "You can nap on the carpet or *Mami*'s bed since it's big like you. We'll wait for you, okay?"

"I didn't put him up to that," Sierra says. Her voice is unsure, a bit nervous.

"Sure you didn't." I tease, trying to think of ways I can get out of this.

"Okay, maybe a little," she admits. "They asked me if we hung out and I asked if he wanted me to invite you and it's hard to say no to cute little boys…"

"And you don't want me to say no." Why won't she let it go? He just wasn't going to be good company.

"I know visit days are hard for you and I want you close."

Out of all the things I thought she would say, that wasn't even on my radar. I smile for the first time since I left her. How do I even say no to that? Even if I wanted to... In that moment I know. I want, no, I *need* her close too.

"I'm on my way," I say before I can talk myself out of it.

"See you soon." The smile colors her voice in a warmer tone.

The line goes dead and I drive for the next thirty-five minutes in silence. It's like I'm in a trance, single minded in my goal to get to her. I can't even entertain my earlier goal of going home. I don't want to be alone or in the dark anymore.

I force myself to stop at Sugar Bakers for some cookies and the grocery store for ice cream. I can't show up empty-handed. By the time I knock on her door, I'm a little jumpy all over again. Not because I feel tense and anxious but because I'm going to see *her*.

19

Matt

He's here.

Eddie's voice rings out through the closed door, bringing back memories of going to Atlanta when Hayden was little. She would yell my name, run through the front yard and leap into my arms.

Eddie doesn't leap but he smiles and hugs me. "Thank you for joining us."

"Would you like something to drink?" Emmi asks as I shrug off my jacket.

I almost laugh at the proper hospitality but their mother, behind them, is preening with much pride. "Yes, please."

"We can give you juice or water. *Mami* doesn't let us touch the adult stuff," Eddie chimes in.

I smile at them. "I get it. Juice is better anyway."

They run off to the kitchen. Sierra takes my jacket off my hands and yanks me by the shirt, pressing her mouth against mine. Then her arms go around me in a tight hug. Her face is warm as it presses to my cheek and she doesn't let go. I keep my gaze peeled on the kitchen but she doesn't seem to worry that the kids will come back any minute.

"Are you okay?" she whispers against my neck.

I nod.

She lets go to look at my face. The frown says it all: she doesn't believe me. "Come on."

I follow her to the kitchen, inhaling the aromatic mixture of herbs. I take one of the stools, the same one I sat on the first time I was here. She goes to stir something on the stove. Emmi hands me a tall glass of juice with a napkin wrapped around it and I get a small smile from her.

"Did you have a good time in New York?" I ask and want to slap myself right after. I shouldn't bring up bad memories.

But she shrugs. "Not really but I'll move on."

I'll move on. Jesus.

"Your mom is happy you're back. She's missed you so much."

"I know..." She sighs.

"And I'll tell you a million times. I don't care if you say I'm smothering you," Sierra shoots over her shoulder.

"*Mami*, can I call Ayo?" Emmi asks.

Sierra looks at the microwave clock. "Yes, but talk in the living room. We eat in forty-five minutes, and remember you and Eddie have to set the table."

She runs out of the room and Eddie comes to stand in front of me, his eyes sparkling like his mother's when she's excited.

"Matt, you can come play a game with me," he says.

"Can you give us ten minutes first?" His mother asks. "You can go get started."

As soon as he's out of sight, she turns to me. "You don't have to go play. I can make an excuse."

I can't disappoint Eddie. He looked so excited. "I'll go. It's been a while since I played video games."

She smiles at me. "You're sweet. But tell me, how did it go?"

I dismiss the flash of tension that grips my belly when my thoughts go back to JCI, to my brother, to his understated recrimination. I shrug. "Same ol'."

She shakes her head. "What's same ol'?"

Some Mornings

I don't want to talk about it. That's why I normally drink or sleep the afternoon away. I try to focus my attention on something else. But I'm tired of holding this all to myself and she won't let it go. "Wally's always contrite when he comes out of the hole."

I take a sip of my juice. She waits.

"He always has a big plan. This time he wants to start taking college courses and get a degree in law. He wants to be a good example for Hayden and prove to me he's not a total fuckup. His words not mine."

Her gaze warms. "Maybe he means it."

"He always does."

She moves closer and takes my hand over the counter. "But you heard it too many times."

I nod. "I shouldn't be like this. I should just be supportive but I can't help it."

"You're entitled to your feelings, Matt. It's not like you're not standing by him, but you've been burned. It's natural for you to be cautious, if not downright skeptical."

I shake my head. "He wants to do something with himself. Shouldn't I just be encouraging?"

"Yes, and you are, but asking people for accountability is not a bad thing."

There's a weight in my chest. The same heaviness that's always there when I question his behavior instead of just accepting and believing. "I don't want to patronize him or have expectations he's going to shatter."

She lets go of my hand and comes around the counter. "Then don't. You can be truthful with yourself while still being encouraging. You can also call him out on it."

"The one time I tried to do that, he reminded me of the truth. I'm the brother that got to live free."

Her gasp is low. "You can't let him say those things to you. It's not fair."

"It's the truth."

"In a way, yes. Because you made the right choice. You listened to your mom and didn't go and fuck up your life."

I snort. "She gave me no choice."

Her hands go to her waist. "Come on, Matt. You could have ignored her or broken out of the house and gone to join him. But you didn't. You chose to listen like you always did. Remember, back in the day? If she told you not to go somewhere, you never went."

"But he was waiting for me." The words whizz out and I can't take them back.

Her eyes scrunch up. "What do you mean?"

"He told me to come with him that day. I went inside to get my hoodie and my mom closed the backyard door and stood in front of it. Wally could see it all. He kept signaling for me to come but mom held on to me. He shook his head when I wouldn't come out and left."

I'm cold inside, like ice is sliding over my bones. I'm not trapped inside my mom's arms, but I swear I feel the tightness around me.

I can't lose you too, Matty. I just can't.

She repeated that so many times and I couldn't push her away. I never could. Not my mom.

Sierra turns me around on the stool and steps between my legs. Her arms going tight around me, her breath on my neck.

"You can't feel guilty for not going. No way. You would have been in jail," she whispers against my skin. "Your life is worth so much. You were meant to be a protector, not behind bars."

"He felt that what he did, he did for our family."

She pulls back to look in my eyes. "How did that help your family? How did that help your mom? She lost two kids in a couple of days. One to death and the other to the system. How did that help you? It left you to carry the guilt and the grief and the responsibility. It was selfish. All he thought of was himself and his anger. He didn't think about how that would affect any of you. How it would affect his daughter."

I've told myself these things many times, even after I've told myself to suck it up.

"You take care of both of your brothers' daughters and you are

Some Mornings

there for him. He doesn't get to throw that in your face."

I look away from her. "He could've died."

"So could you if you had gone with him. You made a choice for you and your mom. And now you're saving lives and helping people stay safe. He made a choice to kill and he is doing time for it. You have to stop carrying the sentence with him."

Her words are like a knife, ripping through my flesh, re-opening the wound. I see red and I want to lash out, tell her she doesn't know a damned thing about me and my family.

I can't. Because I know it's the truth and she's looking at me with liquid, caring eyes. I hold her against me again.

She rubs my back and presses her lips to my cheek. "Let yourself be free. There's no shame in making the right choice."

I swallow a few times but the knot doesn't loosen. I breathe in her floral scent, holding on to the sweet notes in her perfume until my heartbeat slows to a normal pace and the air flows easier in and out of my lungs.

Her hands don't stop making circles on my back. I want to thank her but the words won't come out.

"Matt, are you coming? It's been more than ten minutes. The clock on the cable box says so," Eddie asks from the door.

We both chuckle.

"He'll be right there, baby." But she doesn't let go of me for a few breaths.

"I think our time is up," I manage to say.

"Nope. Not even close," she says and there's something in her voice that tells me we're not talking about the same thing.

I follow Eddie into the living room. Emmi is on the phone on the far end of the couch. She's whispering.

"Ignore her. She doesn't want me to hear their stupid girls' stuff," Eddie says and hands me a controller. I don't have much experience but as he powers on *Mario Odyssey*, I can't help but grin.

"I used to play this game with my brothers," I say. "Well, the old version."

"It's my favorite. You're so lucky you have brothers," he says, shooting what can only be described as a scornful look at Emmi. Then he shows me what I need to do.

It takes a lot of tries for me to get two moves right, which Eddie finds hilarious. He's outright laughing at my attempts, and before I know it Emmi joins the lesson. She's a little more patient and detailed with her explanations. Still, it takes practice before and after dinner and I end up feeling like an old guy who just doesn't get it. When I pass my first world, both kids clap enthusiastically and Sierra shakes her head.

She brings us dessert and we pile on the couch to watch the game. I haven't been teased like this in years. I haven't spent this much time with kids since the last time I went to see Hayden and RyanAnne. I haven't been in this kind of loud craziness in longer than I can remember. Sierra is smiling, with her kids pressed to each of her sides. Her hand drifts to the back of the couch and she rubs the back of my head.

This afternoon encompasses all of who she is and who she's always been to me.

Craziness, laughter, way too much emotion, and all the things I haven't had but am desperate for. I don't want to live for visits to the jail and the hell that comes after. I don't want to feel happy only when I visit my nieces. I want the anticipation I had all week for the time we would get to spend together. I want those text messages that makes me smile and make me hard, movie nights and dirty sex.

I want more days like this with her kids. I want a normal thing. *I want her.*

Sierra

The bright yellow walls are full of images of famous people. On the far side of the wall is the half smirking mug of the celebrity chef who takes no bullshit and is so blunt he made an old lady cry on last week's episode. He seems to like the Bang-Bang Shrimp here. On the left, close to us, the image is more natural and relaxed. This chef discovers diners, dives, and mom-and-pop establishments such as this one. He's an unabashed foodie and the big crab cake sandwich in his hand looks to die for. The waitress passes me by with a breakfast platter, a big omelet topped with imperial crab.

The seasoned eggs topped with Old Bay make my stomach grumbles.

"Hmmm. I should have ordered that," I say as if I'm one of my kids.

Across from me, Matt chuckles. "You still can. But everything here's out of this world. You're going to love the pancakes. Duesenberg makes the best."

I lean forward. "Is that all we're here for?"

He shakes his head but his eyes are piercing right through me. "I'm hungry."

I hate the nagging apprehension that slithers higher up my torso. He looks at me this way right before he feasts on my body. Yet, he insisted on coming out instead of going inside after I dropped off the kids. "You look hungry."

I infuse my voice with some heat and try not to betray how nervous I am getting by the second. He seemed to have a good time last night with us. I went to bed almost giddy at the prospect of seeing him this morning, after we'd dry humped on the couch and made out like teenagers once he'd carried Eddie to bed.

I smiled in the dark and fell asleep reliving the way Emmi and Eddie taught him to play that video game. Matt explained to them what an off-tackle play is. He laughed at Eddie's knock-knock jokes and praised Emmi's first design outfit.

I've never been hotter for him. It's by a miracle, and the fear one of the kids would wake, that I hadn't shed my clothes.

Then he shows up this morning, all introspection and stares, and wants to go for pancakes instead of letting me crawl all over him.

Was I completely wrong? Did I misread last night? Should I not have insisted he come over? Did I push too hard?

My heart is sinking lower and lower by the minute. When the waitress places our plates in front of us, he grabs my hand and bends his head to pray. I follow suit. I give thanks for our meal and pray for strength and insight. I ask God to give me patience to let him say whatever he has to say, in his own time, and not jump to conclusions.

I open my eyes and he's staring at me, waiting.

I nod to let him know I finished. He digs into his steak and eggs. I take a bite of my pancakes. The buttery sweet taste hits my palate and my eyes roll back in my head. I swear I just orgasmed or died in a sugary bliss.

Matt frowns. "I swear to God, I better see that look on your face when we get back to your house."

Relief spreads through my belly. *We're going back home. We're going to get naked. He's planning on making my eyes roll back.* I swallow. "Oh, you're coming in?"

God, I'm pathetic.

"Yes," he says nothing else and that's unnerving as hell. It's the last straw.

"What the hell is wrong with you today? You're this hungry, egg-eating, weird-acting person I don't know what to do with. Did I push too hard yesterday? I just wanted you to have a good time—"

His hand closes over my gesturing one. "I want you."

"Then what are we doing here? I mean, these pancakes are to die for but I would rather have a mouth full of you."

His lips dissolve into a smile. One so wide and loaded it splits his face and twists my insides. "I can't wait for that either."

"But?"

"I really want you, Sierra..." He says, and his breath gushes out. "...and I want more. I don't want to just roll on the floor of your house. I want to take you out and see more of you. I want more days like yesterday and this past weekend."

My heart tumbles in my chest and for a second I don't think I heard him right. I clear my throat. "Wha...what?"

His gaze doesn't waver, it intensifies. "I want to do this." He gestures between us. "I want to be all in."

"But..."

"But?" he asks.

"I thought you were going to say that yesterday felt like too much, that we should take it slow. I thought maybe my kids and I scared you?"

He shakes his head. "Are you kidding me? Your kids are amazing. They made me forget my visit to the jail. The three of you distracted me. That never happens. I usually need a few days to bounce back from visiting JCI." He breathes, his chest puffing out. "Since my mom died, I've been like a rat in a maze. Between work and the visits to the jail, it's a vicious cycle. I feel like my world rotates between taking care of him and the girls. When I'm with you, I'm more than that. I want to explore that to its fullness. You know what I mean?"

My heart is trying to shove its way out of my chest. I know what he means. I feel like so much more with him too. I'm not just a mom or a piece of ass. And I guess, like my sister says, there are natural progressions and this feels like one. But there are so many things I don't know about him and he doesn't know about me. I wouldn't know how to tell him, anyway.

I clear my throat. "So aren't we a little too old for you to ask me to go steady?"

He laughs and the pressure in my chest eases a bit.

"I guess I'm not scared that you'll tell me to fuck off, like I was in high school. Okay, I'm lying. That still worries me, because you can be volatile, but I'm willing to risk it."

I nod because I get it. But... "I want to try but...the kids, Matt. I can't afford to introduce you and risk that you'll go away. The divorce did a number on Emmi and Eddie. I can't keep hurting them."

He frowns. "Hold on. Let's take this in parts. You're not hurting your kids because you decided to divorce their dad."

"It wasn't my intention. God knows I held out as long as I could because I didn't want them to suffer. They love their dad, even if he's a functioning deadbeat."

His hand closes over mine. "I know. I'm not trying to take his place and I won't ever hurt them. I just want the chance to be closer with you and them."

It hits me all at once.

"Oh my God. You want to be my man."

I must sound as horrified as I think because he smiles.

"We don't have to label it if you don't want to. But, yes, I want to be exclusive."

"I'm not sleeping with anyone else."

He nods. "I know but it's more than that. I want to be there for you like you were there for me yesterday."

"Jesus, you want a relationship."

I sound dumb as hell.

"You make it sound like a bad thing," he says.

"It is. I don't know how to do that anymore. I haven't had that since before my kids were born. My marriage was a shit-show."

"I haven't been with anyone in a while, either. We can learn again, together."

I'm pretty sure I'm gaping at him. Between the tightness in my chest and the ball of tension in my belly, I'm at a loss for words.

Almost two months ago, I told Saona I didn't want anything like this. I've been telling myself that for too many years. But since Matt came back into my life, I can't deny how good it feels to be excited about someone. To depend on a person who is reliable.

I can hear my mom's voice telling me I shouldn't be introducing a man to my kids. But they met him and he's been there, sweet and respectful. And I like him. I love how respectful and correct he is. He's good to his family and has this sense of responsibility to his nieces. He's always looking out for them and sending them money, making sure they get what they need. And I'm crazy about how he treats my kids. Why shouldn't I give this a chance?

His gaze stays on me and he doesn't move. He asked to become my escape and he has been that and so much more. I'm scared but the truth is I want to.

I shove a fork full of pancakes into my mouth and chew them as slowly as I can. After I swallow, I nod.

"Okay, go ahead and ask me to be your girlfriend."

"Nah. That time passed when we were sixteen. Sierra, I want you to be my woman."

20

Matt

Her kisses feather over my belly, leaving a wet trail that, to my annoyance, doesn't go straight down but lower and sideways. I swear I feel every ridge of her puckered lips. I buck up my hips, trying to guide her, letting her know where I need her. She doesn't sway. Instead, her fingers join the frenzy. Her nails scrape over my thigh, sending jolts up my spine.

"You said you wanted a mouth full of me," I half groan, half grumble.

She pauses, her breath hitting the cool moisture left by her lips.

"I'm getting there."

"Can't you get there fast—"

Her fingers trail the inside of my thigh, only a tiny distance from my dick and my begging balls. She brushes her knuckles against my gems and goes back to kissing the juncture of my thighs. The feathering against my seam brings up a strong shudder.

"You're so sensitive to my touch." Her smile is plastered on my skin.

"I'm sensitive to all of you."

Her mouth moves left but she stops, looks into my eyes and grins. "I know. I like that."

I want to push her on her back but her breath is fanning down my shaft. *Jesus, I'm going to die.* I've been dying to fuck since last night. I've been dying from the moment she kissed me at the door, pressed her body to mine, and told me how much she wished I could stay and pound her all night.

"Come on, Sierra. Ride me or top me. I can't take much more."

My answer is a long lick from her tongue, one that sends heat through my cock. I don't buck like I want to. She's finally on the right track. Her open mouth glides down my length and my eyes shove closed for a second as I fight the quiver down my body.

I grab her hair and she moans. My fingers flex, yanking back. Her tongue presses tighter to my cock.

"You like your hair pulled?"

Her hips press against the mattress.

"And your mouth fucked."

"Mmmhmmm." She glides farther down toward my base and my dick travels far, tighter, through her hot mouth.

Her right hand comes off my thigh and sneaks between her legs. I want to say no, tell her that's all for me, but I'm helpless. Because she's not stopping. Instead of relaxing, her cheeks hollow tighter.

"I want to see that. Let me see you getting yourself off."

Faster than I can say the words, she switches to the side, bringing her ass closer to me, giving me court-side access. Her mouth back straight on my cock, her legs open so her fast finger can glide down her wet pussy. The pressure mounts in my balls but my eyes are frozen on the index finger circling her clit. I'm enthralled by the lift in her hips to press against her digits.

I can't help it, I join in. At first just petting her with the back of my knuckles. I'm rewarded when she rubs herself against my hand. I pull her hips to straddle my lap and she knows just what to do. She presses on all fours, sending her glorious ass into my face, and everything I've been wanting since last night is right before me.

So I lick and rub and finger. And she takes me deeper, hotter, wetter.

The current shoots down my spine, my leg shaking.

"I'm going to come."

She chuckles. "That's the point. Be my guest."

Jesus, she shouldn't say that as I'm staring right at her ass.

"Sit on my cock. I want to come inside you."

Her mouth comes off my dick and she whips her head around. Her eyes are rounded, her mouth still open, and the seconds tick along with the pounding in my chest. All of which freak me out. Did I say that? *Shit.*

Then her lips melt into a wide smile. "We have no worries."

The relief that spreads through my body is so thick it's almost embarrassing. But I smile back at her. "Let me in, then."

Her hips scoot down my body and she guides me inside her tight heat. Her head drifts back and I get a full look at her in her dresser mirror. Her mouth widens and she wiggles to adjust. I thank God for my big dick as her heat grips me like latex, and for her big tits that sit high, bouncing softly with her every move. I move slightly to the right so I can see her face and chest while we move. I can see all of her while she takes all of me.

"Touch your tits like it's me." My hands go around her hips, steadying her. She begins to move, girding circles around my dick with her hips while her hands are squeezing at her flesh. Those pretty pink nails rake over her nipples and then she latches onto them with her thumbs.

My hips flick up. "Yeah like that," I rasp out. "Pull on them."

"Oh God, Matt," she says, grinding harder, teasing us both.

She leans forward, her hands gliding over my thighs to rest on my knees. I lose my vision in the mirror but I'm rewarded with her ass sliding up and down on my cock. I lose myself in that. It's like I can't lose today. I squeeze it, knead it, enjoying its fullness in my hand.

"I could come just from touching your ass and your tits. You're thick in the exact right parts."

She moans and double taps back against my balls. "So are you, baby. I'm so close."

And so am I. My balls are tight, my cock on the brink of pulsating. I grind my teeth. *Hold so she can go first.*

"Come back here, Sierra," I say with enough force that she freezes.

Then she sits up and drifts back, careful and slow, into my chest. We are now skin to skin. Her back against me, her legs tucked against my hips. My hands are free so I sink one into her hair and turn her head to crush her mouth to mine. I sneak the other between her legs and my fingers find the treasure, her clit wet and swollen. I rub figure-eights between it and her slit. Her moan leaves a tingle over my skin as it fills the bedroom.

Her hips grind fast, her mouth latching onto my tongue, and I need to touch more of her. I need to hold onto something so I don't come. I grab her left tit with my left hand and roll her nipples in my fingers. This is almost too much. She's on top of me, on my dick. I'm touching all of her, her walls, her tits, her clit, and my tongue is in her mouth.

The pressure is too much on my back and my balls. The tingling starts at the base of my dick and shoots up my spine. My hold is slipping. *Please come.*

It's like she hears me because her body goes limp. She doesn't let go of my mouth, even as she moans in the back of her throat. Her pulse quivers and pulsates but she stops grinding. So I take over. It takes four hard thrusts before my insides explode. My legs go numb and so do my arms, so I fold them under her tits, pressing her tight to me.

"Sierra," I whisper against her mouth.

"That was so good," she replies and latches back on to my mouth. My body begins to coast as my dick pulses and surges inside her. I don't think I've ever come this hard.

Then again, I think that with her every time.

Some Mornings

Sierra

I smile all the way to the bar. Not even the bad drivers and rubberneckers can shake me from my mood. My body is light—sore in the right spot, for the right reason—and I can still taste Matt's tongue on mine. The sex today was out of this world. He's becoming all my fantasies with each passing day. Even when I'm in the shower by myself, I think of him and get off to him.

His text message comes through as I'm about to get out of the car.

All I can think about is being inside your pussy again. How am I supposed to work?

I smile harder, if that's even possible. I text him back.

I want that too. Let's not wait two days. I'll keep it fresh for you.

His reply is swift. *I'll be there in the morning.*

I sent him three emojis. A kiss, the eggplant, and the splash of water one.

He sends one more.

Jesus. I'll hold you to that. Make sure you set the alarm when you get inside the bar.

He's such a stickler for safety. Not that I would ever forget. Up until now, I'd lived in apartment buildings. Locked doors and chains are part of the Bronx norm. My dad taught us about security early on in life. Since I was the eldest sister, it was always my job to check the door.

I head inside the building and engage the alarm again. The wall behind the bar has been marked to be torn down to merge the room with the other side. They're going to add a plywood, makeshift wall so we don't have to close the bar for longer than a week.

I go through the books and last night's ledger. I have to fight my brain because all it wants to do is relive today. Everything was so perfect, like his nervous admission that he wants something more. Even as I taste the fear of what this could mean, I can't deny how good I feel. He wants me, not just to fuck but more. It surprises me that I want that too.

I need to call my sister. I can't wait to hear her squeals of happiness. She's such a dreamer, always has been. I need her to share that optimism with me because that's how I feel. Like I'm in a dream.

I don't even get to my calling app, because the phone goes off and one word breaks the connection between me and my excitement.

Mom also known as Mood Killer. Monsoon on a sunny day parade. A raging headache building from the bottom of my neck.

I hesitate, telling myself I'll call her later. I have to finish the books and it's not an emergency or anything.

You've been putting her off for a while. It's bound to blow up in your face.

She's been trying to talk to me but I've been too busy with Matt and the kids. I haven't had time for her negativity and I don't want to engage in what I know will be her main topic of choice to criticize me with: my new boyfriend.

I sigh, tell myself to stop being a coward, and hit answer.

"Bendición?" I'm proud that my voice is cheerful and reflects none of my struggle to answer.

"*Dios te bendiga,*" she replies.

Her God bless you sounds more like, "So you finally decided to answer my call" and I'm not here for that. Not today.

"How are you, *Mami*?"

"I am well, thank you for asking. I'm as well as can be expected, since I'm alone. I miss my daughters and grandchildren. Seems like I'll have to make a trip to Baltimore to see you, since you're unwilling to come to me. You haven't come back since you moved down. I only see Saona for a couple of hours here and there, and she travels to New York constantly."

Tension snakes into my lower belly. *Because you're fucking difficult as hell and that's all my sister can stomach.*

I say none of that. "I'm sorry, Mom. I've been busy with work and the kids—"

"And the new man."

Since she's not going to play nice, I might as well be myself.

"Yeah, I've been spending time with Matt too. But I think you know very well he is not my sole reason not to go to New York. I didn't want to expose the kids to getting their feelings hurt over their father not paying them attention. And I was right, look at what happened this weekend."

She humphs in that way my sister and I have always hated so much. It shows her displeasure with our choices and signals the approach of her less than desirable opinion or advice.

She doesn't make me wait to hear it. "Had you been here, they could've finished enjoying their weekend at my house. You could have been here to soothe them right away. Things would have been better."

Yeah, her house has always been the place where people go to feel better.

I roll my eyes because she can't see me. "Better how, *Mami*? Saona brought them home the next morning and I didn't have to go make one of those *scenes* that you hate so much at Edwin's house. I have been talking to the kids and following up with a counselor. Emmi is really hurt. I want to concentrate on helping her get past this."

She's silent for a couple of seconds and my stomach coils. I know this woman too well. She's manipulative and obviously she's intent on working an angle.

"Maybe part of this is confusion," she says.

"How so?"

"Well, I'll tell you." Her voice is informative and will undoubtedly make me regret my question. "I understand you have needs as a woman, Sierra, but don't forget you are a mother first. Just because that guy is your new man, it doesn't make him the father of your children. He doesn't need to drive them to school or spend time with them like he's Edwin. It's bound to confuse them even more when it doesn't work out."

My heart drops into my stomach. *She found the right angle.* "When?"

"You know what I mean."

"I do. You don't think this will last and, honestly, I don't know if it will either. What I do know is that I am a good mom. Everything you've told me, I've already told myself plenty of times. I wouldn't expose my kids to just anyone."

"I'm glad you are thinking with your head, then. You and your sister were always the most important thing to me. I protected you as much as I could."

No, you stopped living your own life and tried to live through us. To rectify your mistakes through our marriages. I swallow the words but they don't get past the knot forming in my throat.

"I just don't want you to hurt your children by making mistakes. Enjoy your time with that guy but don't bring your kids into it. Leave things be for a while. This guy is not a father, is he? He can't know what parenthood is."

I clear the knot from my throat. I want to tell her about him taking care of his nieces but that's his private life and none of her business. "His name is Matt. You've known him since he was a kid and he's a good guy. He's always been respectful of me."

"He was a thug when I knew him. I know he's a cop now and I'm glad he made something of himself. But my worry is you. You're impulsive and a hot head. I don't want you to forget your first duty is to your kids."

It's a well-placed dig and it perforates my side. "I do put my kids first, over everything. But don't I owe it to them and myself to be in a stable relationship?"

"Is that what that is, Sierra? A stable relationship? How well do you really know him?"

And that does it.

"I gotta go mom. I need to finish the books."

She chuckles in that way Dominican mothers do when they want to grate you further. "You always have something to do when I'm telling you things you don't want to hear."

"I have to get these books done before Jax and the workers get here."

"Fine. We'll finish this later."

Not if I can help it.

21

Sierra

Saona's face materializes on my screen and I struggle not to frown. My sister is lying back against her pillows. There are bags under her eyes and her skin is not rich and glowing like the other day. Yeah, no one ever tells you about that other pregnancy glow. The one where your skin, no matter your complexion, shows a tinge of green from nausea. It's real...shitty.

"I'm sorry I didn't answer you. I was..." she presses a hand to the base of her throat. "...you know."

I nod. "All too well. I was so happy because I thought maybe you wouldn't have to go through this. But even feeling my teeth with my tongue used to make me nauseous when I was pregnant. With both the kids."

"It's terrible. Jax made dinner. It was so good and I ate too much. Thank God he was gone by the time the barf-fest started. Oh and speaking of queasiness, I hear you and Mom talked today."

I groan. "Good God, don't remind me. I really should only text with her. Since she can't type that fast it's harder for her to spew her venom."

My sister snorts. "That bad?"

"Worse. You had to hear her, Saona. She killed my high from earlier on. She had to remind me I'm a mother first and should be thinking like one."

"As if that's something you need to be reminded of."

"Apparently, I do. She suggested I keep Matt on the low and not bring him around the kids."

Saona's face scrunches up. "What is wrong with her? She should be happy you're giving yourself a chance with someone."

I laugh. "Really? Do you not know her anymore? Between her and everything else, it has been the afternoon from hell. My head is pounding from all the hammering and drilling on the bar. I had to rush across town to get the kids from their extended time at school. On the way, I get a phone call from Edwin who feels guilty now about last weekend."

Saona rolls her eyes. "Now he feels bad? When his kids are four-hundred miles away?"

I shrug. "He's trying to make Christmas plans. I'm side-eyeing the fuck out of him but I owe it to the kids to see where this goes."

Her hands rub over her belly. Her eyes take on that glossy look. That's how I used to feel when I was finally getting my belly to stop raging. I used to fall asleep soon after.

"Go rest, *Manita*. I can call you tomorrow."

She shakes her head. "I feel like shit and I'm pretty sure I look like it, too. I'm too tired to sleep and Jax is not here, anyway. It's hard to sleep without him."

I love that she's so in love and happy with someone who deserves her.

"Anyway," she continues, "I had my own encounter with Mom today. That's how I found out about yours. She can't understand why we're not going back to New York to spend Thanksgiving. I am not traveling again this week and Jax can't go anyway, with the bar construction underway. I barfed right after she informed me that she's coming down for Christmas."

Her skin does take an unhealthy turn, like she's about to throw up

Some Mornings

again. I'm not pregnant but even my stomach roils at the thought of my mom being less than three states away.

"Fuck. We are trapped," I say.

She nods slowly, her reluctance a reflection of my every thought. "We can't tell her not to come. That would make us..."

"...shitty daughters," I finish for her. "Not to mention, we would be deeper on the crap list and God knows what we would have to do to make it up to her." My brain is racing in search of an alternative.

"This is God-awful. How is it that we dread spending time with her this badly? I'm so jealous of Jax and his mom's relationship. Being around her is a joy. She's so easygoing and supportive of him. She bends over backwards to make me feel included and treats me more like a daughter than Mom does. She spends time taking shots at Jax and questioning what he's doing to bring himself to 'my level.' I feel terrible when I make him spend time with her."

"You don't make him, *Manita*. He's your man and he has to—"

That's when it hits me. Matt is my man now and he'll have to be around Mom. My belly tightens. Why didn't I think about this before?

"Shit, Saona, Matt will be forced to be around her, too. Just today, she said he used to be a thug. Can you imagine if she brings that up?"

"Oh my God, that's right. He has to come to Christmas."

"Yeah, he doesn't have any other family here. I mean, I haven't talked to him about it. I guess I shouldn't make assumptions that he'll want to."

"Where else would he want to be but with his woman?" The smirk that blooms on my sister's face is downright bratty. Like when she was a kid and, for once, knew something I didn't, or when she had something on me.

"Stop that." But I'm smiling too. It's a new thing for me to be this giddy over a guy. And it doesn't suck.

Today, whenever I found myself too immersed in my mom-induced angst, I would turn to my phone and find a text message from him that changed everything.

I'm thinking about you.

I can still smell you and taste you.

Work sucks. Send me a pic of you to cheer me up. Make sure your boobs are in it.

That last one made me laugh. All his messages brought my world from gray to color.

"I like to see you smile like that, Sisi. It's different."

"Yeah. I'm trying to hold on to it. Even as the world conspires. Emmi and Eddie are excited to be in the Christmas play in school. Rehearsals start next week, and you know what that means. Driving them around, looking for costumes early. It's going to be insane."

"Well, at least the bar is closing for the week."

"True. But let's not mention it to Mom. The last thing we need is for her to try to come earlier and stay longer."

"Oh God, no." She yawns. "Let's do a girls' day next week. We can go get our nails done and do a little retail therapy to prepare for Mom."

I laugh. "Yes, let's, but now you go to bed. Our baby needs some rest."

She smiles. "It is our baby."

I hang up the call and head to check on the kids. Both are sleeping and Emmi is hanging half off the bed. She's a restless sleeper sometimes. I fix her and tuck her in. Eddie is also sound asleep, thank God. I jump in the shower, where I can't help but think of Matt.

We showered together before going to work this morning and how I wish he was here to press me against the tile again. When I get out, my phone is flashing. It's a text from him.

You up? I'm in the area.

Matt

I step out of the car and stretch. I've been riding around for hours. Wicker had the night off for a family emergency so I've been riding solo. I make my way to Sierra's porch and sit on the steps. I don't want to ring the doorbell and risk waking the kids.

My eyes are burning a little. I really should have stopped at Royal

Farms and gotten some coffee. I'll make that a priority when I head back downtown. I couldn't even think of putting anything in my mouth after earlier on. God knows the rank of B.O. is still sticking to my palate. It was a pleasure to drop off that homeless family at the motel, but Wicker is going to have my ass if I don't get the smell out of the patrol car. I left the windows open to see if it gets better. I'll send it to wash and detail after my shift.

The door opens behind me.

"What are you doing out here? Come inside," Sierra whispers loudly.

I shake my head. "Come out for a bit. I need the night air."

"You're going to catch your death sitting outside without a jacket in this weather."

Warmth spreads through my chest. No one has said that to me since my mom was alive. "Go get a jacket and join me."

"Okay." She heads back inside and returns in a couple of minutes.

She steps down and sits next to me, pressing a travel mug to my hand. "I figured you needed this."

Everything hits me at once. The delicate scent of her body wash, a fullness in my chest I can't fight, and a smile that makes my face hurt.

I place my hand on the back of her neck and kiss her. She tastes sweet. A sweetness that's been living on my tongue all day. "How did you know I needed this?"

She shrugs like it's no big deal. "You're working through the night. I figured."

I move my lips past her cheek to her ear and place a loud kiss there, lingering so I can smell her hair some more. "You figured right. I am close to crashing."

"How come you're alone today?"

"Wicker had a family issue with her little brother."

"Ah. I hope he's okay."

"Kids are dumb sometimes. She'll set his ass straight." I take a sip of the coffee and my eyes pop open. "That's the stuff."

"Why are you patrolling on this side of town?"

"I had to drop off a homeless mom and her kids at a motel nearby. They were almost attacked tonight."

"Oh. How old are the kids?"

I shake my head, tempering the rage from earlier on. "Five and six. Some drunk assholes started messing with them."

"What dicks. Are they in jail?"

I nod. "Yup. Assault and battery. I hope they spend the holidays there. They beat up the father. He'll be fine, though. The poor kids and the mom were frantic. She jumped into the street to wave me down."

"I fucking hate people," she says. It's such a Sierra thing to say but she doesn't mean it. She's always taking care of others.

"Assholes are a part of the job."

One of her arms goes around my waist and she wraps her other hand around my shoulder. "I'm sorry you had to deal with that."

I try to shrug it off like it doesn't mean anything. As if her empathy and closeness don't make my whole body warm. "It's the job."

She brings her face closer to mine. "Did the job pay for the hotel?"

My face tingles. "No one should smell like that or have to live out in the cold with their kids. It's barely anything to put them up for a week."

Her smile is blinding right before she presses her lips to mine. "You're a good man, Matt."

"I'm not that good. All day my mind has been more on you than my job. On all the things I still want to do to you, your body, your..."

I let my eyes drift down her form.

"That's 'cause you're good at a lot of things, including multi-tasking."

We both chuckle and she looks away, like she's nervous.

I tuck a strand of hair that fell from her bun. "I like you like this."

She presses herself tighter to me. "I like it, too. I was talking to Saona about it today."

And then she tenses.

"What's wrong?"

"My mom is coming down for Christmas."

My spine stiffens. Her mom—who never thought I was good enough, who makes her life miserable sometimes—is coming. *Jesus.* Then I remind myself I'm not a sixteen-year-old wannabe thug.

"It will be okay." I almost sound convincing.

She snorts. "I guess you really don't remember my mom. I already had a long talk with her today that made me want to drink half the bottles at the bar. And now she'll be here for almost a week and will split her time between here and Saona's house."

How I wish my mom were alive, pain in the ass or not, but Sierra's relationship with her mom was always difficult and the apprehension in her voice is real.

I rub a hand down her leg. "Hey, I know she's difficult but you know what? She's still your mom and we're going to make it work. I can come and take you out of the house when it gets too crazy."

She chuckles. "Leave my kids so we can go *gallivanting*? She would die. Plus, she'll want us close so she can cock-block and make sure you get the intended dosage of her bitter tongue."

"Damn." The word slips out of my mouth.

"Promise me something," she says.

I nod. "Sure."

"If she offends or annoys you, you'll tell me. Don't just internalize it and disappear."

I frown. "I couldn't if I wanted to. Nothing's going to push me away from you."

She looks away. "It's going to be hard, Matt, but I can't do anything. She's my mom."

"I know that. But I think you're over-worrying. We both know how she is and we'll just have to remember that."

She sighs. "She's gotten worse over the years. Now, she has new weapons. There are grandkids to use for leverage, and both Saona and I have failed marriages. You're the guy that's not my kids' father, and Jax is the reason Saona left New York. You're both in for it."

"Are you trying to scare me away?" I'm half laughing.

She gives me an are-you-stupid look. "No, I'm letting you know because now that you're my man, my judgmental mother is your problem, too."

"I'll hold you to that." I nod. "Let's go back to the part where I'm your man."

22

Sierra

I'm swearing at the lights between the school and my house for turning red. I'm rushing, trying to get home way ahead of Matt. I want to change into the new underwear I ordered and lotion my body. I want him to find me like a treat. He had a rough night at work but instead of going home to sleep, he wants to come home to me.

"I want you for breakfast," he said, setting off a quickening between my folds.

I want to look like brunch for him, something a little spicier that can get him drunk.

I pull up to my house and the first thing I see is a familiar Acura sitting outside, and my chest shrivels. I'm seeing things. I want to tell myself I'm being ridiculous, but the navy blue and gold license plates let me know my mind is not playing tricks on me.

It's José's car.

What the fuck is he doing here? I have enough fucking problems with my mom coming down, and things with Matt are going really well. I don't need this shit.

I pull into my driveway and throw my SUV in park. I tell myself to calm down because I need to be rational, but not an asshole, as I send him on his way before Matt gets here. The last thing I want to do is to have to explain José to Matt with José here.

I jump out of the car and by the time I go around, he's waiting for me outside.

"Hey..." I say instead of *I don't know what the fuck you're doing here but you need to get the fuck out now* like I really want to.

His eyes trail down my body with his we're-about-to-fuck grin bright on his lips. "Hey, stranger. Long time no see."

I don't have time for this shit but I breathe. "Yeah, I know. What are you doing here?"

The grin holds. "You don't answer my calls for months, but I'm not one to hold a grudge. So, when you sent me your address, I came right away."

What the fuck?

"What are you talking about? I didn't send you my address. I was clear with you last time we talked. I wasn't going to do this anymore."

He takes a step toward me. "I see you're still trying to play games. You don't have to, Sisi. You're not married and I'm clear that I'm just a toy to you, anyways."

"You're not a toy to me because I'm not playing. I don't know what this is all about but you need to go."

The grin slips from his face this time. "Your friend gives me a message with your address and says to come visit you. I do that and all I get is more games."

"First of all, again, I'm not playing any games with you. Second, what fucking friend? We don't have friends in common."

"That chick, Mirella, from my building. I saw you talking to her once."

Shit. That's Edwin's cousin. What the fuck would she do that for?

"José, I wouldn't send you messages with anyone. If I wanted to give you my address and invite you over, I would have called you. I have your number, even if I don't use it. Why would you just come down here without speaking to me first? Even on the days I was messing with you, I never just showed up at your house."

His face turns dark. It's a side of him I haven't seen since high school. "I called you a thousand times. You must have me blocked or something. Had you answered, we could've cleared all this up."

It doesn't scare or deter me. "Again, the question is, why would you just show up at my house, where I live with my kids?"

"I don't know. I thought maybe it was something you did now. Like all those times you would say don't call me and picked up the phone anyway."

Shame flushes all over me. He's right, I did pick up his calls after my divorce. I didn't want to see him or sleep with him, but he was validation that I was still desirable. He made me feel good.

"I'm sorry. I really am. We've been friends for a long time. I don't want to end like this, but I have a new life now and I'm not the same person who used to be with you. I meant everything I said in our last call. I don't want to do this anymore. I'm sorry Mirella did that. I'll have a talk with her bitch ass. I'm even sorrier you got led on. I'm sorry for everything, José."

He nods. "Look—"

The rumbling of the engine fills my street and a car pulls up behind mine. Ice shoots up my veins, freezing me in place. José's gaze shoots straight to it but I don't turn around. Because I know who that is...and what it means.

Matt.

José doesn't look back at me but mutters, "I guess one of your *kids* just got home."

"Just go," I say.

But Matt's car door opens, and I turn around as he steps out. His gaze is unreadable but it doesn't take a genius to know what he must be thinking.

"Matty?" José says.

Matt is next to us in my next breath. "Hi, José. Long time."

He extends a hand to his old friend.

"You're a fucking cop now?"

Matt laughs. "Yeah, go figure."

"Seems like nothing's changed. We're both still like sharks, swimming circles around the same girl."

My stomach drops. I don't know what's more cringe worthy, José's words or the smile that forms on Matt's face. It's nothing like the guy I've been seeing for the past two months. He doesn't look at me, not once. He doesn't move either. But when he speaks, it's like he gets all up on José's face.

"Everything's changed now. I'm not circling anymore."

José's eyes go wide and he looks from Matt to me and then back to him. "I can see that."

"Then why are you here? Were you invited?"

The blood drains from my skin. My heart is pounding so fast I can barely breathe. *Oh, Jesus in the sky. Help me.*

José looks at me. "I thought I was, but she's made it clear I'm no longer welcome."

He turns and walks away, slamming the car door as he gets inside. In seconds, his vehicle disappears down the street, but my panic doesn't. It rises up my chest and into my throat.

I should have talked to Matt about José, but damn if I ever thought he would show up like this. I turn to him and he's standing there with that look that says nothing, but he's waiting for me to explain.

I take a breath. "Let's go inside."

He signals for me to go ahead. At the door, I'm so rattled I drop my keys.

Matt picks them up, unlocks the door and leads me inside. I shrug off my jacket and go into the kitchen. He follows me in silence. I don't know which scares me more: what I have to tell him, or him being so calm about it? Is he like a psycho whose rage is bubbling inside and he's going to flip out?

I put on a pot of coffee since he just got off work. The last thing in the world I want to do is have this conversation with him. I don't want to tell him about José and me. Nor do I want to see the look in his eyes when he finds out what I did.

"Sierra..." His voice startles me. It's so dry and heavy. "I'm tired and not in the right mindset to wait. Tell me what José was doing here and we can decide where to go from there."

Matt

The small catch in her throat threatens to undo the tight leash I have on my anger. But I'm calm, and even as I'm chewing on nails inside, I keep myself together like I always do. I've learned what happens to people who let their emotions take them too far. I also don't know what I saw. He wasn't inside her house. I know she just came from dropping off her kids. He told me he wasn't welcome. Still, history tells another version. She'd thought I was him when I'd first called her and she's kept in touch all these years.

"Nothing happened with José and me today. Nothing's happened between us for well over a year."

"A year." The words slip out of my mouth, simultaneous with the thought that she's been divorced exactly that long. *She used to fuck him.* "He was your rebound guy."

Her face goes pale and she shakes her head. "He was the guy I got back at my husband with."

"Got back? As in..."

There's a slight tremble in her lips, but she sticks her chest out, crossing her arms in front of it. "Edwin cheated on me every day of our marriage. One day, I got tired of being the fool. The one who wasn't getting hers. I ran into José and I don't need to tell you the rest. He was the booty call that made me feel good for an hour. Sometimes for an afternoon."

My stomach feels heavy and I'm frozen. If she'd head-butted me, I would've felt less dazed. This is a sucker punch if I've ever felt one. The words "Sierra cheating with José" keep circling and there is so much I should say but I don't know what.

Her eyes well and she blows out a breath. The seconds tick and I want to look away. This conversation is fucked up. Maybe I should go home and come back another time.

She clears her throat. "Look, I'm not proud of this. I'm so ashamed, I've been hating myself for it. I always felt like shit when I got home, but I thought I was getting Edwin back. I thought I was being a sly bitch, a badass who no one took for granted. But the truth was, all that did was make me like Edwin. I hated him so much for cheating and humiliating me but instead of leaving him and putting a stop to it, I stooped to his level."

Her arms loosen up and she presses her hand to her stomach. "I didn't see that until I was forced to face myself over a year ago at my sister's house. She found out about my mo—" She presses her lips together. "I found out about someone cheating on someone I really care about and it was like looking in a mirror. The person I loved removed himself from the situation, walked away from the marriage. That's what I should have done. But I was so indignant about Edwin cheating and obsessed with how I could do the same and get my revenge. All I did was shame myself. I couldn't stand it. It had to stop."

She takes a step toward me and stops. "I can't imagine what you must be thinking about me. You must be asking yourself if this is something you need to worry about. I want to tell you that I would never do that to you. Even if you cheated first—"

"I wouldn't." My words come out sharper than I mean for them to.

She winces. "No, you're not the type. But I want you to know you have no worries. I know what I did was wrong. I would remove myself from any relationship before I did that again."

My face tingles. I don't know what to say or where I stand. This is way too much. I had different plans. Eat her, fuck her, sleep with her in my arms for a couple of hours before she had to go to work. But this shit came up and now she's sad and embarrassed and I'm...

What the fuck are you, Hunter? Am I pissed? Disappointed? Curious? Jealous?

Jealous? Yeah, I'm fucking jealous. I have been since I pulled up to her driveway and found José there. It was a fucking flashback to me always tripping over him. He was always after her, like a dog in heat.

And now I find out she used to fuck him. Like she fucks me. He's had her over him and made her come until her legs trembled.

Stay focused, Hunter.

"Make me, understand. Why not just leave? Why José? Why was he here? Do you still want to fuck him?" There's so much I need to know.

She stares at me for a second and I hold my breath. Because I swear, I see the fuck-off in her eyes. I can almost hear her saying I don't have the right to her history. It was before me. Except, don't I? Shouldn't I not have to wonder why she would cheat?

She runs a hand through her hair. "I suspect Edwin is the reason José was here today. He cheated on me from the beginning. I just didn't know about it until I was eight months pregnant with Emmi. His flavor of the month called me to tell me he was in her bed. That he'd been fucking her for months. She was asking me how her pussy tasted, since it was all over his mouth."

Heat shoots over my chest. The Sierra I've always known never would have stood for that. "How the hell did you handle that without catching a case?"

She cackles. There's no joy or fun in it. It's dry and too loud.

"If it hadn't been for my sister, I would be doing time. I chased him with a kitchen knife. Saona managed to calm me down. I went into labor right after. I didn't want him anywhere near me. Not in the delivery room or home when I got back. My mom convinced me he had rights and pressured me to let him be there when his child was born. She said I shouldn't deprive my child of having her father there. That I had to start thinking like a mom. I relented, let him in...and kicked her out. Saona was by my side. He was nowhere near me in the room."

She's staring down at the sink. "After Emmi was born, she was so beautiful and, thank God, healthy. My mom, his mom, everyone got in my head. That beautiful girl needed her dad and I needed to be a mom first, so I had to stop being so unbending. Edwin lapped it all up and campaigned for forgiveness. You had to see that shit.

"Anyway, I was dumb, and so in love with my baby I wanted her to have everything, so I took him back. Things were quiet for a while. Other than being a functional deadbeat father, and the occasional gossip from the grapevine, all was well. Then, one day I got a call telling me to check his phone and the"—she air-quotes—"'coworkers' that kept calling him."

She doesn't even have to say what's next. I already know.

"He had gotten smarter and put his side pieces under his colleagues' names. No wonder his boss called him late so many times. He would work late and overtime all the time. Anyhow, I broke into his phone and read his text messages. His boss liked to deep throat him and slurp him like a breakfast smoothie."

"Shit."

"I should've been mad. I wasn't. I just felt stupid and naive, like a fucking fool. I told myself I was going to leave but the next day, I found out I was pregnant with Eddie. Imagine how much better that made me feel. Anyway, I took it all. Kept my mouth shut...and my legs. Never let him touch me again. So I couldn't fault him for sleeping with all of the Bronx after that. I didn't care, either. I just wanted to get back at him, to humiliate him and make him suffer like I did."

Her emotions color every word and I get it. "I would want someone who hurt me like that to hurt too."

Her shoulders sag a little and she gives me a look of such relief that it's almost uncomfortable to watch.

"Thank you. I'm glad you can see where I was coming from. It was stupid. The week after we divorced, he married one of his side chicks. And you know the rest. He's having a baby with her while not being there for Emmi and Eddie. You should've heard him yesterday, making Christmas plans he won't keep."

"I'm sorry he did all that to you. Don't beat yourself up. He deserves far worse than what you did."

"He does. But I ended up hurting myself much more." She's not even looking at me but past me, like she gone somewhere in her head.

"Come here," I say and she obeys, still with her gaze somewhere else.

I pull her between my legs and hug her tight against me. "I'm going to tell you what you said to me the other day. You need to forgive yourself."

23

Sierra

"Matt's at the door," Eddie announces and runs back into the hallway to open it.

"Excuse me." I ignore the murderous look in my sister's eyes and rush after Eddie. By the time I get there, my son has opened the door.

"Happy *Noche Buena*. Grandma's here," he whispers.

Matt smiles. "I know. I came to say hello."

"Really?" The puzzle in his voice makes me chuckle low.

It dries in my throat when Matt looks at me. He looks delicious in his blue button-down shirt and slacks. I climb on my toes and press my lips to his.

The "Ew" that comes from Eddie is almost comical.

"Give me a minute with Matt, baby. Go in the living room."

"I'll get you a beer, Matt. Uncle Jax is having one too."

"You're going to need it," I whisper and press my mouth to his again, slipping my tongue to caress his for a second. "You never dress this nice for me."

He grunts. "This is for you. Want to come to my house and rip it off me, later on?"

I can almost feel his skin under my hands as I feel my way up his chest and help him shrug the shirt from his shoulders. "If she sleeps over tonight, I'm escaping to come to you. Now come on, before she gets impatient."

When we go into the living room, my mom is talking to my sister while Jax sits on the other side of the sectional. My brother-in-law looks as cheerful as the new widow at a funeral.

"I don't want you to be an out-of-wedlock mother."

My sister's smile must be held together by glue because it doesn't slip from her face. But her eyes threaten to laser my mom to smithereens.

"Mom, in this day and age it doesn't matter when you get married. What matters is that Jax and I are happy together and committed to each other and our baby."

Mom's mouth opens but she turns to look at Matt. Her eyes give him the once-over and her lips purse, as if she could find nothing wrong with him, but the jury's still out.

He closes the distance and offers his hand. "Happy Christmas Eve, ma'am."

Jesus, the way he says the word makes me tingle everywhere. Maybe I should make him call me that in bed. When I'm on top—

"Doña Minerva," my mother says, her hand lifts up at molasses speed to shake his.

Fuck. Why does she ruin everything?

Matt smiles. "*Doña* Minerva."

His pronunciation of that is so good it makes me smile.

"You look very different these days, Matthew."

Kill me now.

"Yes, *Doña* Minerva. I am a different person."

"He's one of Baltimore's finest," my sister says, moving out of her seat to come hug Matt. "It's so good to see you again."

She gestures for Jax to come closer. "You remember Jax, my—"

"Baby daddy?" I say and my sister and I both laugh.

The men know better.

"That's not funny, Sierra."

I shake my head. "*Ay Mami,* I'm kidding. He put a ring on it. Our baby is going to have a great mom and dad."

"Our baby?" Matt asks.

I hook a thumb toward my sister. "Saona's knocked up and it's half mine."

"Half?"

I roll my eyes at Jax. "Okay, a third."

Saona goes to sit next to Jax and Matt, so I have no choice but to sit by *Mami.* The kids are playing a game together.

"Matt, come play with us," Eddie says.

"No," my mom answers. "*Los adultos están hablando.*"

Adults are speaking. Yeah, that sounds like a treat.

"Matthew, I am sorry to hear your mother passed away."

He stiffens next to me. "Thank you."

He may be worried this conversation could segue into Wally and Ryan. My hand squeezes around his.

"How long have you been a police officer?" Mom asks.

"Eight years now."

She leans a little closer. "Do you like what you do?"

He nods. "I do."

"I must say, I was surprised. That didn't seem like a career path for you."

The heat rises up my face. *What the hell?* My mouth falls open going through a repertoire of words, none appropriate for my mother's ears. Why is she like this? I finally find the words but Matt's hand squeezes mine.

"*Mami.*" Saona's voice is sharp. "That's inappropriate."

"Why? He and that other *bueno-para-nada de* José used to run around, hanging out on the roof and stairwells. I'm just saying I'm glad it all ended well for him."

"Matt was always a good kid. Respectful and always helped his mom. Just because he hung out with—"

He squeezes my hand again. "It's okay. If I were your mom, I would've had doubts too. You can go ahead and ask me anything."

Some Mornings

I look around the room, anywhere but at him or her. The horror in Jax's face mirrors my sister's and mine. But Matt is undeterred.

"I want you to know I'm a different person and I have good intentions with Sierra."

A wave of heat flows down my chest. I wish we were alone. He needs to be saved from himself.

"Oh, good." My mom is just as determined to question him. "Where do you live?"

"Two exits from here. I have a house and the doors are opened to you."

She gives him her best parlor smile. "Thank you. Have you ever been married?"

"No, ma'am."

"How come?" she asks.

That's enough. "*Mami*, chill out."

"I'm just trying to get to know him better, Sierra. I want to know who my daughter and grandchildren spend their time with. You understand that. Don't you, Matthew?"

"I do."

"Good. We'll continue to talk but you must be thirsty right now. Maybe you would like a beer? I didn't think it was appropriate for Eddie to get alcohol."

He's taken aback. "Yes, thank you."

Jax springs to his feet. "Come, Matt. I'll go to the kitchen and show you where they are."

I can't even blame them for how they almost run from the room. The minute they're out of sight, I turn to my mom.

"*Mami*, come on. Stop giving him the third degree like that."

Her eyes narrow on me. "Someone has to. You are way too eager around him. I've seen your sister act like a young girl, and it's just as unbecoming, but you can't afford to be this way." Her gaze drifts to my kids.

"What is it that you want from me? All I did was hold his hand. You're acting like I straddled him."

"Watch your mouth." Her tone drops ten degrees.

I sigh and rein in my temper.

Saona moves to sit next to me. "Sierra's right, *Mami*. You always do this. You did this when you first met Jax. Do you remember what happened because of your meddling?"

"It's not like you let me forget, Saona. But I'm your mother and I will be thinking with my head while you're not. Someone has to watch out for Sierra and those two little innocents."

Jesus Christ, I need a drink.

Matt

Her mother still thinks I'm a hoodlum. She's only taken her eyes off Sierra and me to send looks of reprehension to Saona and Jax. They're so happy and it's clear they're tempering their affection so her mother is comfortable.

"Matt says that Emmi and I can't ride in the back of his car because that's where the bad guys sit. It would be really cool though."

"I don't ever want to see you in the back of a police car," Minerva Torres says. Her face takes a soft, loving tone when she's speaking to Emmi and Eddie. There's none of the censuring tone she uses on her daughters or the polite one, laced with distaste, she uses on Jax and me.

I've caught Saona's fiancé's eye a couple of times. His nod is as strong as the "hang in there and don't take it personal" words he shared in the kitchen. He told me how happy he is to be quitting his job and dedicating his time to his bar now that they're having a baby. That's what keeps him from losing his mind around Mrs. Torres.

"How are the renovations to the bar going?" she asks.

Sierra presses a hand to her temple. "Awful. If they don't stop hammering and drilling, I'm going to lose my mind."

"You'll get to work from home next week. I'll be there to supervise," Jax says, his arm drifting to the back of Saona's chair.

Mrs. Torres follows the move and clears her throat. "That will be good for you, Sierra. You can be home when the kids get home from school."

Sierra doesn't take the bait. She doesn't even shift in her chair. Did she hear her mom?

"They're off from school but usually I am home," she says.

"*Mami* picks us up from school," Eddie says.

"Adults are talking." But her hand ruffles his hair.

He smiles up at his grandma. "I should be seen not heard, right?"

"Can we be excused," Emmi asks? "Eddie and I are already done."

"That's because you both ate too fast. Eating is not a race," Mrs. Torres admonishes.

Both kids nod, their eyes on their plate.

Sierra and her mother stare at each other. After a few minutes, the older woman rolls her eyes.

"Fine, go watch TV. I hate it when you sulk."

"Take your dishes to the kitchen," their mother says.

"Can Matt come and play *Mario Kart* with us?" Eddie asks.

Jesus, yes. Let me go with them.

"Matt's not a child. You and your sister go play."

Eddie shoots me a hurt look.

"Later," I mouth to him and he smiles.

As soon as they're out of earshot, her mother leans in. "You really shouldn't let them do whatever they want, Sierra."

"They're kids, *Mami*, and already dealing with yet another disappointment because their father bailed on Christmas. Give them a break. Besides, no kid wants to be at a table, where they need to be quiet, listening to boring adult conversation."

"They're old enough to get *costumbre*. At that age, the two of you already had manners like little ladies. Everyone talked about how well behaved and proper you were."

The sisters exchange a brief look.

"And we were miserable," Saona says. "We hated going to visit relatives' houses and sitting still for hours. It was hell to be in living rooms, pretending we were not there."

Sierra nods. "It was like being a caged animal."

Jax's phone pings and he excuses himself. "Juan says it's getting busy at the bar tonight. I'm heading down." He kisses Saona in the lips, ignoring the hrrrmph from her mother. He says goodbye to the rest of us.

"I'll see you both later."

"I'll be staying here tonight. I want to spend more time with my grandchildren."

I give Sierra all the props in the world. She doesn't move, stiffen or breathe. Her tone is pretty neutral as she says, "Of course, *Mami*. You can sleep in my room. I'll sleep with Eddie."

"You still do that? He's a boy and he's growing fast."

"I think it's time for dessert." Sierra stands up and collects the rest of the dishes.

"Excuse me." Her mother follows after her.

Saona and I are left at the table. She's working on another serving of rice.

"I can't seem to get full these days."

"You're eating for two."

She snorts. "Or four. That's what it feels like." The smile half slips off her face and she looks at the chair her mother left empty, and then back at me. "I want to tell you she's not usually like this but I would be lying. As you can tell, she can work all our nerves. But I'm happy you are here and you're with my sister."

"I don't think your mother shares that."

She rolls her eyes. "Who cares? We love her. She's our mom but we know how she is."

I look toward the kitchen. Sierra and her mom are having an animated but hushed conversation.

"If we let her, she would tell us how to live."

"Maybe she's just trying to be a caring mom." I think about how caring mine was.

"Or…maybe she's trying to manipulate us."

Sierra comes back and places a cake on the table. I hate the tension in her shoulders and how hard she's clenching her jaw. I close a hand over her wrist. Her gaze snaps to me and holds.

I caress her wrist with my thumb. "You okay?"

She relaxes a little and nods. "I'm used to this."

And yet, her body is rigid like a wooden board and her face is strained. I wish I could stand up and hug her, kiss all the tension out of her. I settle for pressing my lips to her wrist and tugging her down to sit next to me again.

"I'll cut the cake."

I cut a piece for her, one for her mom, and a double slice for Saona.

"You're my hero," Saona smiles. "I'm going to the bathroom before the cake." She hurries out of the room.

I lean into Sierra's ear. "I'm going to pound the tension right out of you the first chance I get."

The slow smile on her lips sends a wave of relief through me.

Their mother returns with coffee. "Do you take cream, Matthew?"

"Yes, ma'am."

She goes back to the kitchen. I take advantage and turn Sierra's face to me, pressing my lips to hers. It's quick but I slip her a little tongue and bite her lower lip.

As her mom's steps shuffle back, we pull apart.

"God, this feels familiar." I say. "Who knew so many years later we'd still be sneaking around your mom? I must say, I like today better. I get to kiss you when I want to and so much more..."

Sierra chuckles. "Thank you for being such a good sport about this."

Sierra

I can't stop smiling as Matt insists on walking my sister inside the bar. He wouldn't let Saona get out of the car by herself. He's back within minutes.

"That guy's crazy about your sister. They're...intense."

"Yeah, I'm happy they found one another. They're made for each other and he's such a hard worker. Not at all like her mooching ex. They argue a lot but I've never seen her happier."

He puts on his seatbelt and stops to glance at me. "They must make up a lot, hence the pregnancy."

I laugh because I can still hear my sister's words. *We don't fight enough to be mad at each other but we screw like we've been pissed off for a long time.*

I settle for, "They do okay."

"Yeah, what they have seems so special."

He's silent as we coast to the city, but his hand rubs over my thigh. His eyes are on the road and he seems lost in thought. I look out the window so I don't look like a freak staring at the side of his head the whole time. I can't even imagine what's on his mind right now.

My mom has been an absolute pain all night. I was so happy when he offered to drive Saona, I jumped in to say I would go with them. My mom encouraged us to stay out for a bit. I'll pay for it with a headache tomorrow—I always do—but it's worth it to be alone with Matt.

"We fight a lot, too," he says, pulling me away from my thoughts.

"We do."

His hand rubs all the way down to my knee. "We make up a lot too."

Where the hell is he going with this?

"We do that too."

"He's restless without her. I can tell. He looked so relieved to see her."

"Yeah, they're gaga for each other." But there's a funny burn in my chest.

"I know how he feels," he says without looking at me. "I'm restless without you."

The burn turns into a damned rumble in my chest. One that rattles me. "What are you saying?"

"When I'm at work, I can't wait to get out so I can see you or call you. Months ago, I was so used to my routine, but now I can't think of getting back to that."

"I get that. I like being with you, too, but where is this coming from?"

He shrugs. "I don't know. Jax and your sister are so free to be themselves and touch each other. Today, I wanted to be able to touch you like that when you were so tense. I mean, you can tell they temper it a bit."

I place my hand over his. "They do because my mom hates it. She would've hated it most of all because of Emmi and Eddie. She would go on and on about how I am supposed to set a better example."

"You set a good example. You're a wonderful mom."

"I could do better, as you saw today." I don't know if I'm being sarcastic or not. "And you're biased because you're with me."

"I'm crazy about you, that's true. It doesn't take away my objectivity. I told you I'm a cop who sees ratchet shit all day, every day." His fingers go back to that idle stroke on my leg.

"Matt, why are you telling me all this?"

He takes the exit closest to his house.

"I hated how your mom made me feel today. But all I had to do was look at you and your kids and I could take it. I told her I have the best intentions with you. I meant that—"

"I know—"

"—And someday, there will be more to this. I can see it coming. Can you?"

The walls of my chest start pushing toward each other. I suck in a breath. Jesus, this is moving fast. "I...I...try not to think about it."

"Okay." That's all he says as we roll down his driveway.

I need to explain it better.

He jumps out of the vehicle and walks around to open the door for me. We walk into his house.

"I thought we were coming here for a quickie." *Jesus, Sierra.*

"That's part of it." He shrugs off his jacket.

And this is what happens when I try to lighten the mood.

"Don't be mad at me," I say, shrugging my off my own jacket.

He turns around and there's real surprise on his face. "I'm not. I say a lot of things to you I probably shouldn't say."

I frown. "Why shouldn't you say them?"

"I think they make you uncomfortable. I don't want to do that."

"I'm just not used to it. You say what you mean. I'm like that, too, to a point. I say what's on my mind..."

"But you don't trust," he finishes.

It irks me. "Neither do you."

"I trust you, though, Sierra. I open up to you more than anyone else. I always have."

It shuts me up because it's true. Since we were kids, he's always talked to me. I always knew things about him, about his family, that no one else did.

We sit on his couch and he grabs my hand.

"I trust you, too, Matt. I've never let anyone else that close to my kids."

"But are you letting me that close to your heart?"

"I already have, dummy," I blurt it out. *Shit, I didn't mean to say that.*

But why did I?

Because you have let him in.

"I don't want to be the only one who needs here."

Don't say it, Sierra. Don't say it.

"You're not. I need you, too. You make my life better, happier." I push closer to him, kissing his cheek and the corner of his mouth.

"And you make me feel alive." Then his lips move over mine and he's pulling me closer to him.

Next thing I know I'm on his lap, with his hands rubbing over my back, his tongue inside my mouth. My fingers press against his shoulders and I'm trying to get a lot closer. My heart is beating so fast it can't be normal. I am caught up in this moment because it feels huge but it's so normal for us.

"It's too much. I'm feeling too much."

"Me, too," he says, pressing soft kisses, one after the other, on my lips.

I lean my head on his shoulder. "I like this. You and me."

He presses a kiss against my forehead. "Yeah, it's good."

This feels so good, so comforting. I wish I could just stay here with him.

"Don't let my mom scare you off…"

He shakes his head. "I won't. Nothing's going to make me run this time."

"I would miss you too much."

24

Matt

I finish the knot in my tie and grab my wallet from the dresser. One last check and I think I look okay. Sierra asked me to wear a white shirt so she can picture herself peeling it off me all throughout Christmas dinner. I liked the idea and I would do anything to alleviate the tension of her mom's visit.

I can't believe how much tension *Doña* Minerva brings into her life. Sierra and her sister are always playing defense. She told me today should be better because it's at Saona's house and Jax's family will be there. Her mother should behave "quasi-better," with Jax's mom there.

She told me they'll wait for me to eat because she told them I had to work. I love that she knows how important it is for me to go see my brother. My mentor, Sergeant Ron, managed to pull a few strings for me, so I can see Wally today. It will be great since we have not spent time at Christmas in a long time.

I need to tell her how much I appreciate her keeping his situation a secret. If I leave in the next few minutes, I'll have ample time to come back before it gets dark.

I head downstairs, going through the mental list of things I need.

Some Mornings

The insulated dinner containers to keep warm the sweet potato pie I'm bringing to dinner and the cookies for the kids are on my counter. I grab them and head out the door. I'm loading the containers into the trunk of my car when the old Impala makes its way down my driveway.

Ron Mason, retired sergeant, mentor, friend, and in many ways, savior. My smile is instant, even as my brain is groaning, "Crap you're going to be late."

I finish arranging the packages and remind myself I need to put money in Wally's commissary. He should be running low by now. I walk around my car and wait for Sergeant Mason. There's 75% more gray in his hair than when I first met him but very few lines on his brown skin. He doesn't look like a man in his sixties. At the most, he looks about early fifties. He crosses the distance in quick steps, his face set in a somber tone. Reminds me of all his lectures throughout my youth and when I went into the academy.

Wait. Why is he here?

"Sergeant Mason."

He smiles. "You're the only one of my mentees who calls me that to this day. How are you doing, Matt?"

"I'm okay. How are Bernice and the grandkids?"

"Sad because you're not joining us today, but excited about the new girlfriend. She can't wait to meet her. You should start warning your lady to expect tons of questions."

I chuckle. "Sierra can handle herself."

"Ah, so that's her name. I'm looking forward to meeting her too." Then his face sobers again. "Matthew, you're a smart boy. Have always been. You know I'm not here for a visit on Christmas morning."

My belly tenses a little. The only time he uses my full name is when something big is going on. "What happened?"

"Junior is on his way home for dinner but he called me because he wanted me to talk to you first, before you heard it on the news or were already on your way to Jessup."

The walls of my belly begin to push together. Junior, his son, is a corrections officer. "Something happened to Wally."

A somber cloud hovers over his eyes.

Dear God. Don't let my brother be dead.

But Ron shakes his head and sighs deeply. "He got into a fight with an inmate, but he's alive..."

Relief spreads through me and I almost sag. *Thank God.* I'm about to say it out loud but his hand presses on my shoulder.

"Matt, Wally killed the guy."

It's a punch to the gut, one that has me taking a step back. *Jesus. Oh, Jesus.* I think of his resolve the other day, how he wanted to turn his life around. He wasn't going to try this shit. He wouldn't have done it unless he had to. "It was self-defense, right?"

Ron stares straight into my eyes. He's never lied to me so I brace myself.

"No. The fight had already been broken up by other inmates but Wally managed to push him into a cell and stomp on his head."

It knocks the air right out of my chest and I sag back against the hood of my Camaro. "No."

"He's been transferred into segregation. Right now, they're investigating, but so far, the snitches are pinning it all on Wally. They say one of his buddies inside held the door closed while he killed the guy."

"Why?" I ask.

"I don't know, son. Junior said the inmates are on lockdown. He was off duty and had clocked out when it happened. He couldn't get in to see Wally before he was transferred. His co-worker has been passing him information. He wanted to make sure we could give you as many details as possible."

It has to be a mistake. "I talked to him yesterday. He's been in a different state of mind. He was happy about Christmas and seeing Hayden for New Years'. He wouldn't do this to her because he won't be able to see her—"

My throat swells, stretching out until I can't swallow. I press my fists into my eyes and breathe. My breath is shaky and hot. *He won't be able to see Hayden now.*

"He murdered someone else. How could he do this?"

Some Mornings

Sergeant Mason's hand presses into my shoulder. "Matt, your brother lives in a different world than we do. His mentality is different. Everyone keeps hoping prisons rehabilitate people, and it does for some."

I push off the car. "Why is my brother not one of those people? Why would he dig a deeper hole for himself?"

For all of us.

He shakes his head. "I don't know, son. But what I don't want is for this to mess you up."

"How can it not? He's my brother. I promised my mom I would look after him and the girls."

He nods. "And you're doing that. You help support those girls and you've been doing right by Wally. But your brother ain't right. He never has been. You've done what you can, Matt. Now, like back then, you have to let the system deal with him."

The system. Another life sentence.

"I can't abandon him. He's the only brother I got left, the only family other than…what do I tell Hayden?"

His shoulders sag. "You don't have to abandon him, but you see that? It's the difference between you and him. He didn't think of her or you. You think of everyone." He shakes his head. "Don't tell her anything tonight. Let her enjoy the holiday. Tomorrow, you talk to her mama and decide how to tell her."

I nod. "I'll fly down there. I don't want to do this over the phone."

Shit, I was supposed to take Sierra and the kids out this weekend. I'll explain. She'll understand. We got a real good thing going. Sergeant Ron is right. I'll deal with this but this is not going to mess me up. I'm going to dinner and letting Sierra take my mind off this. After dinner, I'll get her alone and tell her. She'll help me get through this.

―――

Sierra

"I guess we are going to eat later than usual."

I manage to keep my eyes from rolling. "*Mami*, since when do we eat early?"

"We don't but what are Jax's mom and aunt going to say? I was talking to them and they tend to eat early."

Oh, so now she's worried about Jax's family when she can't even stand Jax.

I place the rice serving on the table. "They're okay. They insisted on waiting, as they're excited about getting to know Matt."

Unlike you, they're supportive and not a pain in the—

Her long humph still buzzes in my ears, even as I move around the kitchen. I wish there had been time for me to see Matt before the dinner. I've been low-key tense about his visit to Wally. I don't want his brother to make him feel guilty about enjoying Christmas like any other person because he's locked up in there. I feel bad about Wally but Matt carries too much weight on his shoulders.

"Hello?"

I blink a few times at my sister. "What?"

"Why are you so distracted?" Saona's tone is half annoyed, half amused. It's in her sharp eyes and hint of a smile.

"I'm sorry. I'm thinking about Matt."

The hint turns into full smile. "Of course, you are."

"Not like that." I elbow her. It's soft because I am super careful now that she's prego. "He had to do something before he came here. I hope it went well."

I look toward the dining room to let her know that I don't want to talk about it because of Mom.

She nods and leans close to my ear. "Can you fucking believe she is trying to use Jax's mom and aunt as an excuse to gripe about Matt? Ridiculous."

I nod. "Not really surprising. By the way, we're all set in the dining room. Your house looks amazing."

She smiles, stretching out her glowing cheeks again. "I want everything to be perfect for our first time hosting. Next year, you'll host and I'll help."

"And the baby will be part of it."

Some Mornings

She laughs. "Yes, can't wait—"

The knock on the door has us turning to the living room. My heart takes off in my chest because I know it's Matt and I'm so relieved that he's here. I rush out to greet him and almost trip over my own feet at his body in that white shirt and slacks. *Just like I asked.* He's simply delicious from head to toe, except for that smile that's not quite his and the heightened color on his face.

My kids get to him before I do. They give him hugs and Eddie whispers that he finished the children's cop book he gave them. They thank him for the Christmas presents.

I move to kiss his cheek. They're cold, as if he's been standing outside for a long time. "Hi," I say, looking into his eyes.

"Hi," he replies but looks down at his feet.

Shit, what the fuck did Wally say to him now?

I squeeze his hand and take him around the room, introducing him to Jax's mom and Aunt Iris. He's smiling and polite but something's on his mind. I walk with him to the closet in the foyer so he can put his coat away.

"Are you okay?"

He starts to shake his head but then he nods. "Yeah."

"Do you want to go outside and have a moment alone?" I say it tongue-in-cheek, hoping to coax a real smile from him.

He doesn't smile. "Your mom would freak."

I shrug. "Who cares?"

"We'll talk later." He puts a hand on my shoulder. "You look beautiful, by the way."

If it were possible for me to brim, I would be brimming with pleasure. I chose this dress for him. It's red and hugs my body and all those curves he loves so much. "Thank you."

I wish I could take away whatever it is that's weighing him down. He was so animated when we talked this morning. It was odd that he had not texted me all morning but I knew he was busy, and my mom had been riding us since six in the morning.

I'm nabbing the first chance to get him alone and talk to him.

Dinner goes by in a blur. I love Jax's family. His mom and aunt are so warm. They're the opposite of my mom, who has her nose in the air because the menu wasn't vetted by her. We're all doing our best to ignore her. It gets to be so much that Jax's mom and aunt excuse themselves, along with the children, and go upstairs once we're done eating.

"Matthew, did you go see your brother today?"

My blood stops cold and I don't look at Matt, but I feel his whole-body stiffening.

"Mom…"

"What? I'm just asking. It's Christmas, even inmates need to see their loved ones today."

Oh, Jesus Christ.

"I did not see him today." Matt's tone is flat. There's nothing there, except I know better. Unless one presses, he won't share.

"But they allow visitation. I would think your mother would have wanted you to go see him today. I'm sure your job would have understood."

My mom is an expert on pressing.

Matt clears his throat. "I did plan on seeing him today. It was not possible."

What could've happened? I'll find out later. For now, I need to keep my mom off his back. "I am sure Matt had his reasons. Please drop it."

"Watch how you talk to me, Sierra. Everything I do is bad. If I don't talk to him, you will pitch a fit. If I ask him anything, you want to jump down my throat. I can never do anything to please you and your sister."

"Mom, let's just have an enjoyable Christmas. We're all together and next year you'll be a grandmother again. It's a happy time for our family."

I could kiss my sister, but my mother is less than impressed.

"Hmmm. Fine. I gave him the benefit of the doubt, to see if he would be mature enough to tell me about his family history. He wasn't. I will keep my mouth shut, but you should know hiding that your brother is doing life for double murder won't make it go away."

Someone at the table gasps but the heat that's blowing through my veins is too fast. I push my chair back but Matt's hand clamps on my leg. "How did you know that, Mom?"

"I've known for years. People in our building talked about it."

What the fuck? Where was I? "Why didn't you tell me? Matt and I were friends and you knew his mom."

"Why would I? I didn't know if Matthew was following his brother's path. I had no reason to think he wouldn't, given what I saw when he was younger."

Jesus. She's fucking evil.

Matt's hand presses harder on my leg. "My brother did commit double murder but he's doing time and paying for it. I didn't say anything because I don't talk about it with anyone except for a couple of people. I don't advertise it and I'm not proud of it. My life is different than his, like I promised my mom it would be."

"But you're not thinking how this could affect my daughter and how you're both going to explain that to my grandchildren."

And with that, my heart drops down my chest.

25

Matt

My head is pounding and my skin itches. It's like that moment right before I face an armed perp, except this is worse. All a perp can do is hurt me or kill me. I feel like this woman is damaging in a bigger way. She can take more from me.

"Mom, stop," Sierra yells.

Her mother shakes her head. "I will not. Someone in this family has to think with her head. It's obvious that you and your sister don't. At least Saona had the good sense of waiting to have kids. You don't have the luxury of being mindless about this."

"I'm not. My kids are what I love the most but I'm also a woman and I have the right to a chance at happiness."

She looks at me and for a second the world stills and I can ignore her mom like she's white noise.

"A chance at happiness, Sierra? *No seas cursi.*"

She takes her eyes off me and I wish I could pull her face back to me. "I'm not being a sap. Everyone should have a chance at that. You can't blame Saona and me for not letting a failed marriage mess up our entire lives. You should have done the same."

"I had daughters to think about. I wasn't about to expose them to some man who wouldn't respect the two of you like a father should."

Something explodes inside me. *What kind of guy does this woman think I am?* The hell if I will let her insinuate that about me. "Are you insane? I wouldn't hurt Emmi or Eddie. I'm a police officer. I would take a bullet for those kids. Who the hell do you think you are?"

I'm louder than I meant to be. The shock is reflected in her face and worry in Sierra's. The only person I care about right now is her. I don't want to yell at her mother. I lean over. "It's better I leave."

She wraps her hand around my wrist. "No, just ignore her. We all do."

I shake my head. "I can't. I shouldn't have come today."

I stand up and excuse myself. Saona and Jax are trying to get me to stay but my skin is way too hot and I only have the door in sight. Sierra catches up with me at the closet.

"Please don't go. Please. Don't let her do this. She's wrong. I don't think that way. You know it. I trust you with my kids. You're a good man. That's all that matters."

She means it. It's all over her face, in those pleading eyes. She trusts me with her kids and I want nothing more than to be there for her, for them. "I know. It is, but I need some space tonight. Something happened today and I'm just not in the right place."

"Matt, I don't want you to go. Whatever it is, we can go to my car or yours and talk about it. Or I can leave as soon as I help out with the kitchen. My sister can watch the kids for me."

My heart fills with warmth and something so big I only find in her. I almost say yes. I want nothing more than to take her arm and run to my car to spend the rest of the evening with her in my arms. But II can't let her do that. "Your whole family is here and I can't take you from Emmi and Eddie today. And I need to be alone. We'll talk tomorrow, okay?"

I don't wait for her answer. Instead, I press a quick kiss on her lips and head out the door. The temperature has dropped even lower and it's downright crisp out. The walk down the block to my car helps me clear my head. I check my phone and there's a message from Sergeant Ron.

I pulled some strings and called in big favors. You can get in to see him but it has to be late tonight. I'm coming with you.

I text him back with my thanks and tell him I'll pick him up.

I'm glad I didn't get the chance to drink anything tonight, because I'm planning on speeding. I make it home in record time, even for a cop. I change into jeans and a black T-shirt. My phone vibrates five times. I don't even have to look at my screen. I already know they're messages from Sierra.

Are you okay?

I really wish you had stayed. You didn't have to go.

Everyone knows how my mom is. I can't believe you forgot what a pain she is.

I'm saving you leftovers and dessert for tomorrow.

No excuses, I need to see you.

I'm an asshole. She's worried about me. I need to do better, now that we're together. I could have her here with me. She offered to leave and come spend time, and I turned that down. I text her back.

I appreciate it. I'm sorry I lost my temper with your mom. I'll make it up to you.

I open the calling app. I should tell her what's happening but I just stare at it because a thought comes to mind.

You're not thinking how this could affect my daughter and grandchildren...

Her mother's words stay with me because, once again, something someone in my family does is affecting things with Sierra. I know she won't take it well that I left and shut her out. But how do I explain what happened? It's the fucking holidays and I'm half torn because my brother committed yet another criminal atrocity. I can't tell her and that's going to cause even more problems between us.

She made it clear that I need to tell her these things but I can't. It would ruin her day. Not to mention when this hits the news, she may have to explain to her kids everything that happened. What if they think I would do the same thing? What if they're afraid of me?

Not to mention, her ex-husband would try to use this against her.

Maybe her mother's right. Maybe I need to put some space between us. I don't want to put her in the position of having to explain to her kids what Wally did years ago or, worse yet, what he did today.

But how can I even think of putting space between us? She makes me feel alive. Like I'm more than being a provider for Wally and the girls. I'm almost normal around her.

Fuck that. I'm not putting any space between us. What happened is not our fault and I will not let it affect us. I will make it up to her by taking her and the kids out.

Matt

The office walls are crammed with books. There are books on prisoner education, motivation, and support. Front and center is the hardback with the warden's smiling face. *Dare to Rise: Life is Possible Outside Prison Walls.* Copies of the book are also on a pile labeled "loaners."

Footsteps echo outside the door and the man on the book cover turns to me. "Do not touch him, even if he starts to cry."

This man does not know my brother. As contrite as Wally can be, he'd never let anyone see him weak.

The warden continues. "I can't leave you alone, for obvious reasons. Ron and I will stay here by my desk. You go sit at the conference table. Two officers will stay by you to make sure protocol is not broken."

Sergeant Ron presses a hand on my shoulder. I look at him and he nods.

Seconds later, there's a knock on the door. I've been dreading the moment they bring my brother into the office since I'd left my house to pick up Sergeant Ron. I know Wally will be contrite but how can I react in a way he needs? I need to be honest and real with him. There's very little to be positive about right now. I'll just tell him that we need to move forward. I need to find out what happened, so I can speak to the lawyer and see what can be done for him.

When the door to the office opens, I'm standing by the table. I lock eyes with my brother. A brief smile crosses over his lips. "Matty, how the hell did you pull this off?"

"Hi, Wally." As much as I try, I can't make my lips curve. All I can think is how he'll never see the world outside this place. How we'll always have to be divided, and only see each other during visiting hours on certain days. God only knows when I can see him next.

The guards guide him to the table but Wally turns to look toward the warden's desk. The second he spots Sergeant Ron, his lip half-curls. "Ah, I see how you got in here. Magnum P.I."

"Hello, Wally."

He turns back to me, his gaze sharp, and I can almost hear the accusation. He doesn't make me wait to hurl it at me. "You had to bring him in."

I refuse to get rattled by him this time. "Sergeant Ron's the one who got me to see you. You should be grateful for that."

He turns his mouth to the side and mutters, "Thanks."

I sit down and the guards guide him two chairs away from me.

"I can't even sit next to my brother. What the fuck is this?"

"Rules," the guard on his right says.

Wally rolls his eyes. "Sup, Matty?"

I get right to the point. "Why?"

"Why did I kill his ass?"

There's no remorse or emotion. He could be referring to a bug he swatted. I nod.

"He was after me. You saw him last time. He was mean-mugging me and talking shit. When you talk shit, sometimes the shit gets smeared on your face."

What the fuck? How's that a reason to kill someone?

I shake my head. "Just because he was talking shit? You had plans to go to school and do good things in here, and you threw that all away because someone was talking shit?"

His eyes go flat. "You don't know what he was saying, Matty. He threatened you. Said some of his friends outside could make sure you didn't make it home after your shift one day. I wasn't going to let him threaten my brother's life."

It doesn't make any sense. "What's to stop his friends from trying to hurt me now that you've killed him?"

His forehead wrinkles. "You're not even grateful."

I blink a few times, unsure I heard him right. "Grateful for what? That you caught another fresh sentence? That you killed someone else?"

He sneers. God, there's so much disgust in his eyes. "That I am willing to do anything to protect you. That, like always, I have to be the brother who takes the fall so you can live the good life."

Heat explodes all over my face. "Are you fucking kidding me? How is this protecting me and making sure I live a good life?"

"People know they can't mess with you or anyone in my family. I would kill as many times as I need to for you and Hayden."

I push to my feet and one of the guards takes a step forward. I take a breath and raise a hand. Then, I sit down again. "We don't need you to kill for us. We need you to rehabilitate yourself. To be the good person we know you are. We wanted to one day see you walk outside."

"That was never going to happen, Matty. You knew it. I knew it. You're a good hype man, but even you can't sell that. You're meant to be the free brother. I'm meant to be the sacrificial lamb. That's how mom chose it."

Fuck no, he wasn't going to blame mom for this.

"Mom didn't choose this. She didn't make you go—"

"No, she didn't, but she made sure to save her favorite and let me fuck up my life to make sure Ryan's killers didn't get to go free. She let me sacrifice myself. You would've been here, serving time, too, if you had the guts to do what needed to be done."

"That didn't need to be done. It didn't fucking help anyone. If I were in here with you, who the hell would have taken care of your child and Ryan's? Who the fuck would be depositing commissary money and visiting your ass? You talk about being the sacrificial lamb? I'm the one who's always taken the fall for the two of you."

I try to stop but I can't.

"My life is always changing because of the two of you. I fucking left the Bronx and all my friends. I'm supporting your kids. Until recently, I didn't have a fucking life between jail visits, parenting Hayden from afar, and work. I had to nurse my sick mother and watch her die. And you think all you did was because of us? For us? You're a selfish asshole."

He grins. "Wow, Matty. It took you long enough to throw all you've done for my kid in my face. I am grateful for all you've done for her. That's why I wasn't going to let anyone threaten my brother. I don't mind taking the fall for us, bro. Let's not fight. We're all each other's got."

The change in him is so fast it takes me off balance. *What the hell?* He always does this shit. Today, I'm not feeling or patronizing it. I stand up. "I'm going to go, Wally. I'll come back when visits are allowed again. The lawyer is coming by to see you tomorrow."

I nod to the warden. "Thank you for letting me see my brother."

I walk out of the office and Sergeant Ron follows me. We check out in silence but the minute we are outside the prison, he places a hand on my shoulder.

"He's not going to change. You have to."

And I will. This is the last time I let Wally ruin anything for me.

I drive back like a bat out of hell. If Ron notices, he doesn't say anything. When I drop him off, he repeats what he's always told me, "Remember, son, we are who we choose to be."

That's why I drive past my exit and take Sierra's. I need to see her. I'm not going to wait until tomorrow to tell her what happened. I open my phone app to call her. I don't want to go into her house but maybe we can take a drive if she's still awake.

Then I remember she's at her sister's house. *Fuck.*

I have five missed calls from Danielle, Hayden's mom. She never calls me this many time. *Jesus, she must have found out.*

I tap on her name. She answers on the first ring. "Matt, thank God."

"Hey, sorry. I had my phone in do not disturb—"

"We know what happened to Wally. Hayden didn't take it well —" her voice breaks. "We're in the hospital. She tried to hurt herself."

She starts to sob and my heart starts to pound quickly. In the distance, a horn blares and makes me jump. I'm at a standstill in the middle of the street.

"Matt?"

Jesus. Hayden. No.

"I'm here. Is she okay?" I move to the right lane and drive slower than usual.

"They sedated her. It was horrible. She was hysterical, asking why would he do that. She said he's a bad person and how can that be her dad? I am so scared. I don't know what I'll do when she wakes. Kids never understand these things. I hate him so much right now. I've had to spend Hayden's whole life explaining to her what he does and why."

I breathe and grip my steering wheel tighter. I can't fault her. Not when I feel the same way.

"Danielle, I'm going to call the airlines and get the first flight out. Hang in there. I'm coming."

I make a U-turn and go back home. I'm not going to see Sierra tonight. She doesn't need this. Or all the messy trouble I bring into her life.

My gut twists because I know what I have to do when I get back from this trip. I need to let her go. She needs to be free from this drama I drag along with me.

But when I turn into my driveway, she's waiting inside her truck for me.

26

Sierra

My whole life I've prided myself on calling guys back in my own time and never being the one to call them first. I don't chase them. They chase me. And look at me now. This is stalker territory. There's no other way to see it. I've been sitting here for the better part of an hour, waiting for Matt to come home. His last text didn't make me feel at ease.

There was something in his eyes tonight that bugs me. He also said something happened and I just have a really bad feeling. I need to know what it is.

I text Saona to make sure everything's going well. I'll have to make it up to her for leaving her alone with my mom and the kids, even if she insisted. I'll deal with my mom tomorrow. I refuse to engage her because that would be letting her in my head. I don't want to tell her what's really on my mind. *And in my heart.* Hopefully, we can just coast the next two days and she will be out of our hair for a while. This week's ordeal has bought me at least six more months, if not a year, away from her.

Everything's fine here. Thank God for mom (Jax's) and Aunt Iris. Kids

Some Mornings

are teaching Uncle Jax how to play Mario Cart *and Mami is being the usual.* She adds an eye rolling emoji at the end.

I owe you. I reply.

Tell Matt he owes me too. He should've ignored her like we do.

I send back four exclamation points and a thumbs up.

I go back to waiting, tapping along to the radio to *I do*.

Cardi croons about doing what she pleases. Nothing more, nothing less.

It would have been my song, back in the day. I did what I liked. I sweated no one. Men had to sweat me. Yeah, that seems long gone. This guy has me in knots, waiting for him to show.

I'm ready to leave when Matt's Camaro turns into the driveway. There's a slight pause, then he drives down and parks next to me. That's when courage flies out the window. I feel stupid and clingy. Shit, would he think I'm crazy if I just back out and go home?

Yes, you would look like a complete loon. And you're in a relationship with him. All the old rules fly out.

I suck in a breath and throw the door open. By the time I get out, he's already around his car.

"Hey, I'm sorry I showed up like this. I just wanted to make sure you were okay. I wanted to see it for myself."

"Don't apologize for coming. You're always welcome. Let's go inside."

He holds my elbow as I make it up his porch steps. My heels click against the wood and I wish I had put on the flats I carry in the trunk. All that time sitting there and I didn't think about them.

He stops at the door. "Hold on, let me check first." He opens his phone screen and I get a clear shot of his security app. He enters the security code, but uses his key to get through the door. He ushers me inside.

"Is everything okay?"

He closes the door and turns to me. That's when I get a clear look at his face. He's pale as hell. His lips are red like he's been biting them.

"What happened, Matt?"

"Wally killed a guy in jail today because he threatened to do something to me. Hayden is not taking it well. On the way here, her mother called me. She tried to hurt herself."

"What? Oh my God."

"I'm going to grab the first flight out to Atlanta. I need to be with her right now."

I nod. "Of course you do. She's going to need you now more than ever. That poor baby. What do you need me to do? How do I help?"

"I don't know. I don't even know how long I'll be gone…"

I grab his hand and squeeze it. "I understand. You have to take care of Hayden now…and yourself. I'll be here when you get back."

I throw my arms around him as tight as I can. He hugs me back and I breathe him in, hoping he can feel how much I care. I wish I could go with him to see his niece. Maybe I can for a couple of days. My sister wouldn't mind watching my kids. Should I offer? I open my mouth but his next words stop me.

"I can't keep bringing this around you and your kids."

Wait, huh? Bringing what? Maybe he's confused. He's got a lot going on. "It's okay, Matt. I get that this is delicate. We're going to take care of you. When you get back, I'll make you a nice dinner and the kids will play video games with you."

He shakes his head and his arms fall at his side. "We can't. I can't do this to you or them."

Now I pull back. *What the hell is happening?* "What are you talking about?"

"We should take a step back. My family is in shambles right now. Hayden needs me. I wouldn't know how to explain this to Emmi and Eddie. They're young and if Hayden, who has been around this for so long, is having a hard time handling it, can you imagine your kids? They're dealing with so much with the divorce and I don't want to make things worse."

"Matt—"

"I shouldn't be an added burden to you, either. I should be helping you and supporting you, not bringing you shit that your family has never dealt with."

This sounds familiar as hell.

I scoff. "What the fuck? You sound like my mother. A relationship is about sharing the good and the bad. I want to be there for you, help you solve things, not just take from you."

There's a pause and he shakes his head.

"Maybe that's it. We shouldn't be in a relationship."

It's a sharp jab to my gut. I press a hand to it. *He's looking for excuses. He wants out. Maybe today with my mom was too much.* I smile because I don't know what else to do and because I want to just tell him to fuck off... "Oh, I see. You want to go back to morning fucking."

He moves so fast I don't even register it. His hands are grasping my shoulders and he brings me close, just not close enough.

"No. That's not what I want, Sierra. That was never my sole intention with you. That just happened and I took what you were willing to give me...I'm not trying to downgrade what we have."

And it hits me hard. He's ending things for good. My eyes threaten to well but I blink it away fast and sharp. "You're breaking up with me."

"I don't want to."

"Then fucking don't." I can't believe the words coming out of my mouth. I don't beg.

"Don't you get it? I don't want any of this near you. My brother fucking killed someone and has no remorse. He did it for me because he thinks he's protecting me. The guy threatened to have someone hurt me out here. Wally thought killing him eliminates the threat. How do we explain that to your kids?"

"Together. It's a *we* conversation but you're making it into a *you* thing. You're making the decision to break up and what I say doesn't matter."

Stop, Sierra. Just walk away.

"I can't do this to you. It's better we give each other some space."

Yeah, time to go.

My throat tightens and I take a step back, away from his touch, and clear my throat. "Okay, Matt. I understand."

I stroll past him toward the door but he gets there before I do.

"Let me walk you out."

Anger flares through me. *At least let me walk away on my own.*

"Why? What's the point?" The words come out more forceful than how I mean to say them, but I am barely hanging on. *It's over. We're over.*

"I don't think there's any real concern, but I want to be sure no one's out there watching."

That makes me feel like shit. He's still being a nice guy. A nice guy who's fucking dumping me when I care so much about him. When I came to be with him, to try to help him through whatever he's going through.

I let him lead the way, concentrating on my feet. I don't want to keep looking at everything I'm losing.

He holds my car door open for me and I get in, but he doesn't close it.

"I'm sorry," he says, sounding like shit. *Like I feel.*

I make my lips curve, summoning the smile of the girl who chased no one, the one who hadn't cried when she'd gotten divorced. "Me, too. I'm just glad you didn't disappear in the middle of the night this time. Have a safe flight, Matt. Give my love to Hayden."

I pull the door closed and manage to have enough control to back out of his driveway at a decent speed. It's almost scary how calm and in control I am. It's like I'm my old self. Except my heart is shattered into a thousand pieces. Some left behind, lying on his living room floor.

The pain won't let me breathe.

Matt

My eyes don't even strain as they should against the bright sun. I'm so used to the night-to-day transition, from so many years of working the beat. I didn't even realize the sun had come out. My eyes have not left Hayden since I came here.

It's crazy that this was the little girl I'd held just after she was born. It's hard to reconcile the seven-year-old with the missing front teeth who'd smiled so brightly on her first day of school photo with this young woman. Her beautiful face, a mixture of my mom and hers, is troubled, even in sleep. The peace and heavy slumber I remember her for is not there. As a little girl she would fall into a deep sleep anywhere. It was always funny. She's sleeping now but it's uncomfortable, due to the meds.

My heart is still heavy from her sobs when she'd woken up around four in the morning to find me here.

I'm never going to see my dad again. They're going to fry him in the chair. Everyone's going to taunt me because he won't stop killing people.

I had to explain that wasn't going to happen because Maryland does not have the death penalty, and that she can still go visit him. The hardest part was trying to explain to her that she had to pick the opinions that matter. I wasn't going to sugar coat shit for her the way some had tried to do for me. It's rough out there when a family member kills someone. There's a guilt like you did it, too. And a stigma that maybe you're a killer, too. The hardest part is shoving the assholes into a box.

My phone vibrates and Wicker's name flashes on the screen. I tap Danielle, who's sleeping in the chair next to the bed, to let her know I'm stepping out into the hallway.

By the time I get to the waiting area, I have to call Wicker back.

"Hey, sorry about that."

"Are you okay? I got your text about being away for a few days." Her voice is subdued and lacking her usual energy. "Hunter, I heard about your brother. I'm sorry."

The police grapevine is worse than TMZ.

"Yeah. He fucked up again."

"He did. But you didn't."

My breath stalls. I've never talked to her about Wally and Ryan. I figured she knew about it.

"I know that," I say, like it's a conversation we've always had.

"Good. How's Hayden doing? Tell me what I can do."

I'm grateful to her for not making this into a huge deal and maybe that's why I tell her everything. "She's not taking it well. One of her mother's friends, who has a relative serving time in the same prison, called Danielle and told her what happened. Hayden was close by listening. She took a bunch of pills last night. They have her sedated. When she wakes up, she cries. I don't know how to fix it or make it better."

"You can't, Matt."

I frown at her use of my first name. She never calls me that. "I know."

"But you can listen to her and share your experience. You're going through the same thing with Wally, since you were almost as young as she is. You can trade stories and tell her how you handled it. Don't bullshit her, tell her the truth. She'll appreciate that more. You're her father, without the burden of having brought her into this world. That gives you leverage. Kinda like me and my brother. I helped raise him but I'm not our mom, so he listens to me more."

I nod though she can't see me. "That makes sense. But won't the truth make her want to hurt herself more?"

"No. If she's going to try it, she will do it regardless, but more so if you lie and she catches you. When Teddy was going through the shitty stage, I had to be real as shit with him. Because every time I lied, he would do worse things. So learn from me."

"Thanks, Dahlia. And thank you for not dwelling on my brother's stuff."

She snorts. "Since when do you call me that? I'm pretty sure that's crossing the line."

"You called me by my first name just a little while ago."

"Oh. I guess I did. Anyway, I know you don't like to talk about the whole thing with your brothers. I respect that. There's shit I don't even like to talk about with my mom and brother. Anyway, handle things there so you can get back to work. Your spicy *Mami* will make it all better. You better let her."

She means Sierra, and it hits my belly. I've been trying to concentrate hard on what's here to avoid thinking about her.

"We broke up," I blurt out and regret it immediately.

"What? Why? You went to Christmas with the family and everything. Right?"

"I did but this happened right before and I don't have the mind for that right now. I can't drag her and her kids into this." Why can't I stop talking?

"Hunter, you're crazy about this woman. Don't ruin that. You're not the one who killed someone. You're the opposite of everything your brother is."

Her words burn like rubbing alcohol on a festering wound.

"I have to go back in the room, Wicker. Thanks for everything."

She hmmphs. "We'll talk about this when you get back."

"We won't," I shoot back.

"It's over, Hunter. You opened up. I'm not letting you shut the door. Give my love to Hayden. Let me know if you need anything. I can go check on your house if you need me to. Open your faucets or something."

"Yeah, I may be here 'til the new year. I'll let you know."

"Take care of yourself." She hangs up and I stay in the hallway for a few breaths.

I'm contemplating texting Sierra and letting her know I made it okay. Would she even care? She looked like it was no big deal last night. She even smiled before she drove away. I don't blame her. I'm the one that broke us up, but did she have to look so, well, so put together?

My insides were all torn and twisted, and she looked beautiful and poised. Like I was just cancelling a coffee date and not our everyday texts and calls. Like it doesn't matter that I won't be pounding her pussy for hours in the morning. Like she won't miss us hanging with her kids.

I shove my phone in my pocket. It's better this way, even if it doesn't feel like it. Doing the right thing never does. Still, I'm hurt like a motherfucker. With Sierra, I felt alive. She was like oxygen. You don't know how much you miss it until you're gasping for it.

And now, I can't breathe again. But how could I, when I gave up air?

27

Sierra

I feel like absolute shit and if I weren't a bit nauseous, I would be horrified about how awful I look. The mirror in Saona and Jax's guest room doesn't lie, though. Written all over my face are the Jameson shots Jax and I drank while sitting on the renovated floors of the grill. I also feel the shame of getting dumped and the foul mood that's predicting what my day is going to look like.

I'm pretty sure I smell like that bottle of Jameson, so I strip out of my clothes and jump into the shower. We got ready for Christmas dinner here yesterday. I change into my yoga pants and T-shirt. I don't need my kids smelling alcohol on me and asking questions. It will be hard enough to explain to them everything that happened.

I brush my teeth with my finger and a washcloth, using enough mouthwash to wipe away the evidence of my pain-numbing night. At least on the outside. My head is a rattling mess and my emotions are like the wreckage of a Category 5 storm.

Every hit of shame has me wanting to scream, "Fuck Matt." But I don't want to think about him. I want to handle it like I did back in the day and hop on someone else. Well, I kissed someone else when I thought he'd ghosted me. He hadn't done that this time and I'm wondering if it would have been better if he did. Let me wonder, instead of being honest and having it hurt even more. Because it's stupid. I don't care what his brother does. I care about him. Only him.

And now I don't know what to do with this hurt. I'm not used to feeling this way. Even when Edwin cheated, I was pissed off and embarrassed. But I don't remember if I felt deep-down pain? Maybe I erased it. He fucked up so many times, who can remember?

I want to hit something. Maybe I should go to the gym when I'm not feeling so queasy and join a boxing class.

I get out of the bathroom and head downstairs. My kids are in the dining room sitting in front of empty plates. They've already finished breakfast and guilt hits me like a stone. *Jesus*, I'm upstairs dwelling on a man who doesn't want to be with me and I'm not even getting up to make my kids breakfast. *What the fuck is wrong with me?*

I need to shake myself off. I'm going to spend the day with them.

"Good morning," I say to Aunt Iris, who is making more food over the stove and my mom who is sitting on the far side of the table. I don't look at her. I kiss my kids. "*Mis amores*. Did you eat?"

My mom answers for them. "Yes, Miss Iris made them breakfast. They're still in their pajamas because they didn't want to wake you."

I don't miss the rebuke in her tone or acknowledge it. Instead, I go hug Aunt Iris. "Thank you."

"You're welcome. Now, sit down so you can eat." Her warm smile and tone brighten my mood a little.

"You guys, go get dressed," I tell my kids and remove their plates. Then I go sit on the farthest chair from my mother. I need to get out of here without engaging her.

"You got in very late last night."

I say nothing. I don't have anything to say to her.

"She's young and we had the kids. She's a great mom and deserves to have some fun." Aunt Iris says in a breezy tone. She winks at me at the end.

God bless her beautiful soul. I smile at her.

My mother side-eyes her.

"A mother is always a mother first. Her children are sleeping at home and she's out celebrating with her new man and dragging her sister out there, who is pregnant and should be resting through the night."

The bile rises up my throat, upstaging the delicious taste of Aunt Iris' eggs. "I wasn't out with Matt. Saona, Jax, and I were hanging out at the grill. And let me make your day, month and year. I no longer have a 'new man' as you like to call him."

Her eyes widen but other than that there's barely a reaction.

Aunt Iris shakes her head. "But the two of you are so in love."

My stomach drops at the word love, but I don't get to think about it because my mom climbs up on her soap box.

"I must say I'm not surprised. His mother wasn't married, and God knows that brother of his already had a baby out of wedlock when he was still a kid."

She's so judgmental. "Mom, you were a single mom at one point. *Papi* divorced you. Remember? I'm a single mom, too. We can't afford to judge people."

So much for not engaging her.

She presses a hand to her chest. "How dare you talk to me like that. It's not the same. I was a married woman, and so were you. We didn't just have kids—"

I'm feeling mean and I just want to rub her face in everything. "Out of wedlock? I was pregnant before Edwin and I got married. God knows I didn't want to marry him, but you forced me."

"You were a decent girl from a good family. Edwin did what was right for your reputation."

I snort. "What reputation? This isn't the 19th century."

"You're trying to take your breakup out on me today. I'm always the bad guy whenever you make the wrong choice. When you or your sister pick men who are not at your stature."

Aunt Iris' eyes flash with a fire I can identify with so well. She throws the spatula into the sink and turns toward my mom. I stand up and move between them. Mom never knows when to stop.

"Jax is a good guy and so is Matt. It's funny how you don't approve of them but would welcome with open arms the cheating assholes we were married to before. Is it because they used to pass you money on the side?"

She pushes to her feet faster than I've seen her move in a very long time. I don't even get to register what she's going to do when her palm crashes against my cheek. Pain explodes over the side of my face, making my whole head swing to the right. My hand flies to cover the spot as the urge to pay her back in kind spreads through me.

"I don't care how old you are, you will not disrespect me. You and your sister made vows in front of God. They shouldn't have been so easily disregarded. I'm only trying to save you and your kids from that family. That boy was a little hoodlum. Everyone in the building knew what his brothers did. What they sold on the side. Those habits don't just die. He was never good enough for you. I raised you for a better purpose."

I take a step back from her, catching a glimpse at Aunt Iris' horrified expression.

"You insult him, *Mami*. You say he wasn't good enough for me. And you know what? He made something of himself. Unlike me. All I became was a housewife whose husband couldn't keep his dick in his pants."

"You're a college graduate and a professional," she replies.

"And he's a police officer, a good man who doesn't do drugs and is not jumping in bed with everyone. He's good to me. No one's ever treated me like I'm more than my face and body. He does things for my kids their father won't do, like spend time and show interest in the things they like. He encourages them."

"You know what? I don't know anything about the kind of man he is right now, but the kids want to be with their father. Don't blame me for that."

"You're right, you don't know him. And I do blame you, for encouraging that when there is just no way. You treated Matt like shit. And all for nothing. Edwin has a new family."

She stills my hand. "But he would come back if you let him."

"No, he wouldn't. He's married to Dania. Why would I want him back, though? He didn't respect me."

"For the kids. Because a mother always thinks of her children first."

"That's what I'm doing. I'm putting them first. I don't want them to see their father disrespect their mother and their mother getting hers on the side. I am teaching Emmi she doesn't have to take a cheating husband and Eddie that you don't cheat or disrespect your family, you stand by them."

"Sierra—"

"And I have a lesson for you too: Stay the hell out of my life. You keep trying to atone for your guilt through Saona and me. Trying to save your marriage through our old fucked-up ones. It's not going to work. You can't take back how you cheated and broke *Papi's* heart. It doesn't matter anymore. For one, *Papi* is already dead, so it's too late. And two, you should just get a life of your own so you can butt out of ours."

Her mouth flies open and her hand to it. She takes two steps back. "I'm your mother. You can't talk to me like that. You can't—" she slurs.

Her mouth goes and she's staring at her arm.

"Mom?"

Her knees go out and I grab her just before her head hits the table.

Sierra

Jax puts his arm around my shoulders. "She's going to be okay, Sisi."

I try to stop shaking. "I need to get a grip."

He does that brotherly squeeze. "Not just yet. Give it some time. You had a big scare."

I scoff. "You mean, I almost killed my mother because I went off on her like a beast."

He shakes his head. "No, you were mad and with all the reason. You had no way of knowing this would happen. Your mom is always doing this kind of thing to you and your sister. Saona's gone off on her more than once, too."

"Yeah, but she didn't give her a stroke. I did. Because Saona knows how to do this. She's not a freaking elephant stomping on shit. Why didn't I just keep my mouth shut and walk out of the room?"

Jax squeezes my shoulder. "Because she provokes you. All the time. And she put her hands on you. Aunt Iris told me. No one would keep their mouth shut after something like that. She disrespected you. She always does that to you and Saona. You guys take it and act like lightning will strike you if you say anything. This was bound to happen when you keep it all bottled up."

I look at him. "Who are you, Iyanla Vanzant? Oprah?"

"I'm more like a sexy Doctor Phil. And stop looking at me like that. Mom and Aunt Iris love watching OWN."

I shake my head. "I love your mom and aunt so much."

"And they adore you and your kids."

I stand up. "I'm going to check on them."

"I've been texting with them. Everything is okay. The young were teaching the older how to play *Mario Kart*. Now the older are teaching the younger to make cookies."

I smile, picturing his mom and aunt playing video games. The smile is short-lived, as my sister comes rushing out of the room. Her face looks like she could kill someone.

My heart drops into my stomach. *Oh Jesus. Did my mom die?*

"She's so fucking impossible. Even when sick, she's so annoying. She knows more than the doctor with the fucking medical degree. She wants the Vapor Rub, so she can put it up her nostrils, because she's convinced the air is too cold and crisp in there and she's going to catch a cold and die." My sister drops her head on Jax's shoulder when she's done with her rant.

The relief is so big and fast, it almost makes me weak. "So, she's going to be okay?"

Saona puffs. "Did you doubt it?"

I can only nod.

"Oh, Sisi. You know *yerba mala nunca muere*."

"What the hell does that mean?" Jax asks.

I chuckle. "It's an old saying. Weeds never die out. You know... because she's too mean to die."

He looks horrified, so my sister and I laugh.

She kisses him and turns to me. "Come on, she wants you in there."

I press my index finger to my chest. "Me?"

She nods. "Yes. Did you think you're off the hook because you almost killed her?"

My palm presses to my throat. "Saona—"

My sister throws her arms around me. "I'm sorry. I couldn't help myself. She's out of danger and I'm just so relieved I'm being inappropriate. Let's go. And brace yourself because you know she's about to get extra."

She's not wrong. The first thing I see when I walk in the room is my mother's reproachful look. I fight the burn that rises up my chest and force myself to keep walking in. I don't stop until I'm next to the bed.

Saona stays by my side. We need to protect each other.

I reach for my mom's hand and to my surprise, she latches onto it, tight and warm like when I was five and Saona was three. She would take us to the park while *Papi* worked. Maybe I remember her differently because that feels like another person.

"How are you feeling, *Mami*?" I ask.

"As well as can be expected for someone who could've died."

And welcome back.

"Mom, you didn't almost die. It was a mild stroke. The doctor said you were lucky and you need to take better care of yourself," Saona says.

Mom's gaze would obliterate my sister if it could.

Oh, yeah, she's all the way back.

I need to take the pressure off Saona. "I'm glad you're okay."

"Are you really?"

I nod. "Of course I am. You're my mother. I love you."

No matter how fucking hard you make it.

Her eyes grow misty. "I don't lie to myself. I've always known you loved your father more than me. That you would have rather it was me gone and not him."

What the fuck?

"Jesus, Mom. Why would you even say something like that? We would have preferred not to lose either of you."

She dabs at the corners of her eyes. "I'm not blind. I see the way the two of you can't stand to be around me. You moved down here to get away from me."

Saona sighs. "Mom, I moved down here to be with Jax because my job is flexible. Sierra moved here because she needed a job, a good school district, and a better life."

She sniffs. "You don't even answer my calls most of the time and when you do, you rush me off the phone."

I can't take this manipulation tour anymore. "Because you're difficult. All you do is criticize what we do and how we do it. And you refuse to understand that we left our past marriages behind."

I force myself to stop talking but my sister shows no mercy to her.

"And you're mean and judgmental. Last night was awful. You ruined Christmas."

"That's not what I was trying to do," she sniffs again.

"That's what you did. You had no right to bring Matt's family business in front of everyone. I knew all of that. And I know about..." I take a breath because I'm not telling her about what Wally did yesterday. Even if Matt and I are not together, she doesn't need to know that. She doesn't need to keep judging him. "...I know about his family history. I was willing to work with that. If I didn't think he's a good guy and different, I wouldn't let him near my kids."

"Fine. You can go back to him."

"Thanks for your permission," I say, letting the bitterness speak for me. "That ship has sailed. The breakup wasn't all your fault, so don't worry. And let's get off this topic. You need to rest, anyway."

"You're going to stay with me, right?"

"Nope. You're going to rest, and your beautiful daughters are going home," the attending doctor announces from the door. A dimple hollows his cheek and his hair is perfect. He should be on *Grey's Anatomy*.

He shakes my hand. "I've already met your sister but I'm Dr. Ellison. You can call me Joshua. You can go home and rest. Your mom will be in good hands. When you come back tomorrow, we're going to have a nice little chat with her about taking better care of herself, so this does not turn into something more serious."

Thirty minutes later, we walk out of the hospital. Jax is waiting for us with the car in the front.

"How is she?" he asks.

"So good she was trying to manipulate us," my sister answers.

"Oh, wow." His expression is almost comical.

I put on my seatbelt and lean back on the headrest. "And all that's about to change."

28

Sierra

My nerves are wracked, my head's all over the place, and my insides are barely holding on. I've never been so happy to see my house. I wouldn't have been able to go another five minutes putting on a brave face for the rest of the family. Jax's mom and Aunt Iris watched me like a hawk and fed me like a Christmas hog. Jax kept the kids busy with games and whatever he could find while my sister made up reasons for me to stay around.

"Why don't you just stay over?" she finally asked, betraying her worry.

I hugged her and told her I needed my house and my own bed for a few hours. We would be back in the morning to go see Mom.

I'm going to have a long shower, watch thirty minutes of TV with the kids, and then we're all going to bed. I wait until they have had their showers and are playing with their Christmas toys, then I sneak to my own bathroom.

It's hard to keep my mind blank but I concentrate on my mental list of things to do. My sister and I talked about keeping Mom here until she is better and ready to go back home. We are both worried about her alone in New York. The horror that crossed Saona's face at the idea of her moving in with one of us made me feel a million times better about the queasiness in my belly. I don't think I could survive that but at the same time, that's our mom and she needs us.

I would give anything to have five more minutes with my mom.

Matt's words come out of nowhere and I hear them clear, like he is standing beside me.

Fuck. No. I've spent the whole day trying not to think of him. The scare with my mom has had me too worried to think. And even though I know the breakup was the reason everyone tried to keep me at my sister's, I made it a point not to think of him. But here are the thoughts of him, prying open the wound without mercy.

I rinse the shower gel from my body and put on my robe. I hurry through my routine and get out of the bathroom. I find my kids sitting on my bed, comfortable against my pillows with the TV on. I smile at them.

Until my son opens his mouth. "When is Matt coming over? I want to show him my new game."

The pang in my belly is instant and painful. The smile slides right off my face. "He's... He had to go out of town for a little while."

Emmi stares at me. "Where did he go?"

"He went to see Hayden, his niece." It's not exactly a lie. I don't want to lie to them.

"Oh," she says and goes back to staring at the TV.

"Can we FaceTime him?" Eddie asks. "He said we were going to get to meet her."

"No, baby. He's spending time with her." *Good. That's really good.*

"Only two minutes. I don't think he'll be mad."

Jesus. I don't want to explain this to them right now, when I'm so deep in this shit, but I can't lie to them. I understand what my mom was saying when she asked what if it doesn't work. It didn't and now I have to explain it to my kids. But it doesn't have to be today. It can wait.

Don't drag the lie, Sierra. It will only hurt you all more.

"We have to talk, guys."

I sit on the bed by Eddie and across from Emmi, who's already

Some Mornings

staring at me with way too much suspicion. They're probably remembering the last time we had to talk. Edwin had been there, but he'd let me do the talking...and take all the blame.

"I don't know when Matt will come around again. Right now, he's dealing with a lot of stuff with his family..."

"Mommy? Did Matt have to go away because his brother got in trouble again?"

My insides tremble but I manage to keep my face from contorting. *Jesus, how does he know that?*

Emmi shoots a glare at her brother. "Eddie. We're not supposed to know that."

I clear the knot from my throat. "You two really need to stop eavesdropping."

"Well...it wasn't exactly eavesdropping. *Abuela* was telling Aunt Iris before you woke up. She said she saw it on the news."

It's always my mom.

"Matt's brother did get in trouble and it's been very difficult for Matt. So we need to give him time and space to deal with it. He may not come back for a very long time."

"You broke up." Emmi's words, more like an accusation, put an end to my attempts to be gentle.

I nod because I need to admit it.

"Why?"

"We're both dealing with a lot of things. He has to take care of his niece and your aunt and I have to take care of *Abuela*."

God, my throat hurts. I smooth a hand over it as my daughter death-stares.

"But we like Matt," Eddie says.

"I know, baby. I do too. I like him a lot."

"Then, why did you push him away?" Emmi asks. I'm taken aback by the harshness in her words.

"I didn't."

"You push everyone away. Daddy, *Abuela*, Matt...That's why *Güela* says you're bad. We don't ever get to like anyone because you take them away."

Her words stab right through me, breaking something, and I can't seem to stop the pain in my chest. "I didn't want to push him away. I love him."

I double over and I don't know when I start to cry. It hurts. Each sob rocks my body. It's too much. Then I feel the hand on my shoulder, and I look up. My daughter's face is in front of mine. Her eyes are full of tears, too.

"*Mami*. You never cry."

I straighten up and try to catch my breath, breathing through my open mouth. I need to get a hold of myself. My kids didn't see me like this when my marriage to their dad ended. They shouldn't see me like this, period. I'm the mom, the one who has to be strong.

"I'm really sad," I manage.

She crawls up on my lap and hugs me. It's the most heartbreaking moment of my life. I'm supposed to comfort her, not the other way around. But I cling to her because I need it. Soon I'm in bed with a child on each side of me, pressed against me.

I can't stop the tears, no matter how much I swipe at them.

"We hate Matt now." Eddie declares.

"Why do you say that, baby?"

"Because he made you cry. He hurt you."

I look from him to Emmi, who is nodding, and shake my head.

"Matt's going through a lot right now, but he's a good guy. People don't always break up because someone's bad. Sometimes life just works out that way. It's not meant to be. He likes you guys a lot and you do him. That has nothing to do with him and me."

"But he won't come around because you're not together."

I wish they weren't so smart.

I nod. "That's true. But you never know. Sometimes you stop seeing people for a long time, but that doesn't mean the way you feel about them has to change."

I press my lips shut because the meaning of what I just said hits me full force. I'm going to keep loving him, even if I don't see him anymore.

"So maybe one day he'll come back?"

Or with time I'll forget about him.

"I don't know," I tell my daughter. "He's going through a bad time."

"Then we should pray for him." Emmi says.

We do. I try not to cry but fail.

Matt

"Hayden?"

Her name is sharp on the doctor's lips and it works. She turns around and looks at her for a second.

"I was just thinking..." She looks at the fish in the koi pond. "...I was right. I ended up just like him. Like daddy."

There's a sharp pang in my belly. *No, she can't think that.* I open my mouth, but Melissa raises a hand. When I look at her, she shakes her head.

"Why do you think you ended up just like your father?" Melissa asks. There's no notepad in her hands today and she's a little more casual than when we see her inside the office. She's not in a suit. Instead, she's wearing jeans, flats, and a blouse. She had warned me today's session would be different. I already see it.

Hayden shrugs. "He's in jail. I'm in jail. Even these fishes are in jail."

Everything inside my chest is shrinking right now. I wish Danielle were the one here. Hearing this is way too much.

"But you're not in jail, Hayden. You're just in a hospital." Her voice is so even, so soothing. Even when Hayden has pitched a fit or screamed, this woman's voice never raises.

"All my stuff was taken from me. Even my hair clips. I can't check my Instagram or Snap with my friends. Isn't that what they do to prisoners in jail?"

"I can appreciate the similarity. Here's another one. The reason they take the belongings from prisoners is also to protect them. And the prisoners get cut off from the world partly to rehabilitate them.

We took your stuff because we don't want you trying to use any of that to hurt yourself. We also want you to get better before you hit the *Gram* again."

My niece turns a frowning face on her doctor, and then shoots me a can-you-believe-her look.

Melissa's nonplussed. "I guess you don't believe me."

"Not completely."

The doctor chuckles. "Good. That means you're not a pushover."

"Don't you want to ask me about my feelings?" Hayden's somewhere between annoyed and curious.

"Are you ready to talk about them?"

Hayden rolls her eyes and turns around. "Duh. It's been six days. I came in here last year. It's a new year, I want to go home."

Six days. Jesus, that's all it's been? It feels like at least a month. Between her therapy, daily talks, and the hell of waiting to see if the attempt was a one-time thing, time has slowed into a cyclical vortex.

"If I tell you, I go home?" Her tone is half-manipulative, half-hopeful.

I squelch the urge to pad that hope because, as Melissa told us during our session alone with her, Danielle and I need to stop cuddling and catering. We need to be real with her.

"It's a huge step toward it."

"It's not fair you're holding me hostage unless I tell you how I feel."

Melissa stares at her until Hayden relents.

"I don't want people to find out. They'll judge me and think I'm the same. That in time I'll become like him, a murderer."

The word is like a blade sliding over my skin. When will this wound stop bleeding?

She sits on the floor by the pond. "I wish we could move. Somewhere where no one knows us. Where they can't find out what he did...again."

"You're a smart girl, Hayden. You know anything can be found out with social media. You also know, given by your use of *I wish*, that running is not the answer to this."

"Then what is? Because I have to go back to school and face everyone. What if someone throws it in my face? I don't have a boyfriend anymore and he's pretty pissed. He would probably—"

Her gaze flies to mine and then away. There're so many emotions lying between us.

I would beat that little fucker and his dad senseless if he did that. "Is he pressuring you in any way?"

She shakes her head. "He told me I was trash just like my dad when we broke up."

"He's a little asshole, isn't he?"

We both stare at Melissa.

She shrugs. "I may be a psychiatrist, but I've met plenty of assholes."

Hayden smiles. "He's definitely an asshole."

She looks at me as if expecting the rebuke. I should, but that kid just smiled for the first time in days and I want to see more of that. I also don't want to get in the way of the progress Melissa seems to be making.

"I thought he loved me. He knows all about Daddy. We were going to college together, so I figured it was okay to tell him. Then we broke up and he turned on me."

"It's hard when people betray us."

She snorts. "He was so scared I would tell…" She tilts her head my way.

"I always knew he was a little bitch."

Melissa shakes her head and I swear she's about to blast me. Instead, she sighs. "Why didn't I have an uncle to scare my past boyfriends to death?"

Hayden giggles. It's the most amazing sound I've heard in days.

"I like the relationship the two of you have. I don't condone violence, but your uncle seems like he would do anything for you."

Hayden looks at me and nods.

"I would." I would kill anyone who hurts my girl. And that thought makes my stomach pitch because isn't that why we're here? Because my brother would do anything to protect me?

"What are you thinking, Matt?" Melissa is staring at me with dissecting eyes.

I want to lie but I can't. I think of Wicker's words. If I bullshit, Hayden will see right through it.

"I would do anything to protect Hayden. Wally perceived a threat and he acted on it. The difference between us is mere action."

My niece's eyes widen.

Melissa leans forward, her elbows resting on her knees. "There's a huge difference. Most people with the capacity to love think that way. Because any harm to the people we love is something we feel like it was done to our own flesh. We also understand impulse control. You're a police officer, a man that lives to serve and protect. You know what happens when people lose command of their impulse control and decide to take the law in their own hands. You also know people's lives depend on your ability to control your reactions."

I nod.

Hayden looks at her hands. "I get so mad sometimes. I wonder if it's only a matter of time until I do something to someone."

It ruptures something inside me. I'm off the chair and on the floor next to her. "You're not."

"How do you know?" she asks.

"Because I waited all this year and it hasn't happened to me—"

My throat swells, fast and painful and I can't breathe. I try to draw breath in vain. I just can't.

"Really? You think about it too?" Hayden asks.

All I can do is nod.

"You're not alone, Hayden. Matt has lived with this for longer than you have. He was close to your age when it all began. But like you, he still needs to learn that Wallace Hunter's actions are just his. They're not yours. They're not Matt's. They're not your mom's."

Hayden shakes her head. "But people don't understand that. They think and accuse and bully."

"The only way to stop a bully is to take away their power. I've been a thick girl since I was younger. No matter what I did to try to take the attention from my big butt, it never worked. Kids would taunt me. Older men would leer at me. It stopped the day I looked in the mirror and said, 'My ass is big. So what?' That day, I pulled on my tightest pants and didn't tie a sweater around my waist."

"Did people stop messing with you?"

Melissa shook her head. "They bugged me even more for a while but the more they yelled, the more I sashayed my hips. The only people who got to see me cry and see me sweat were those who had earned my trust. And they cheered me all the way."

"We've got to lean on each other, Uncle Matt."

"Yes," Melissa agrees. "Concentrate on you and the people who matter. Because letting people project onto you doesn't work and neither does carrying their crosses. You can empathize and be there without letting them drag you down."

I'm pretty sure she added the last two sentences for me.

29

Sierra

The Altima drifts into my lane, way too close to my driver-side headlights, making my stomach pitch forward. I swing my head to the right, make sure there's not a car beside me, and swerve into the middle lane. The Altima misses me by a hair, but my heart has joined my stomach way up in my throat.

"Motherf—"

The swear dries in my mouth when I glance into the rearview mirror. My kids' heads are still buried in their iPads, with their headphones on. They're unaware of how close we came to a crash. I grip the steering wheel and take a few breaths to compose myself.

The traffic on I-695 is especially atrocious tonight. It's like all of Baltimore is out to celebrate tonight, but they left their driving skills at home. I can't wait to get to Saona's to drop off Emmi and Eddie. These bad drivers are giving me anxiety. I fire up a prayer to San Miguel when I finally take the exit.

I hate how quiet Emmie and Eddie are. Every glance into my rearview makes my stomach churn more and more. All day, I've been harboring my reaction to their responses when I told them their dad wouldn't be picking them up for New Year's. They were quiet for like thirty minutes and have been resigned ever since. My heart shattered when Emmi said, "It's okay. We're used to it."

I had to give her the routine speech about life and how things come up. I am tired of telling my children we need to leave room for the unpredictable. They're kids. They shouldn't have to learn shit like that when it comes to their parents.

But like *Mami*, Edwin is not going to change unless forced. I'm the one who has to change how I deal with him. So, all day I've been plotting this call, even as I've tried to make it better for my kids.

I played video games with Eddie, while Emmi worked on the design book Matt gave her. I told her she could call Ayo but she hadn't wanted to. Instead, she helped me choose my outfit and makeup for work tonight. But they're not as excited today as they had been last night.

And all because of fucking Edwin. *Because of another broken promise.*

I can't wait to talk to him. I'm going to tear him a new asshole. He didn't even have the decency to call but sent me a text. *Hey, Dania's not feeling well. Gotta stay close to home. Tell them I'll come by next week.*

He's been dodging my calls all day, but he's going to talk to me when I drop the kids off. I don't care how many times I have to call him.

"*Mami*, at what time do you get out of work?" Eddie's voice yanks me from the mental dressing down I'm giving his father.

"We close at four in the morning, baby. We'll sleep at *Titi* Saona's and do breakfast, then go home. Why?"

"I'm going to miss you."

I smile. "I'm going to miss you too but tomorrow we can hang out together. The grill doesn't open until late."

"That's good. We can play more video games. I like it when you play with me."

Oh, fuck. I hate that damned game. You have to press too many damned buttons.

"Of course, we can play more games," I say. *Because I would jump off a bridge to see you smile again.*

Emmi jumps in. "I'll play too."

"Sounds like a plan. You guys be good for *Abuela*, Nana and Aunt Iris."

"We're angels. Nana said so," Eddie says.

I love that they've started calling Jax's mom "Nana," not only because it grates my mom, but because it makes Mama Hamilton so happy.

Ten minutes later, after dropping them inside, I head to my car, already dialing their father's number. Edwin doesn't answer. I call again and again until he does.

"Are the kids okay?"

The unease in his voice comforts me a little bit. At least he cares a little and I won't need to start the call with a, *Listen motherfucker*.

"They're fine, Edwin."

A second ticks by. "Then why are you blowing up my phone? I'm having dinner with my family. You know how Mom gets about phone calls at the table."

Apparently, his family doesn't include his already-born children. So much for him caring. "We have to talk."

"I told you, Sisi, I'm—"

"I know, at dinner with your family, but Emmi and Eddie are part of your family, too, and we need to talk about them. Don't worry, I won't be long. I just need you to hear me out."

"Fine, say what you're going to say."

He's such *a dick.*

"It's December 31st, the end of the year, Edwin, and things need to change. Starting tomorrow, I need you to get on the ball, because I want all your back child support by March 1st or I'm reporting you to the courts."

He sucks in a breath. "Sisi, Uh...you can't do this—"

"Yes, I can, and I'm not finished. Since the divorce, I've been lenient about this because I didn't want to aggravate things and because secretly, I hoped that if I didn't pressure you, you would be there for Emmi and Eddie. But you're not even making the effort. You keep breaking promises and their hearts. There's no way I'm going to be kind to someone who doesn't treat my kids right."

"There you go again. You always gotta run out and be all extra, Sisi. I told you that you'll get your money—"

"Yeah, you did but just like the promises you make to Emmi and Eddie, you don't ever deliver. I'm tired of covering for you, with your kids and with the courts. I can't make you love them or be there for them, but I will hold you to your financial responsibility."

"Fuck you, I love my kids."

It doesn't even get a rise out of me. He's already done his worst to me. "Then stop breaking every promise, and make an effort to see them. Start by showing them that you care if they eat, if they have clothes to wear, if they have money for their school projects. Let them know they're not being replaced by your new baby."

I hate the catch in my voice at the end. He doesn't deserve it.

"Fine, I can do that. Can you just hold off on the reporting to the courts?"

Fuck this. That's all he's worried about. It's like he can't even be a father unless someone makes him.

"No, I cannot. It's been over a year and I'm not rich. There are things I've had to put off, like buying a house, because you're not holding up your end and all my funds go to cover it."

"You know what? Fine, you'll have your fucking money. Is that all?"

"Again, it's your children's money, and no, we are still not done. There's no love left between you and me but we'll always have Emmi and Eddie tying us together. We need to make this work, Edwin."

"Yeah, we do. I'm really planning on coming down there next weekend."

Yeah, I won't be holding my breath.

"One more thing. I've never called Dania and told her all the things you did in our marriage or the signs she should be looking for. Because one, I'm not that person. Two, I just don't care and three, I still have some respect for you because you're my kids' father. I expect you to show me the same kind of respect and courtesy."

"What the hell are you talking about now?" His tone is that mixture between indignant and dodgy that triggers my bile. It's the same tone he'd use when I would confront him about cheating.

This fucker knows exactly where I'm going.

"You sent José to my house."

"Why would I send the man you were cheating with to your house? By the way, it was real nice of you to hook up with someone in my cousin's building."

Ah, so he knew. I always wondered.

"I hope you don't expect an apology from me, after how many times you cheated on me and with how many women. Anyway, cut the shit. I know it was you who sent him."

"I didn't—"

"You did. He got the address from your cousin, Mirella, who only could've gotten it from you. I just want you to know that I know. Don't ever try to meddle in my relationships again, Edwin."

"Whatever. Are we done?"

I shake my head like he can see me. "So to recap, I need your back child support by March 1st or I'm reporting you to the court. You're not going to make promises to my children that you cannot keep. Oh, and the old Sierra may be gone but she's not so far that she can't come back. Make sure you tell Mirella that. Happy New Year's, Edwin. Now we're done."

30

Sierra

I turn my face up and send up a silent prayer of thanks that I've never had to work as a waitress and that I'm only doing it to help out tonight. When Jax said we were reopening The Birthmark on New Year's Eve, Saona and I told him this was going to be pure hell.

We were right.

Every family, couple, and group without plans have ended up in here. All the staff, and even my sister, have been scrambling around to pitch in where we can. The place has been jam-packed all night and the people don't seem to want to leave once they come in. It's really a good thing, but I don't know that we'll survive it.

I wipe down another table, seat yet another group with no reservation, and lather, rinse, repeat.

"Sit down for twenty minutes, prego," I tell Saona.

She shakes her head. "If I sit down, I don't think I'll be able to get up again."

"You don't need to get up again. We can handle it." It's a lie. We need everyone right now because this place is nuts.

She's about to protest but I grab her by the arm and start moving toward the office, when a uniformed officer walks right into our path.

Recognition makes my pulse quickens. She's Matt's partner. Did something happen to him?

She must see the worry all over my face because she says, "He's fine."

But why is she here?

"Can we talk?" she asks.

"You're hurting me." Saona tries to yank her arm free and I look from Wicker to my sister.

"This is Matt's partner."

"Ooooh. Is everything okay?" My sister rubs the skin of her elbow.

"Yeah, he's still a pain in my ass."

"Come with us," I tell her and head to the office. "Saona, sit. I ordered you dinner and you're going to stay put."

"I'm pregnant, not sick."

"Oh, this is your sister? And you got knocked up by the bartender. Way to secure the bag," Wicker says, making Saona laugh.

"Thanks. I hear you're a fan."

"Yes I am, and congratulations, girl. But just so you know, I would never make a move on a taken piece." She hooks her fingers in the loop of her service pants.

Saona smiles. "I appreciate the honesty. Would you like some wings?"

Wicker nods. "I am on break, but I'm paying for them and taking them to go. I don't want anyone to think anything untoward."

Saona nods. "This time, but you have to come back and have some on the house, as a friend. I'll go place your order or you'll never get it."

Wicker hands her a credit card, thanks her, and turns to me. "I passed by and noticed the place reopened, so I figured it would be a good time to let you know that Matt's okay."

That's nice of her. Then I remember that she helped Matt with advice and gifts for my kids. *She really is nice.* "What about Hayden?"

"Eh. They have their good and bad days. Yesterday was good. They had a breakthrough. Today she's been a fucking obnoxious

Some Mornings

teenager who, again, doesn't understand why they want to have her in observation for a few days longer."

I nod, my heart aching for him. His nieces mean the world to him. So many times a day I want to text and ask how he is.

I settled for telling him the kids and I are praying for them the other night. His, *thank you that means a lot*, broke me. I wasn't expecting anything but I wanted to keep texting him, keep talking to him.

I'm not used to this radio silence between us. Every day, every moment drives home how permanent this is. "I'm glad things are looking up. Thank you again for letting me know."

Did he ask her to come? A glimmer of hope ignites in my chest.

"Hunter is super private with his stuff and he would stop trusting me if he knew I came here, but I thought you should know. If you care about him, you're bound to be worried."

"I do and I am."

Wicker nods. "Give him time. He's used to sacrificing everything for his brother. Not that he told me, but I'm a woman and a cop, so not everything needs to be told to me. Like he never had to tell me the two of you went way back. He tried to pretend, but you can't hide much from your partner."

I don't know what to say to her, so I say nothing.

"He'll be back in a couple of days."

I still say nothing. He's not the one telling me or asking me to be waiting for him so I don't know what my reaction should be.

She stares and waits. I do the same.

She chuckles. "You're both hard-headed. How the fuck are we supposed to get you back together?"

I shake my head. "You're not. Some things are not meant to be. And this is for the best. I have little ones and he has nieces to worry about."

"What does that have to do with the price of pork in China? Hunter is being a hurt idiot. His brother has this kind of hold on him. Plenty of parents with children date other parents with children."

"I know that. And we tried but it didn't work."

"It was working just fine before Wally fucked up again. I've never seen Hunter that happy. It was fucking disturbing sometimes to see him in such a good mood at the end of a shift."

I can't wait to get out of here so I can have you for breakfast.

Those were our mornings. He would walk through the door and we would tear at each other.

The memory is way too vivid. The pang of raw desire is instant and I struggle so my legs don't rub together. God, I miss all of him.

"Yeah, we had a good time, but I can't dwell on that. It's over and we are both moving on."

Wicker looks around. "Where the fuck are ya going? He's miserable and lonely as fuck over there and I bet you're not having a blast. Look, all I'm saying is, this is something you both can work through. But someone's going to have to make a move and he's kinda stupid about these things. Now that my sermon is finished, Pastor Dahlia is going to get her wings. Your sister is signaling me. Happy New Year, Sierra. Here's my number, in case you need it."

She hands me a card.

"Happy New Year, Wicker, no, Dahlia."

Saona comes back with a platter of food. "I gave her someone else's order. It was ready first. Plus, those people are too drunk to notice."

I nod.

"Jax said make sure you take a break. So, sit down and tell me what else she said."

I take the seat behind the desk. I can eat and check how we're doing on sales. I hit a few keys to wake up the computer. "She doesn't want me to let him go."

"Me neither. I like him for you."

"But he made a decision, *Manita*. I'm going to respect that because I would want him to respect what I decide. I know all too well what it's like to have my choices taken from me. Plus, I can't worry about him right now. Not when there's Mom's situation to think about. I'm working more hours, and my kids need me to be on my A-game."

"But you love him."

It cuts deep but I cut myself deeper. "I do, but he doesn't love me. If he did, he wouldn't make so many excuses not to be with me."

"You just admitted you love him," Saona says, surprise coloring every word.

"I did. Acknowledge, feel the pain, and let it go."

That's what I plan to do.

31

Matt

"She's a fucking bird, I tell you."

Another day, another call to Morris Place. In the past four months, we've been here four or five times. Since the call came today, Wicker has been on a mad rant.

I'm half listening to her, half bracing myself for our forage through Calvary Street. The last three calls have not been as bad. I haven't kept my neck so stiff and have even allowed myself to look around.

"I'm really tired of going to that house. I know it's hard for domestic violence victims, but she needs to fucking leave his ass. Where is her family? Why are they not staging an intervention?" Wicker is so hell-bent on raging that she takes the turn at full speed, only to slam on the brakes as a walker shuffles to cross the street.

We get propelled toward the dashboard, my stomach going first. "Shit. Sorry, Hunter."

I shake my head and try to regain my breath. "It's okay. You know I think it's sweet you worry about them."

"Ugh, don't use words like sweet. Ever since my ma baked you that pie, you've been fucking weird."

I laugh. "No, I think it's since you used my first name. It's like we're friends." I love to mess with her.

"Fuck you, Hunter."

I'm about to rib her some more but a glint to the right catches my eye, and it registers too late. My head is already turning and my gaze makes a beeline for the neon sign from the chicken place. *Come to Kenny's* switches to *Best Fried Chicken in Baltimore* followed by *Ask for our Chesapeake Drip Sauce.*

The car moves forward but I'm still staring. In the background Wicker is still griping.

"Hunter? Are you listening?"

I turn to look at her and blurt out the only thing on my mind, "My brother, Ryan, used to work there."

She turns to me with a frown and then shifts her eyes back to the road. "Where?"

"At Kenny's. He got killed in the alley behind it."

"Shit, Hunter. I'm sorry."

"Thanks. It was so long ago."

"That doesn't mean squat. I'm still hurt over my dad and that was eighteen years ago. Some people we miss forever." It's in her voice, that blatant pain that doesn't stop nagging at the soul.

"I'm sorry about your dad."

"Thanks. One of these days, we'll go to a bar after our shift and trade stories."

"We'll go? *Hell no.* "After a night shift or an afternoon one."

She laughs. "Afternoon. The shit I drink is bound to fuck up my insides in the morning."

"Deal," I hear myself say.

She turns into Morris Place. "Here we go."

This time we are the first two officers on the scene. The perennial crowd is, as always, gathered here whenever we get called for a disturbance. The eldest son's friends are in the crowd and one rushes to me the minute we're out of the car.

"His mom opened the door and Tyler said his dad came in there, mean as always. He locked all the kids in the basement. He can't hear much."

We walk up to the door and Wicker turns to me. We nod to each other. I count to five and go through my routine.

Say Mom's name.

Pat my vest.

Unfasten the safety strap from the holster.

Fingers hover over the service piece.

Listen for Wicker's breath.

She knocks and the seconds start to tick. We don't have to wait long this time.

The lock clicks and the door creaks open. The suspect's face appears. Same pale skin, same bloodshot and shifty eyes. This time with a smile. "How can I help you officers?"

"Mr. Blanton, someone reported a disturbance in your home."

"Ain't nothing going on. All these nosy fuckers need to mind their own business. Stacy and I argue like any couple."

Bullshit.

"Be that as it may, we need you to step out so we can take a look and make sure Mrs. Blanton and the children are okay," Wicker says.

"They're all fine. Stacy's in the kitchen making lunch and the kids are playing."

Wicker nods. "Great. We still need to check for ourselves."

"Don't you need a warrant for that?"

"You damn well know we don't. Step out of the way," she says.

He does.

"Do you have any weapons?"

He shakes his head, but we cuff him. "Don't move," I say.

We walk down the hallway in complete silence. The wife is nowhere to be seen. Every time we come, she's always at the end of the hallway, waiting for us to come rescue her and her kids. Something's not right.

My hand reaches for the Glock and I open my mouth to tell Wicker to retreat but I'm not fast enough.

"Freeze," Wicker yells.

But the loud pop fills the room and the cracking sound follows. One second, Wicker is standing in front of me, the next she's flying back against the wall. Her head smashes against it.

She's been hit.

My heart explodes in my chest and I scream her name. I move to the side, trying to cover myself while I assert that she's okay. The thumping is too loud and mingles with echoes of the shot bouncing around the room.

In my next breath, there's a man with a gun right in front of me. His gun is aimed at my chest. In my peripheral view, a shadow scurries. Not for the first time, I'm on the other end of a gun. But this time it goes off, the flash followed by the pop, then the explosion and the thick stream of smoke. Eyes intent on mine with determination and intention of the man. *He's trying to kill me.*

As I'm falling back the pain explodes through my chest and against my ribs.

All I can do is return fire. If I leave him alive, he's going to finish off Wicker.

Pop. Pop. Pop. Pop.

And down I go. My back hits the floor and another wave of pain resounds through me. I fight the fall, so I don't hit my head on the floor and end up half on my side. My forehead bounces off the ground.

Pop. Pop. Pop. Pop.

More shots ring out. I don't know if or where I've been hit. I don't feel it. There's no sound except the reverberation of every shot and the smell of sulfur coating my palate. My chest is burning like I took a sledgehammer hit. I need to get up.

"Marina," I manage, hoping God hears our code word. My mother's name is my one-word prayer. I say it one more time because I need to get up and get to my partner. Hayden can't lose anyone else. And I need to talk to Sierra one more time. I need to tell her I'm sorry and tell her that she makes me happy.

"Sierra," I say her name like another prayer. One for God to let me see the future. To give me one more chance.

I manage to turn myself around. Wicker is sitting against the wall, her eyes closed. Her hand is on her gun and both are resting on her thigh. I call her name but can't hear anything. I reach for my waist and pull out the radio. "Officer down. We're at five-oh-one Morris Place. Officer down."

I scream her name again and push on my elbows to crawl to her. There's blood on her shirt, the smell of it mingles with the sulphur and my fear. I can't breathe.

With my trembling hand, I touch her neck. My heart pounds in my ears and her pulse against my fingers. *She's alive.* I close my eyes and swallow hard as I rip my service shirt from my body. I press it hard against the wound and she pushes back.

"Fuck, Hunter. That hurts."

I've never been happier to hear anything in my life.

"I need to keep pressure on the wound. You got shot."

"No, shit. So did you. I popped that other fucker before he could finish you off."

I look to where she's pointing with her gun and there's a guy slumped on the floor. The one I shot is about ten feet away. On the dining room table, beyond them, are the dime bags stacked in neat piles.

I don't even get to tell Wicker as our brothers in blue swarm the house.

Sierra

"So, I was thinking that next Saturday you and I go to the spa for the day," my sister says, her hand rubbing over her growing baby bump, the smile brightening her whole face.

I don't groan like I want to. It's impossible when she looks so cute with her big belly. I know her intentions are pure...and super transparent.

Some Mornings

"That sounds really good, but we can't. There's so much work here. I need to keep jumping in to help the staff. We are lucky the place stays packed on the weekends but until we hire new staff, I can't take a day."

Her smile doesn't waver. "I knew you would say that, which is why we're going on Thursday. Jax already knows. He's making plans to cover you and will pick up the kids from school. So it's a thing."

"Saona—"

"You're not getting out of this one, Sisi. For months, all you've done is work at the restaurant, do the accounting for your side job, and take care of the kids. You don't go anywhere, just you, or do anything for yourself."

"Because time alone just means time to think and feel shit and I'm not here for that." I blow a mouth full of air. "I'm okay this way. Being busy keeps me sane."

"You can't keep living like that—"

Jax pokes his head through the door. "You need to come see this."

His tone is brusque and hurried, so we have no choice but to rush out after him. The TV at the bar is set to the midday news. The anchorwoman with the stylish bob and the no-nonsense suit is frozen. Her perfectly lined lips are half open. The line across the screen reads: *Police shooting on the East Side.*

Jax hits play on the remote. "Police were called to the five hundred block of Morris Place for a domestic disturbance but found themselves in the middle of a deadly cocaine distribution operation. One officer's been wounded, the other placed on paid administrative leave until the incident is investigated. Mary Murphy is outside St. John's Hospital, where officer Dahlia Wicker was admitted in the early hours of the morning."

Dahlia Wicker. Officer Wicker. Matt's partner.

"Oh my God."

The field reporter is outside the hospital. Two cop cars are behind her and it takes her a couple of seconds. "Laney, I am here in front of St. John's while we wait for an update on the case. We know the two police officers were called for a routine domestic disturbance and someone in the house opened fire on the officers, hitting Officer Wicker in the shoulder and her partner, Officer Hunter in the chest. Fortunately, both were wearing their bulletproof vests. Officer Hunter only sustained minor injuries and, as you said, was placed on paid leave pending an investigation. This is routine procedure as the officer discharged his gun and two of the alleged suspects are dead. Officer Wicker was shot in the shoulder but is in stable condition."

My pounding heart leaps through my throat and I don't hear anything else. Matt was shot. His partner got hurt.

"Jesus. He almost died. Oh God."

My sister throws an arm around me. Until then, I hadn't realized I was shaking. His name was like a canon to the chest. Saona takes me back to the office. Jax shows up a minute later with a glass of water.

"Matt's okay and his partner will be okay too. Just breathe, Sisi."

"He could have died."

"But he didn't. You heard it. He just got minor injuries. His partner is in stable condition. I know you're scared but the key part is that he is okay. Now breathe." Saona's speaking slowly and I'm so glad she's here and that I didn't find out while I was alone.

I would have lost it. I close my eyes and pray.

Thank you, God, for protecting him.

My sister's hand closes over mine. "Why don't you call him?"

Yes, that's a good idea. I want to hear his voice and see for myself he is doing well. I pull my hand from hers, open my desk drawer and pull out my phone. I unlock the screen and then stop. Does he even want to hear from me? What if he's going through work stuff and I'm bothering him? I don't need to be bugging him, just because I would be reassured by his voice.

I place the phone in my desk and shake my head. "He must be busy and doesn't need me calling while he's trying to get through stuff."

"I think he would appreciate the call. I bet he's shaken by all this."

"Maybe, but he made a decision not to keep in contact and I'm going to respect that."

My sister shakes her head. "Things like this change everything and you're not asking him to get back together. You just want to see how he is."

She's right.

I unlock my screen again and dial his number. It rings twice then goes to voicemail. *He sent me to voicemail.* I know, I've done that to others so many times. I jump when the phone beeps.

"Hey, Matt, I was calling because I heard about you and Wicker. I hope you are both doing okay. I'm thinking and praying for both of you."

I hang up.

I'm about to fling the phone away when I see a text message alert. It's from Matt. I click on it and see the message.

In the middle of work, will have to talk to you later.

It's one of his decline-call messages. I want to die.

"What is it?" My sister asks.

I shake my head. I can't even tell her. I'm so embarrassed I could die. "Nothing. I'm just wondering if I should have left that message at all."

"Of course you should have. You love him and wanted to make sure he's okay. Even if he's too stupid to see it."

I smile at her. "What would I do without you?"

"Same thing I would do without you: go crazy."

My sister is the best. Our relationship has gotten me through so much. I'm lucky to have that. "I'll go to the spa with you on Thursday."

She laughs. "Of course something nearly tragic has to happen for you to see the light."

I shake my head. "It's not that. There are people out there who don't have someone to care for them and help them. I have that and I'm not wasting it."

She draws a heart in the air.

I pick up the phone and order wings in four flavors and other food from the bar.

Saona's eyes widen. "Are you going to stress eat? Count me in. I can't seem to get full these days."

I shake my head. "I want to go see Officer Wicker and bring her some good food."

"Good. And if you see Matt, you talk to him."

Oh, no. I'm not going to see him. I'll make sure he is gone before I go in and if he's there, I'll leave the food with the nurse and go. I'm not going to make this more awkward than it is.

32

Matt

"Mom, stop fussing with the stuff around the room and sit down. Teddy, go get me some water, please."

Wicker's little brother puts his phone in his sweatpants pocket and walks out. Her mom sits down and pulls out her Bible.

I press my lips together. "You do boss everyone around."

She rolls her eyes. "They're only listening because they got scared by all this. I'm so freaking hungry."

"When are you getting out of here?"

"I don't fucking know. I think the doctor must be in love with me or something and he's trying to keep me here."

"In love? Not yet. Attracted? Definitely, maybe."

I turn to the smiling man that walks in the room. He's wearing a lab coat, perfect hair, and carrying a clipboard. The interesting part is the teasing way he's looking at Wicker and even more, the shell-shocked look on her face.

He takes his eyes off Wicker and looks at me. "I'm Dr. Ellison. I'm taking care of Dahlia, here."

"I want to go home," she says, the bite back in her voice.

"I know and, unfortunately for us, it's going to happen in the next couple of days." The doctor goes around the bed and inspects the bandaging. "You're healing fast, which is great."

He stares into her eyes while he talks and, is it me or is she blushing? Her brown skin is glowing, and I don't think she's breathing. I look away and catch her mother's gaze. Her little smile says it all. *I'm not imagining things.*

He touches Wicker's hand. "I'll be back to check on you, Dahlia. Make sure you get some rest. And have the nurse call me if you need me."

He starts to walk out but stops by me. "Has someone checked your bruises today, Officer Hunter?"

I'm taken aback that he knows who I am. "Yes, thank you. And if you're going to call her Dahlia, you should call me Matt."

The doctor shakes my hand and winks at Wicker. "Ma'am," he says to her mother.

"Mmmmhmmm," her mom hums when he's out of earshot.

Wicker is glaring at me.

I tilt my head to the door the doctor just exited. "Is that what you're into, Dr. McDreamy?"

The flash in her eyes is too good to be true. "Shut up, Hunter."

God this is fun. "Only two more days. Plus, it seems like you're... well taken care of here."

"Dick."

"Language, Dahlia," her mom admonishes.

"I really wish I didn't have to go. I'm having a good time."

"Oh. You're leaving?"

"In like five minutes."

"Oh, too bad," she says and types something into her phone.

I don't know if she's being sarcastic or not. It doesn't matter, though. She needs her rest and I'm going to stop by Sierra's job and ask her if we can talk. I don't feel right going to her house. She didn't mind in the past, but that was before I fucked up again.

The past four months without her have been bitter. I want to see her, but I know it's going to be a difficult conversation. I'm prepared for her to tell me to fuck off. I deserve it. I shouldn't have pushed her away. I wasted precious time and, if I had died a couple of days ago, my biggest regret would've been walking away from her again, this time by my own choice.

Five minutes later, I say goodbye. Wicker's mom stands up, as she now does every time she greets me, and says goodbye. She hugs me tight. "You take care of yourself, Matthew, and call the spicy *mamacita*. Too bad you can't wait—"

"Mom, leave him alone." Wicker latches on to my hand. "She's right, though. You should call the spicy *Mami*."

I nod. "I'm going to."

"Good."

"Unless she tells me to fuck off."

Wicker shrugs her good shoulder. "That's a possibility. If she does, you try again."

I nod because I will. I'm prepared to beg, insist, and grovel. In a non-felonious kind of way, of course. I run into Teddy in the hallway.

"Oh, you're leaving?" He looks so much like Wicker they could be twins.

"Yeah," I say. "I have stuff to get done, now that I have some time off."

"You're going to miss the wings. They're so good. No wonder people can't stop talking about that place." He shakes my hand and goes back in the room.

I make it all the way to my parking spot when it hits me. Wings people won't stop talking about. Wicker's face when I said I was leaving. Spicy *Mami*.

Shit.

I rush back into the elevator and am just in time to see Sierra's form sashay down the hallway and disappear inside Wicker's room.

I stand outside the room.

"Thank you for bringing these and for coming," Wicker voice carries. She sounds like the commissioner's wife at the damned Policemen Ball.

"Oh, it's okay. Thank you for letting me know when the coast was clear. Yesterday, I almost ran straight into him."

My stomach drops. *She doesn't want to see me. She made arrangements to come when I'm not here. Jesus, this is going to be tough.*

"Don't mention it. Hunter would understand. He knows I'm a bitch when I'm hungry."

"I don't want to make this more awkward than it has to be. You're his friend. I just wanted to—"

"Show me some love via delicious food? I'm all here for this. It's not like I'm selling his secrets."

Sierra laughs and it's like a bullet to the vest. I miss her laugh, her smiles, her everything. I head back to the elevator with a heaviness I had managed to shake off. I was so ready for this conversation. I knew there was a chance she wouldn't be receptive but now I'm pretty sure she won't be.

I get on the elevator and make it back to my Camaro. The engine roars to life and I'm going to head home, but no. It's not going down like that. Not this time. I'm not giving up on her and I'm not going to walk away. If she wants me gone, she'll have to shove me out of her life.

I drive up and down the parking lot until I find her 4Runner. I park next to it and sit on the hood of my car to wait. Every time the elevator door alarm rings, I'm almost ready to stand up and begin my speech. Each time it's not her.

To keep my mind off it, I group text with my nieces. I took an extra week off in January for Hayden and I went to go see RyanAnne.

What are you up to today? There's no activity on the Gram. Should I be scared?

The rolling eye emoji from Hayden is followed by her cousin's Animoji which screams, OHMYGOD.

One of my life pleasures has become annoying them by replying to anything they post to Snapchat and shocking them with the lingo. Maybe I should freak them out and send them a filter photo. I can use the one that turns you into someone of the opposite sex.

The elevator door opens, and I look up to see a nun exit. I nod and go back to the snaps. The clicking of heels sends my whole body on alert. I look up to find Sierra about twenty-five feet away.

Some Mornings

Sierra

There's a split second, when Matt's looking into his phone, when I consider tip-toeing back into the elevator, getting off on another floor and catching an Uber home. How childish would that be, though?

Instead, I roll my shoulders back and march forward. I shouldn't be appreciating how good he looks there. He's like a living Camaro commercial. Even I would buy that car.

He looks me up and down and pushes himself from the car, like an animal that's spotted prey.

I wasn't expecting to see him, but I made sure I looked good. I wanted the word to get back to him that I'm well.

"Hi," I say, like I'm not at all affected.

"Hi. You're probably wondering what I'm doing here."

I shake my head. "I imagine you came to see your partner."

"You know I was here before." His jaw is set, his eyes bearing into mine like he's daring me to deny it.

I don't bother denying it. "I knew."

"Why would you wait 'til I left to go in?"

I should've expected this. She's his friend after all. "Wicker told you."

He shakes his head. "No. I overheard it. I came back and saw you going in there. I heard when you told her thanks for the heads up."

Shit. He knows too much.

"I didn't want to make this awkward. You made it clear you don't want to communicate with me. Your generic messages say it all. I've never chased a man and I'm not starting with you."

I try to move past him, but he takes my elbow in his hand. I've always loved how strong his hands are. I move away from his touch. God knows I need to think with my head and not my needy-kitty.

"I was in an interview with the captain. I couldn't type a message, but I planned to go look for you. I was about to head to your job to talk to you."

I don't believe him. "About what? Everything's been said."

He shakes his head again. "Just give me some time. Please?"

I lean against my truck. "Okay. Let's talk then, Matt. But be quick, I have to pick up the kids soon."

He frowns. "Here?"

His expression would almost be laughable if I thought any of this was funny. "Where else do you think—"

"A restaurant, a park, anywhere else."

"This is just fine. And for the record, before anything else is said, I want you to know that I am glad you are safe and well."

"But I hurt you."

It's on the tip of my tongue to yell that he didn't. But he did and I love him. I'm not a liar. "I still care what happens to you."

Not a full-blown liar...

He smiles so bright that it hurts a little. It's not the smug smile he gets when he comes. It's the 'after smile,' the one he would wear when he held me after we were both satisfied.

"Thank you."

"You wanted to talk, so talk, Matt." I can't help the hint of annoyance in my voice. Feelings piss me off.

He smiles harder, and then stops. It's so abrupt and disconcerting.

"I shouldn't have ended things with you."

No shit.

But I say nothing, crossing my arms in front of me.

"I let the moment, what I was going through, make that decision for me. I had made a decision that I wasn't going to let Wally's situation take anything else from me. I tried to hide it from everyone. I was embarrassed and I felt guilty that he was in there. And that my mom saved me while he spent his life behind bars."

I relax against my car, while he sits on the side of his, facing me.

"My mom, Sergeant Ron, and you all have told me that I need to stop acting like I'm doing time with my brother. At first I couldn't see why you said that. It wasn't until Christmas, when your mother pointed out in front of everyone that she knew about it—right after I found out that he had killed again—that I saw how much of a prisoner I was. I've been living my life in fear of everyone finding out, of everyone judging me."

"It was your worst nightmare." My chest constricts for him. What a heavy load to carry.

He nods. "Except it wasn't just me. There was you and your kids. Emmi and Eddie are smart, and what if they thought I would harm them? Even your mom thinks I'm capable of not respecting them. I couldn't live with myself if they thought of me as a bad person."

"You know I don't care about that. I never thought you were like your brother. I know who you are, Matt. That's what I would teach my kids."

He exhales and we're silent for a few. He swallows. "I wasn't planning on breaking things off with you. I just needed a little air, and to be honest, some space from your mom. But then Wally said he killed that guy for me and that he was in there because he was able to do the things I couldn't do to defend our family."

"Oh God."

"But it's bullshit. You said it best. All he did was take away another member of our family. He left his daughter an orphan, left RyanAnne without another person to look out for her, broke Mom's heart, and left me to pick up the pieces. He's not sorry, Sierra. For any of it. And I can't do it anymore. I can't carry that cross. It's too heavy."

My hand reaches for his and he squeezes it. "It's not fair, either. You're taking care of everyone. You have to start caring for you, too."

He nods and pulls me toward him.

I tell myself to let go of his hand and move away. This is too dangerous.

"I am trying to take care of myself. I've been talking to Doctor Melissa, Hayden's counselor. We're doing family therapy and we're also having conversations on the side. I'm not letting the visits to Wally send me into a dark state anymore. All that is helping, but it's not enough. There's one thing I need, one person to make life complete for me."

My chest is squeezing so tight, I'm pretty sure I'm lightheaded and imagining things. He can't be referring to me. *Yeah, that's wishful thinking.*

He pulls me even closer. "You. What I really need is you."

Oh, shit. He did say it's me. But I shake my head. I love him but I can't do this kind of thing. My heart couldn't take it and I couldn't expose my kids to that again. "It didn't work, Matt. I'm happy for all these things happening in your life. It's about time you had a life of your own and knew your own value. It doesn't change anything. We can be friends..."

My words drift away when he takes my face in his hands. "Don't say that."

I try to move away but he holds me.

"When I was a boy, you made me look forward to the evenings, to our time on the fire escape and the roof. I never got to tell you what that meant to me, and when I finally made up my mind, Ryan fucked up and we had to run. When I found you again, you made me look forward to a phone call and then had me living for two mornings a week. You were the light in my fucked-up world. Your texts woke me up more than coffee. Every time I left your house, it felt like I was killing time 'til our next time together. Not because I got to fuck you, but because I got to be with you. You can't say all we can ever be is just friends."

"But what if that's all we can ever be, Matt? All we should be? I can't go back to giving you just mornings." Not after we've had so much more. I need to know how he thinks, how far he's willing to go.

"It wasn't enough then. It's not enough now. We never could just keep it casual because I needed to hold you and talk to you. I need more, Sierra. I think you do too. I want to come home to you, sit across the dinner table, talk with your kids, help you mold them into good citizens. I want to go to bed with you every night and fuck you 'til we drop off to sleep exhausted. I want to tell you every day that I love you like no man has ever or will ever love you. But you're the only one that can give us that."

Warmth explodes inside my chest, twisting like a storm.

"Matt." His name is all I can say as I throw my arms around him as tightly as I can.

He flinches.

I pull back and look into his smiling face. "What?"

"I'm hurt. Where the bullets hit my vest."

Oh. "Show me."

He looks around. "It's a parking lot."

I reach for the zipper on his pullover and slide it as far as it will go, to the top of his torso. There's a blackened welt in the middle of his pec. I let out a shaky breath. My fingers ghost over it. "You could have died."

He shakes his head and kisses my lips. "I had the vest. I was safe. I have a cracked rib, but that's it."

"That's it?" My tone is sharper than I meant it to be, but I can't believe he's acting like it's nothing.

"I lived, Sierra. To come back to you. When my body hit the floor, and I thought would die, I said two things. My mom's name as a prayer to God for protection. And yours because I wanted to be alive to be with you. Say you'll be with me."

He said my name.

"Yes, if you promise me, you'll never go away from me again."

He shakes his head. "I don't have anywhere to go. I couldn't leave you again."

I crush my mouth to his, savoring what I've missed not only for the past four months but for most of my life.

"Let me say it right. I love you, Sierra, and I want to be with you and your kids."

I can't help but smile. This wasn't what I ever expected would happen.

"I love you too, Matt. I realized too late I loved the boy who disappeared from my life, but I love the man he has become more. Because you would do anything to protect those you love, even when it hurts you."

He presses me against the car, kissing the breath out of me, his body plastered against mine. "We should get out of here before they call the cops on us."

I laugh. "Actually, the kids will be out of school soon. Let's go get them together. Unless you're busy."

He smiles. "Nothing's more important than you. Come on, let's go get our kids."

EPILOGUE

A year later

I take one last peek down the hallway. All the lights are off. Thank God the kids are all in bed. I haven't seen my husband all day. He's been a true champ with all four of them. RyanAnne and Hayden are visiting for spring break. He took Hayden this morning to visit Wally and after that, he took them all out and about.

I've been laughing every time the question *How do you deal with all of them?* appears on my screen. But the sexy texts in between have kept me on my toes...and wet.

Eddie wants something so his room is all cleaned.
Emmi wants to cut her hair like RyanAnne.
I'm taking all four of them to fro-yo.
I'm about to kill the fucking little twerp hitting on Hayden.
Get ready. I'm going to eat you like this ice cream tonight.

There's a flat tongue emoji and a berry next to it.

And there's something I want...
I'll tell you tonight.

The only thing that kept me at work all day was that I promised Saona I would go baby clothes shopping with her. God knows I love holding my niece and helping my sister make her look even more adorable, but I couldn't wait to come home to Matt. Then Juan got sick and I had to go help out at The Birthmark. I had to settle for texting him back.

I can't wait to get home. I miss U.
My sister and Jax are being reckless.
They're trying to have a second baby.
A second baby!
You want to give me a preview of what you want?
I keep imagining things...

He didn't. He said it's a personal request. I can't wait anymore so I rush to our room to find out.

I find Matt lying against the pillows when I walk in. He's still wearing all his clothes.

"Why are you still dressed?" I can't help but be disappointed. By this time, he's usually naked.

His gaze is on my legs, on the thigh-length skirt I wore out today. "In case I had to go herd the cats. They've been arguing all day."

"You didn't mention any of that. They're all sound asleep."

He shrugs. "I handled it. How was your day?"

I lean against the door. "Long. But I'm so happy. I think it's crazy, but I can't wait to be an aunt again. More babies for our family."

I'm gushing but his sly smile tells me his mind is more on baby making activities than babies. He spent the day with four kids of different ages. Who can blame him?

"Drop the skirt and the shirt, and come here, Sierra."

Raw need rakes its way through my belly. "Oh. It's like that?"

"Now."

The word reverberates through my body. I turn around and lock the door. In my next breath the shirt and skirt go flying. I keep my bra and panties. I know he'll want to peel those off himself.

I make my way to the bed. I want to tease him but then push it further. "Do you know how tired I am?"

Matt shakes his head. "You can't even pretend. You're smiling way too hard."

Some Mornings

I climb on the bed. "Maybe you're like my morning coffee. You wake me up, Officer Hunter."

He raises a brow. I call him by his official title when I want something specific. "Handcuffs it is."

He reaches for the nightstand drawer. I shoot a look at the door. We don't ever do the handcuffs when the kids are home since we both get a little extra with it.

"What if they wake up?"

Matt chuckles. "Someone can't keep her moaning under wraps."

I roll my eyes. "Neither can you."

"I know. You bring out the worst me." He snatches me on top of him. "And the best."

He kisses me, one hand behind my neck and the other on my lower back.

"What is it that you want?" I ask in between kisses, rubbing my crotch against his. He's hard, pressing on the right spot. I could make myself come by rubbing against him.

"You really want to know?"

I nod.

He rolls me under him, spreading my legs wider so he can be right between them. He flicks his hips against mine, sending a bouncing wave of desire through my body. His lips are on mine, then kissing over my cheek, all the way to my ear.

"Can you guess what I want?"

I'm not even coherent anymore. I've been primed all day. "I'm guessing you want to fu—"

The words freeze on my lips. Just like eight months ago when he proposed to me, there's a question on our bedroom ceiling. Just like it had then, it sends shock waves through my body. I blink a few times but it's still there.

Would you have a baby with me?

"Matt," I gasp.

His expression is serious. "Last time I got a ring. I didn't know what kind of jewelry I should get for this proposal."

I frowned. "I think the ones you got resting on my crotch are exactly the right ones."

We both laugh.

"I'm serious," he says.

"I know."

He kisses the corner of my mouth. "Would you think about it?"

I shake my head.

"Oh," he says, looking down.

I take his face in my hand. "I don't have to. Not with you. I can't wait to have your baby."

His smile is the biggest I've ever seen. "Seriously?"

"Five kids, Matt. We're going to have five around here."

"Is that a dare?"

I laugh. "I thought you weren't that guy anymore."

"You take me back, Sierra. Way back."

THE END

ACKNOWLEDGMENTS

Thanks to Deranged Doctor Designs for this beautiful cover. Thank you to my awesome editor Nina S. Gooden and to the sweet Katie Testa for proofreading.

Thank you to the Damned Mob of Scribbling Women: Audrey Couloumbis, Shadow Leitner, and Laralyn Doran—with a very special *thank you* from the bottom of my heart—Cate Tayler for feeding my muse and cheering me every step.

Angil, thank you for rounding up this story and for feedback that's gold-worthy! Your support means more than I can ever express.

A shouted-out THANK YOU to my virtual assistant Kimberly Costa, without whom I would go crazy.

Thank you to my group of supportive friends John, Vivian, Crystal, and Vera Maria, Felia, Marisol, Kakazi, Citlali, Nancy, Robin, The Lake House Writers, The Domingo crowd, and my LPHIDs.

Thank you to, my amazing family. Papi, Mami, my stepmom, my brothers and sister, uncles, aunts, nieces and nephews, and my beautiful Trin. I wouldn't be here without any of them.

Thanks to you, my readers for your support.

ABOUT THE AUTHOR

J. L. Lora is a Dominican-American author. Her stories explore the dark side of good characters, people living in the gray areas of life while playing the cards life has dealt them. She loves strong heroines and their equally powerful Men. She currently lives in Maryland, pursuing her dream of writing compelling, sexy, can't-put-down stories about empowered, badass alpha heroines and take-your-breath-away alpha heroes. You can find her and or chat her up on Social Media.

Sign up for my newsletter and learn more about new releases, events, news, freebies and much more at **www.JLLora.com**.

facebook.com/AuthorJLLora

twitter.com/jtothelove

instagram.com/jllora

bookbub.com/profile/j-l-lora

BOOKS BY J. L. LORA

The Trinity

BOSS

MADE

STEEL

A Love for All Seasons Series

THE SUMMER I LOVED YOU

THE WINTER OF MY LOVE

THE AUTUMN YOU BECAME MINE (Coming soon)

THE SPRING OF MY HEART (Spring 2020)

Standalone Books

SOME NIGHTS

SOME MORNINGS (10.25.19)

EMPIRE (2020)

Free Short Stories

DAMNED — *Companion story to* Made

ALL I WANT — (Epilogue) The Summer I Loved You

EN ESPAÑOL

La Trinidad

Ella es La Jefa (October 2019)

Made in the
USA
Lexington, KY